THE CUT DIRECT

PHOEBE ATWOOD TAYLOR

WRITING AS ALICE TILTON

THE
CUT DIRECT

A Leonidas Witherall Mystery

A Foul Play Press Book

THE COUNTRYMAN PRESS
Woodstock, Vermont

Copyright © 1938, 1966 by Phoebe Atwood Taylor

This second edition published in 1993 by
Foul Play Press, an imprint of
The Countryman Press, Inc.,
Woodstock, Vermont 05091.

ISBN 0–88150–270-7

Printed in the United States of America

10 9 8 7 6 5 4 3 2 1

THE CUT DIRECT

Chapter ONE

FOR half an hour the alley cat had been crouching on the brick sidewalk, staring at the roadster parked near the curb.

Nothing had been able to divert the intensity of his unblinking vigil. He ignored the swirling gusts of bitter March wind that ruffled his fur and moaned around the cupolas of Ward Street's square frame houses. He ignored the Dalton Centre fire engines on their nightly run. Even the enticing mews of a raffish gray tabby left him cold.

Only twice had the cat moved, and then only to escape the petulant kicks of a lone pedestrian, a furtive individual, who had made a double circuit of the block, each time pausing before the roadster to scrutinize it with an intensity no less sharp than the cat's. But now the furtive individual was gone, the echo of those quick nervous footsteps had entirely died away.

Stoically, the alley cat moved nearer the curbing and continued to crouch, and stare, and wait.

One glance at his sinister reverie was sufficient to bring Miss Margie Dodge to a standstill. She tugged at the arm of Cuff Murray, towering above her, and pointed.

"What a queer cat! Stop, Cuff, and take a look. What do you make of that cat?"

Cuff tilted his derby back on his head and obligingly considered the animal until the impatient tapping of Margie's toe spurred him to a decision.

"I think," he said, "it's a tom."

Margie sighed. She liked Cuff. His general physical dimensions were roughly those of a Greyhound bus, but sometimes it seemed to Margie that his mind moved more like a heavily loaded truck. Cuff was, as she often remarked, a fool for facts.

"I mean, what's the cat watching?" she said patiently. "What's he staring at that way?"

"Bus ticket." Cuff picked up a pink slip from the sidewalk and gave it to her. "Ticket to Boston, see? Somebody dropped it running for the bus at the corner. I guess the tom wants to go to Boston. Come on, sugar."

"No, wait," Margie said. "I can't go till I find out what's wrong. That cat hasn't even looked at us. He don't know we're here—what's he staring at so?"

"Maybe the car," Cuff said. "I guess he likes the car. I like it too. It's got uhh. It's a snappy buggy." He cleared his throat. "You don't happen to want that buggy, do you, sugar?"

"No, no!" Margie hastily put out a restraining hand. "You know what you promised about cars! I don't want that car—"

"Nothing's too good for you, sugar." A note of

pleading crept into Cuff's voice. "It wouldn't be no trouble at all. It's a snappy—"

"Listen," Margie said firmly, "tear that roadster out of your eye, Cuff Murray! All I want to know is about that cat—he's making shivers skate on my spine. What's he staring at? You go find out!"

"Aw, Margie," Cuff protested, "how can a guy tell what an alley cat's got on his mind, huh? You can't walk up and ask—"

"Look in the gutter," Margie said. "I'm staying right here, because it might be a rat, and I don't like 'em. Go on, Cuffy."

"S'pose somebody goes by and sees me—"

"If they ask what you're doing," Margie assured him with irony, "I'll tell 'em you're hunting that old diamond tiara I tossed away. Get going—"

Cuff shrugged elaborately and strolled over to the curb. Margie was tops with him, but sometimes she made him think of the desk sergeant over at the Dalton Hills station. Always having ideas.

With great deliberation, Cuff yanked the folded "Racing Gazette" from his overcoat pocket, and spread it carefully over a patch of ice next the cat. He was not going to sacrifice his best pants to this screwy investigation of what alley cats liked to watch. They were his only pants, too, until his landlady got paid.

As he knelt on the paper, he bore down resentfully on the headline picture of Salamander Sal. A horse in whom Cuff had complete confidence, Sal had spent the afternoon's fifth race munching daisies at the post. Because of Sal, Cuff's bank roll now lacked the price of a small lemon coke, a fact which his landlady had already found out and acted upon. Margie had yet to be told.

"Cuff, will you hurry up?"

"Okay," Cuff said wearily. "Okay."

Stretching out, Cuff thrust his head down into the space between the curb and the roadster's narrow running board. The alley cat watched him malevolently.

After several minutes, Cuff got up, replaced the "Racing Gazette" in his pocket, and took Margie's arm.

"Come on. Let's scram."

"Was it a rat?" Margie, who had not missed Cuff's unconscious recoil from the cat, guessed that it was not.

"It's a guy under the car," Cuff said. "He's dead."

Cuff's blunt statement was not an indication of callousness. He personally found nothing in the fact of sudden death to get worked up about, and hoped that Margie was going to feel the same way. To his relief, she didn't scream and carry on. She simply made a little squealing sound and tightened her grip on his arm.

"I felt in my bones—I *knew* something was wrong. I had a hunch when I saw that cat—how'd the man get under the car? Are you sure he's really dead?"

"That guy," Cuff told her, "is a doornail. Come on—"

"But we can't leave him there, Cuff! We got to do

something—say, how'd he get under the car? What should we ought to do first?"

"Sugar," Cuff said, "you listen to me. If we hadn't bothered to look and find him, we wouldn't give the guy a minute's thought, would we? Well, then—"

"But, Cuff, we got to—"

"Sugar," Cuff said earnestly, "you seen the cat, you get this hunch something's wrong. So you're right. Okay. Now I got my hunch. My hunch is, we poke our nose into this, and we land in trouble. So we scram, see?"

"We do not scram!" Margie said. "We do something about the poor guy—"

"What do you want to stick your neck out for?" Cuff demanded. "The guy is dead. He's running for the Boston bus, see? And he loses his ticket, see? And he don't look where he's going when he hunts it, and somebody runs over him with a car, and he gets bumped so hard, he gets thrown—"

"How do you know he was run over?" Margie interrupted.

"Oh, his hat," Cuff said. "And the loaf of bread and stuff beside him. All squashed. He's all covered with mud and slush. He got bumped over by that puddle in the street, and he got hit so hard, he's thrown here under this roadster, see? Now, if you call the cops—honest, Margie, you got no idea what a lot of questions them cops can think of. The guy is dead, and it ain't our— Margie, what you doing!"

Margie was stretched out on her stomach, peering into the gutter.

"He's not dead, Cuff! Come here."

Mr. Leonidas Witherall, sprawled limpidly under the car, blinked up at her, and then hastily shut his eyes again.

A cat, a man with a mustache. A cat, a man without a mustache. A cat, and now a girl. There was apparently no end to this series of bulging orbs that goggled at him so inquisitively, as though he were a man-hole worker or a subway being excavated.

Ruminatively, Leonidas Witherall wiped some gutter slush from his right cheek, just as Cuff stretched himself out beside Margie.

"Sugar, get up and get going! I tell you, I got this hunch. I don't get a hunch very often, but when I get one, it pays to play it—"

"Like Salamander Sal, huh?" Margie derived a nasty pleasure from watching Cuff wilt. "Sure, I know about that, all right. I wasn't going to bring it up, but—look, Cuff, the guy moved. I saw him move."

"Rigor whatever it is," Cuff said unhappily. "The guy is a doornail, and—"

"I am not!" Leonidas Witherall said with great distinctness.

Cuff's head bumped against the running board.

"Huh?"

"I'm very sorry to disappoint you," Leonidas said. "Very. But I'm not. I'm jarred, and bruised, and I am infuriated. But definitely not dead."

"Then you sue him, mister!" Cuff said.

"Sue," Leonidas inquired, "whom?"

"The guy that run you over. Din't you get his

name and address? Not even his number? Gee, mister, you'd ought to of! Did you ever look dead! Say, I never seen a guy look more like a doornail—what a case you got to sue—"

"Cuff," Margie said, "get up and go around into the street, and see if you can help this man get out from under. Can you move, mister?"

"What a case!" Cuff said. "It's a pity you din't get his number—say, this is a real hit an' run, isn't it?"

"I had guessed," Leonidas said, "that it was a hit."

The flicker of a smile played around his lips. Margie grinned at him, and mentally handed him an orchid. The old guy was a sport.

"M'yes, indeed." He didn't bother, Margie noticed, to make any tentative wrigglings. He seemed to know. "Aside from an assortment of cuts and bruises, my only real injury is a sprained left wrist."

"Okay," Cuff said. "Lie easy and I'll slide you out."

As carefully as though he were handling the Portland vases, Cuff slid Leonidas Witherall out and carried him bodily to the curb, where Margie set to work with handkerchiefs to remove the mud and the gutter debris.

At the end of five minutes of effective scrubbing, she stood off and surveyed the results.

The guy was really quite nice-looking, if a little on the elderly side—anything over fifty was elderly to Margie. His long thin face, she decided, was sort of distinguished, like an ambassador in the movies. He had a mustache, and a funny little beard—

"Say," Cuff said suddenly, "ain't I seen you somewheres before, mister? You look like someone I met before somewheres. Say, where've I seen you before?"

"That's just what I been thinking," Margie said. "I've seen him before, too. Like in school, or a library. I seen you, I know. Or your picture. Say, are you in the movies?"

Mr. Witherall sighed. He went through this sort of thing daily. He had gone through it daily for more years than he cared to recall, and for him the game had long since lost most of its charm.

"Was it the movies?" Margie mused. "Or the library—"

"My name is Witherall," Leonidas said, "but I have been told that I look like Shakespeare. I have been told it so often that I see no reason to doubt the statement that I am the spitting image of Shakespeare. I am constantly being prodded in the midriff by Shakespeare lovers who want to know if I am real. The resemblance even disturbs people whose memory of the bard is otherwise hazy—" he broke off and spoke to Cuff. "Are those my pince-nez you've found in the street? Thank you—"

"He means the glasses, Cuff," Margie's voice was stern. "And the wallet, too. Pass over that wallet, Cuff. You just picked it up from the gutter, remember? And the keys. That's right. Hand 'em all over. Say, is that your cat, Mr. Witherall? It's still staring—what *is* that animal brooding about?"

"I wish," Leonidas said, "I could think he had been consumed with fellow feeling for a companion in the gutter, but I think it's fish cakes."

"Fish cakes?" Margie stared blankly at him.

"Possibly the cheese. You see, I've been spending the evening with one of my former confreres at the Academy—Meredith's Academy, on the next street—"

"That's the swanky boys' school that just moved out here from Boston, huh?" Margie said.

"Exactly. Professor Otis's cook is a tender-hearted woman who feels that all bachelors hover on the brink of starvation. As I was leaving, she presented me with vast quantities of food to take back to Boston. Newly baked bread, and innumerable fish cakes, and a large amount of Gorgonzola cheese—er—Cuff, perhaps you'd retrieve the bundle of fish cakes and present them to the cat? He has earned them."

Cuff lined the fish cakes along the curb. The alley cat surveyed them, yawned, and with stately dignity began his long-awaited meal.

"If he could talk," Leonidas observed, "doubtless he would murmur something philosophical about Job, and the rewards of patience. Give him the cheese, too, to top off with. The wrapping and rewrapping of that cheese involved the entire Otis family, causing me to run for the bus, and—"

"Mr. Witherall, how's for a doctor?" Margie interrupted. "Hadn't you better get yourself looked over?"

"No," Leonidas said quickly. "Oh, no. No indeed!"

Margie's eyes narrowed. "You look shaky—say, I know. Cuff, you hop around to the drug store and get some aspirin. And a paper cup of water. I'll wait here with Mr. Witherall—"

"You could phone from one of these houses," Cuff said, "or ask—"

"All of Ward Street's been in bed since nine o'clock," Margie said, opening her purse. "Here, take this and march up to the drug store and get some aspirin and a cup of water. See? And—what's that you muttered about ideas?"

"I said, you keep having them," Cuff informed her as he took the quarter and departed.

Margie watched him stride up the street, and then turned to Leonidas.

"Now, Mister Shakespeare," she said, "what's the big idea? What's the racket? No, don't put on your fancy glasses and pretend you don't understand. You know what I mean. Why did you play corpse for Cuff? And then pretend to come to all of a sudden after you'd looked us over? Who did you expect? What were you lying under that car playing dead so hard for? You were all right. You knew it. What's been going on here?"

Leonidas, watching the alley cat begin his fifth fish cake, leisurely swung his pince-nez from their broad black ribbon.

"You are an unusually perspicacious young woman," he said at last. "Frankly, I felt that your good looks precluded perspicacity—"

"Skip it," Margie said. "Who run you over? What happened?"

"This car here," Leonidas lightly touched the roadster's fender, "ran me down. Ran me down with what

I should unhesitatingly call malice aforethought. The—"

"What! This car? This one here? Listen, Shakespeare, if this car had gone over you, you would be a doornail, like Cuff said. The way you was lying under—"

"I assure you," Leonidas said, "it was this very vehicle. It charged at me over by that large puddle in the street. And when I came to, someone was finishing the job of draping me tastefully under it, over here by the curb—"

"Who?"

Leonidas shrugged. "I was not in any state to be very clear about the person. I only know he wore a mustache. That impressed me, I think, because in that split second when the roadster charged at me, I saw that the driver wore a mustache—"

"Whyn't you yell?" Margie demanded. "Whyn't you do something?"

"Have you ever been run over?" Leonidas asked her courteously. "No? I never have before, myself. It seems that when you are charged and hit by a ramping roadster, something happens to your reflex centers. Your spirit wishes to do many things with which your flesh is unable to cope. In brief, I couldn't do anything. I was frightened."

"I don't get this," Margie said.

"Neither do I," Leonidas returned. "By the time I had recovered enough to think, there were footsteps, and I had a quick flash of that mustachioed face again. And—"

"Listen, Shakespeare! Enough is enough, and—"

"I am not romancing," Leonidas said quietly, and Margie, to her own amazement, found herself believing him. "After what this strange individual said when he kicked the cat, I decided it might be wise for me to remain where I was. It turned out to be very fortunate that I did so. He returned. That I finally convinced him I was dead is no tribute to my histrionic ability. I was literally frightened to death. Then, after some minutes, you and Cuff appeared—"

"Look, whyn't you do something?" Margie said. "About this guy. Whyn't you try to find out what was going on?"

"My dear young lady," Leonidas said, "when a person has obviously decided to erase you by hurling a large and powerful car at you, and when the person gives every indication of being willing to hurl it at you again, if necessary, there is no point in—er—"

"Sticking your neck out," Margie finished for him.

"Exactly. Nor was I in any condition to. My desire to have the person go was far greater than my desire to inquire into the situation. He went, and I am here, and that is still a satisfactory conclusion to me."

Margie thought for a moment.

"Who would be wanting to erase you?" she asked. "And why?"

Leonidas shook his head. "It's very flattering to be singled out for destruction, but I can't imagine why I was chosen. I am a retired professor from the Academy, as I told you. After retiring, I traveled for several years, returning to find that the depression had converted my financial backlog into a single match stick. I have a minute pension, which I eke out by writing, and by hunting rare books for the wealthier and lazier Boston collectors. At the moment I have three dollars and fifty cents in my wallet, which this strange individual made no attempt to take. I am involved in no amorous triangles. To sum it up, Margie, no sane person should kill me for love or money."

"Maybe the guy was drunk. The driver, I mean," Margie said. "Maybe that's the answer."

"I wish I could think so, but he was terribly, terribly sober. Grimly, determinedly, appallingly sober."

"What're you going to do now?"

"Take the next bus back to Boston," Leonidas said. "Thankfully. I wonder, should an alley cat be allowed to eat more than five fish balls without pausing to chew, or reflect—"

"Say," Margie interrupted. "I just thought of something. Am I dumb! The license plates! Take the number, and there you are. The registry can tell you whose car it is, and then—"

"I thought of that," Leonidas said. "But I wonder if anyone would have left behind so obvious a clew? Why bother to drape someone under your car, if the car can be traced?"

"You mean it's probably a stolen car," Margie said. "Or something."

"Or something," Leonidas agreed. "I keep wondering why I was not left in the puddle, Margie. Why was this roadster so beautifully parked here by the curb? Why was I then so picturesquely spread under it— Margie, do you see Cuff coming? I—I feel dizzy—"

Cuff, turning the corner a few seconds later, was met by Margie, anxious and white-faced.

"Where's that cup of water—you big galoot, where's the water? Where've you been?"

"Aw, Margie," Cuff said miserably, "I had this hunch at the drug store, see? And there was this guy spent four bucks, and he hadn't got nothing—"

"So you put my quarter in the slot machine. Yeah. Hustle, you lump—Shakespeare's passed out. We got to get him to a doctor's, quick—"

"There's a doctor on Pine Street," Cuff said. "I just seen the sign. I'll go fetch him—"

"No, you don't," Margie said. "You'd probably stop for a crap game. You come get Shakespeare and carry him there—hustle, you dope!"

The doctor's office in which he came to seemed to Leonidas Witherall the most utterly repulsive place he ever remembered. The first object to meet his faltering gaze was a stained-oak cabinet full of sharp, shiny knives. A dusty skull leered from the top shelf. Leonidas winced, and turned away, and then wished he had let well enough alone. The picture on the opposite wall was a classic but none the less unattractive eighteenth-century print entitled "The Use of Leeches."

The doctor, a sleepy-looking man in an untidy gray dressing gown, occupied himself with the mixture of a number of evil-looking liquids. Leonidas surveyed them with distaste, then leaned back and tried to relax on the uncompromisingly rigid padding of the operating table where he lay. Probably, he thought, those liquids were destined for him. He tried to find some solace in the knowledge that leeches, at least, were no longer fashionable.

"Come to, have you?" the doctor inquired brusquely. "Drink this."

The mixture had been loathsome at a distance; at close quarters it was so disgusting that Leonidas rebelled.

"Why? What for?"

"I said, drink it!"

"My good man," Leonidas put on his pince-nez, "I fainted. That's all that happened. I fainted. I'm sure there is nothing about a simple faint to warrant the consumption of any hideous concoction like this!"

"See here!" the doctor said crossly, "I've just been waked from the first sleep I've had since day before yesterday. I'm in no mood to argue, after pulling my worst deadbeat through pneumonia, and delivering twins to his wife. You drink that!"

"My dear sir," Leonidas sat up on the operating table and fumbled for his wallet, "I assure you that I am no deadbeat. Nor do I care one whit for your lost sleep, or your manners. If you will be good enough to tell me the price of this—er—call, I shall—shall be—shall—"

He stared at the wallet in his hand. It was not his wallet. It was an entirely strange wallet, of handsome pigskin, expensively handsewn. Cuff, he recalled, had given him a wallet and some keys at Margie's command, and he had automatically put them in his pocket. This was that wallet—

"What's the matter?" the doctor demanded.

"This wallet," Leonidas said, opening it, "this wallet belongs to—"

He realized suddenly that the doctor was speaking not to him, but to the agitated woman who had burst into the office, her negligee churning behind her.

"Harry, those two—that couple with this man—I told you to be careful of patients this time of night, after what happened to Dr. Granby—"

"What's the matter?"

"That young fellow—he's taken all the silver off the sideboard—Gramma's silver! And your watch—your best watch that was on the hall table! Go after them, Harry—"

"Cuff?" Leonidas was incredulous. "You mean that Cuff and Margie have stolen—"

"See, he's a confederate, Harry!" the woman said triumphantly. "Cuff and Margie indeed! He's a confederate, it's just like at Dr. Granby's—run after them quick, Harry, I'll call the police. I'll watch this man. You get Gramma's silver and your best watch—"

The doctor raced out of the office as the woman grabbed the phone.

Leonidas, listening to her vigorous call for the police, made a quick decision.

He had no intention of answering for the shortcomings of Cuff and Margie. He had endured enough for one night, and he saw no reason for spending the remainder of it enduring more, probably in some dank cell. Besides, he had that wallet to think about.

His head reeled as he swung his legs off the table. Large black spots leapt at him from the ginger-colored carpet.

Drawing a long breath, Leonidas closed his eyes and picked up the glass of evil-looking liquid. Doggedly and unflinchingly, he drained it to the last drop. Then he jumped for the door.

Whatever the concoction was, it put wings on his heels. He was around the corner of Ward Street before the doctor realized what had happened.

Four blocks away, Leonidas paused to get his bearings.

He was on the pike, the express highway. And—he nearly crowed with delight—there was a Boston bus coming toward him!

He stepped forward off the curb to hail it as a sedan rounded the corner. Leonidas saw the sedan, but the motherly looking woman at the wheel of the sedan did not see Leonidas.

For the second time that night, Leonidas hit the street with force.

The room where he waked up was unfamiliar, but that did not bother Leonidas. He was getting quite accustomed to regaining consciousness in strange places. At least the overstuffed chair in which he sat was more comfortable than the Ward Street gutter, or the operating table of the doctor named Harry.

Leonidas yawned, and then he gasped.

Across from him, in another overstuffed chair, sat

the mustachioed man who had been the driver of the roadster!

"My good man," Leonidas began, and then he stopped short.

There was no use in talking to Bennington Brett. Bennington Brett was dead.

Leonidas stared in horror at the knife handle protruding from the man's chest.

Bennington Brett was not just dead.

You could practically say without fear of contradiction that Bennington Brett had been murdered.

Chapter **TWO**

BUT in the very next breath, Leonidas contradicted himself.

"He has not! Of course he hasn't!" he said firmly.

The sound of his voice made him feel better, somehow. It reassured him, although he didn't know exactly what it reassured him about. His wrist watch had the same comforting effect. He found a positive relief in looking at the watch and finding that it was six-fifteen.

"It's absurd," Leonidas said. "Absurd. Impossible!"

And of course it was. It had to be.

Just a vision. A nightmare. The whole fantastic scene opposite him was the net result of last night's bewildering events, of constantly being run over by cars, of drinking evil-looking liquids in the offices of rude, brusque doctors.

Bennington Brett was not murdered, or even dead. The knife handle was a shadow. He would put on his pince-nez, Leonidas thought confidently, and everything would clear itself up. Everything would be all right then.

Particularly the knife handle.

But the longer that Leonidas gazed at it, even with the aid of his glasses, the more acutely and shockingly real that knife handle became.

The knife handle was no myopic error, no optical illusion, nothing you could brush lightly aside and dismiss as a mirage.

That knife handle was real enough.

So was all the rest.

While he tried to get used to the idea of it, Leonidas found himself suddenly thinking back to the day some fifty years ago, when he sat beside his father on the red plush seats of the Tivoli Amusement Palace. As his scalp tingled, and a dryness pounded in his throat, Leonidas had watched the most famous knife act of that period. With gusto and abandon, the Incomparable Zolu hurled knife after knife at the veiled lady who stood nonchalantly against the pine board. Then, in a triumphantly blood-curdling finale, Zolu thrust the lady into a box and briskly sawed her in two.

Leonidas had always looked back on that afternoon as an emotional milepost. He never expected to attain again such lofty heights of fascinated horror. He never thought it would be possible.

He was wrong.

His reactions to the Incomparable Zolu had been sissy things, compared to the way he now felt. Now his mouth was so dry that his tongue grated against it, and his jaws ached from teeth-gritting, and the palms of his hands were cut in little arcs from his fingernails digging into them. And his head!

Leonidas forced himself to sit down and lean back in the overstuffed chair. Methodically, and with infinite accuracy, he recited "Thanatopsis" in its entirety, including the punctuation. Then he drew a long breath and allowed himself to consider the situation.

The man in the chair opposite was Bennington Brett. There was no mistaking that pudgy discontented countenance that had faced him with unvarying sullenness in English classes throughout the upper and lower schools of Meredith's Academy. No mustache could ever hide the inherent weakness of that mouth.

Bennington, Leonidas decided after rapid calculations, was around thirty-five even though he looked at least forty-five. Since his graduation some eighteen years ago, Leonidas had seen him not more than half a dozen times. Casual meetings, all of them, at alumni reunions, once at a football game, once or twice in the lobby of the Parker House.

The mustachioed driver of the Ward Street roadster had been vaguely and elusively familiar. His identity had been clinched by the gold-lettered name on the pigskin wallet that Leonidas had flourished in the doctor's office, the wallet Cuff had found in the gutter. Bennington was the roadster's driver. Bennington had charged the car at him. Bennington had tried to kill him.

"Why?" Leonidas said to himself. "Why?"

That was a problem bordering on the mystical. It enchanted him. But now, with all the other pressing problems, it hardly seemed worthy of consideration.

How, for example, had Bennington Brett inserted himself here in this room, in the overstuffed chair? How, for that matter, had Leonidas himself arrived in *his* overstuffed chair? And when? And where, when you got right down to brass tacks, where was he anyway?

And then of course there was the most important problem of all, the problem that reduced the others to the status of trifles—who had thrust that knife into Bennington's chest?

Leonidas sighed. First of all, he must tell someone about Bennington.

Clearly, the police were indicated.

Leonidas sighed again. Perhaps it might have been better if he had not run away from the doctor's office. Perhaps the results would have been happier had he allowed himself to be held and questioned concerning Cuff's and Margie's theft of Gramma's silver, and Harry the doctor's best watch. Petit larceny, even grand larceny, was preferable to a charge of murder. And Leonidas owned to an increasingly profound feeling that no matter who happened to have killed Bennington Brett, he himself, Leonidas Witherall, would shortly be a leading candidate for the position of Suspect A. That was the way it always happened in books.

"I shall telephone the police," Leonidas told himself conscientiously. "At once. I have already done wrong in dallying. Certainly an hour, if not more."

It shocked him to discover that his wrist watch said six-nineteen. His dallying had consumed exactly four minutes, including "Thanatopsis" in its entirety, with all the punctuation!

His dutiful attempt to call the police was thwarted in its infancy.

The telephone cord, he discovered after a caustic and unproductive monologue to central, had been neatly sliced.

Setting down the receiver, Leonidas battled with his better judgment.

There was no reason why he should not let himself hurriedly out of the house. He had only to turn door handles to leave behind the whole horrible spectacle of Bennington Brett.

On the other hand, his low opinion of Bennington did not alter the fact that Bennington had been murdered. That to sneak away under the circumstances was cowardly. Not decent. Not— Leonidas searched for a word. Not cricket. To slink off, to skulk away, that was in itself an admission of guilt.

Besides, Leonidas had enough faith in police methods to feel that a hasty departure now might very possibly mean an implacable arrest later, with just so many more explanations to make.

This was no time to run.

This obviously was the time to use his head.

He reached for the telephone book. Before he

began to be embarrassed with questions, it might be well to find out a few answers.

Two minutes with the phone book were unusually profitable.

Bennington Brett lived at ninety-five Paddock Street, Dalton Hills. His number was Dalton Hills 4334. The number on the disk at the base of the phone before him was Dalton Hills 4334. The completion of the simple syllogism gave Leonidas his bearings. He was at ninety-five Paddock Street, Dalton Hills, at Bennington Brett's own house.

Another Brett, Leonidas noticed, was listed as living at ninety-five Paddock Street, and the discovery relieved his mind. It was not Bennington's house after all. It belonged to his uncle, August Barker Brett, a worthy, well-known and reasonable man. Leonidas knew him slightly; occasionally they nodded to each other across the length of an Athenaeum reading room. Their discussions were invariably literary or political, and had never included the topic of Bennington. But Leonidas remembered hearing mutual friends admit with sadness that Bennington was a Trial to his uncle. Some had even gone so far as to call him A Damn Bitter Pill.

Bitter pill or not, Leonidas doubted if the discovery that Bennington had been murdered would be other than painful news to August Barker. But August Barker, being a reasonable and logical man, could understand and appreciate the awkwardness of Leonidas's position. Armed with August Barker's knowledge and understanding, and of course with his prestige, Leonidas felt that he would be better equipped to cope with the Dalton police.

Leonidas set off upstairs to find August and awake him and tell him all.

The house was larger than he expected. By the time he had knocked tentatively at the doors of three empty and unoccupied bedrooms, Leonidas began to have qualms as to whether or not he would find August Barker there.

The fourth bedroom, to judge from the pictures of young, comely women strewn about, was Bennington's. The last room, empty and a little dusty, was without doubt August Barker's. The comfortable red leather chair, the copies of the "Atlantic" and "Harper's" on the table beside the bed, the Dickens prints on the wall, all of them indicated the occupancy of Uncle August.

But Uncle August was elsewhere.

A typewritten sheet of paper, thrust into the mirror frame on the bureau, suddenly caught Leonidas's attention. He walked over and read it, and sighed, and read it again.

February 15-28	Visiting Forster. Palm Beach.
March 1-12	Miraflores. St. Augustine.
March 13-30	Visiting Campbell. St. Peters-
	burg.

In case this schedule is changed, I shall let you know. Either Forster or Campbell can always find me. Miss Tring has both numbers at the office. Consult her before calling me. She has her instructions.

So August Barker was in Florida. Enjoying balmy breezes, unlimited orange juice, and complete freedom from his office, where Miss Tring undoubtedly carried on in a most efficient manner, having had her instructions.

Leonidas walked over to the window and looked out over Paddock Street.

Born and bred in the city, Leonidas barely tolerated the country. For the suburbs, like Dalton, he admitted a hearty scorn. It seemed to him that suburbs combined all the inconveniences of the country, including its inaccessibility, with the more unattractive aspects of the city, including its dirt and to a certain extent its congestion.

Nothing, he thought, could be much more unattractive than Paddock Street at six-thirty of a March morning fresh with the chill of an embittered New England dawn. Heaps of week before last's snow clogged the gutters. A northeast wind bent the scrawny young maples so mathematically set out at twenty foot intervals. Disconsolate ash barrels awaited Dalton's Department of Sanitation. A tired looking dog walked along the gravel sidewalk, sniffing hopefully at each barrel.

Leonidas tried hard not to notice Paddock Street's architecture, but he couldn't help himself. Apparently the builders of Paddock Street had made up their minds that here would be no street of identical houses. Here, things would be different. And with a fine disregard for the limitations of an eighty-five foot frontage, they had made Paddock Street different. From the window, whether you cared to see them or not, were two imitation Colonial houses, two brick and stucco and lathed edifices of bastard English origin, one early American building with practically no windows except a few diamond-paned things, and a starved cement building bound with chromium and laced with glass brick.

"I hope," Leonidas said with great sincerity, "I hope that Frank Lloyd Wright is never forced to look on Paddock Street!"

He could not be sure, but from what was visible of number ninety-five, Leonidas suspected that it had once been advertised as Brick Georgian Modified.

Leonidas turned away from the window.

He simply had to tell the police about Bennington Brett. At once. Instantly!

What, he wondered, would be the reactions of the occupants of the starved cement building when he rang their doorbell and asked them please to report a murder? Would they have a doorbell, or had they gone whole hog in their pseudo-modernity and installed a photo-electric beam arrangement for visitors to walk into?

Curiously, he glanced out of the window. The modern house, he was charmed to note, had a wrought-iron door knocker shaped like Mickey Mouse. It—

Leonidas leaned forward suddenly. A girl was crouching between the ash barrels in front of the white Colonial house. Further along the street, in front of one of the English models, wandered a thickset man with a broadbrimmed felt hat pulled down over his face.

He wandered along till he came directly opposite ninety-five, then he stood and studied the outside of the house intently. He was watched in turn by the girl, who peered around the corner of the barrels like a child waiting for an unguarded base in hide and seek.

The man teetered back and forth on his heels. Once he started across the street, then he returned and continued his meditative study of ninety-five.

Unobserved, the girl crept from her hiding place and disappeared down the driveway of the Colonial house.

Almost at once, the thickset man crossed the street and mounted the steps of ninety-five. The bell rang. Slowly, Leonidas went down to the front door. The thickset man, he kept thinking to himself, looked like all the detectives in the world rolled into one.

"Here," Leonidas murmured, "here I go!"

Before the door had opened six inches, the thickset man thrust a folded paper in his hand.

"I wonder if—" Leonidas began.

But the thickset man suddenly snatched the paper away from Leonidas, muttered something, and ran hurriedly down the steps.

"Wait!" Leonidas said. "Come back here—"

The man paid no attention. Like a frightened rabbit, he scuttled down Paddock Street and out of sight.

Leonidas shut the door.

The suburbs might be unattractive, but you could not say that they lacked either action or surprises.

"The best features," Leonidas said, "of E. Phillips Oppenheim with the general characteristics of a psychopathic ward—my, my!"

Facing him in the living room was the same girl he had seen crouching between the barrels a moment before.

In her hand she held a gun, and the gun was pointed at what any babe would concede to be Leonidas's most vulnerable spot.

"Put up your hands! Oh, don't you look like— I said, put up your hands!"

"M'yes," Leonidas said, "I do resemble Shakespeare, don't I? D'you mind if I put on my pince-nez? I can't really see you without them—m'yes, you are the ash barrel girl, aren't you? Don't you find it cold?"

"Find what cold?" the girl said. "And put your hands up, Shakespeare!"

"Groveling around ash barrels." Leonidas complied with her order. "Chacun à son gout, and all that, but I should personally never feel that playing ring-around-the-rosy with Paddock Street's ash barrels was the ideal, soul-satisfying existence. Possibly I wrong you. Possibly it is a project?"

"Keep your hands up!" the girl said. "What is possibly a project?"

"Barrel groveling— May I lower my left hand? I'd quite forgotten, but it's semi-sprained. Yes, indeed, considering some of the projects I've witnessed and others I've read about, I suppose barrel ducking is not an extreme. Er—my interest is impersonal, but I trust that the salary compensates for the early rising—"

"Look here!" the girl sounded very angry, "what *is* the meaning of all this? What are you talking about? What are you doing—"

"I'm trying," Leonidas said politely, "to carry on a pleasant conversation in the face of almost insurmountable odds. With many questions pricking my mind, with a throbbing wrist, with your hand cuddling the trigger of that weapon you've aimed so directly at me, with Bennington Brett dead in that chair —frankly, I marvel at my composure, Miss Tring."

"How did you know my name? How did you know who I am?"

"I guessed," Leonidas told her modestly. "Your efficiency, you know. You pretty much had to be Miss Tring, or one of Bennington's comely young women. You're very comely, of course, but I didn't feel that one of Bennington's friends would be capable of holding a gun so steadily. I feel they would have shot or fainted by now. And I'm sure they wouldn't have recognized Shakespeare. Miss Tring, what is the most efficient method of informing the police that they have a murder to deal with? I have been trying to break the news—"

"Why did you kill Benny?"

"My dear young woman," Leonidas said, "I didn't. I simply happened to be here. I—"

"Were you here when Benny called me twenty minutes ago?"

Leonidas looked at his wrist watch. It was ten minutes to seven.

"Were you?" Miss Tring demanded. "He called me—said he was in trouble, and for me to come over here at once."

"Did he," Leonidas said, "indeed."

The girl looked at him sharply.

"Shakespeare," she said, "march over to that phone and call the police!"

"I'm sorry," Leonidas returned, "I can't. The telephone wire has been cut. But for that fact, I should have summoned the police myself, long ago. Er—d'you always carry a gun, Miss Tring? Or only when Bennington summons you?"

Miss Tring flushed. "Who are you, anyway?"

Leonidas told her. "Do I gather," he added, "that you have perhaps had—er—trouble with Benny in the past?"

"Trouble!" Miss Tring's knuckles were white as she gripped the chair back with her left hand. "Trouble! That—that utter louse! Not—not even the sight of him there makes me feel any pity! I—I'm glad he's dead, d'you hear me? I'm glad!"

Dropping the revolver, Miss Tring pulled off her hat, flung herself on the couch, and burst out crying.

Leonidas rather absently picked up the gun and put it in his pocket. He had never for a moment believed that the comely Miss Tring intended to use him as a target, but firearms in the hands of a woman were at best foreboding. One never knew. There had been that strikingly beautiful White Russian who ran amuck on the "Princess of Asia," for example. He would never forget her, standing there on A deck among the shuffleboard players, with a gun in either hand. It turned out she was a practicing anarchist, and ambidextrous to boot.

Miss Tring's sobs were beginning to subside. Leonidas offered her his handkerchief, and she mopped at her face and eyes.

"Er—you came in the back way, I suppose," he said conversationally. "You had the keys, perhaps?"

"Yes—oh, Mr. Witherall, if you killed Benny, you had reasons for it! I—I don't know anyone who knew him who didn't. Only we endured him because of his uncle—Mr. Witherall, go on. Go. Beat it. Before I change my mind and turn you over to the police as I ought to. I've got money in my bag—I was bringing it for Benny. Mr. Brett always leaves me an emergency fund to get Benny out of scrapes—take it, and go. Get a western bus out on the pike, and keep changing—hurry, take my bag, and go!"

"Oh, no," Leonidas said. "Oh, my, no. I mean, that's very nice of you, but of course I can't go."

"Why not? You had your reasons for killing him, and—well, I'm glad! That sounds awful, I know. It sounds beastly and cold blooded and inhuman. But my best friend happened to commit suicide last year because of Benny Brett. She's not the only girl he's—look, Mr. Witherall, take that money and go! You killed him, but you—"

"But I didn't kill him," Leonidas said. "He was

there in the chair, quite dead, when I waked up at quarter after six, you know."

"What! But he phoned me! Just a few minutes before six-thirty. My alarm had just started to go off!"

"I've no doubt someone phoned you," Leonidas said. "But not Bennington. Definitely not Bennington, Miss Tring. Are—did it seem to you that it was unquestionably Bennington, at the time?"

She hesitated.

"Well," she said, "he just sounded drunk. I really didn't stop to think, much, about his voice. He's so often drunk. I just leapt into my clothes and grabbed the emergency fund, and my gun—"

"Ah, yes," Leonidas said. "That gun. M'yes."

"If you," Miss Tring said bitterly, "had ever had any experience with Benny Brett in a drunk, you'd carry a gun yourself. A gun and a chair, like a lion-tamer. That's what! Anyway, when I came up the street, I noticed this man prowling around the house, so I sneaked in the back way. The last time I came here with emergency funds, the man prowling around outside turned out to be the owner of a dog Benny had run over for fun."

"Indeed," Leonidas said softly. "Indeed."

"The man," Miss Tring said, "was only a cut above Benny. He really didn't care about the dog, he only wanted money. But the money saved Benny a good beating. I was rather sorry I'd been so quick in getting here. But, Mr. Witherall, if Benny didn't call me, who did?"

Leonidas shrugged.

"Dalton," he said, "is like that. Dalton, the Garden City, the Suburban Paradise, the City of Charming Homes and Happy Laughing Families—really, Dalton amazes me. If I were to tell you my experiences in Dalton since twelve o'clock last night, you frankly would not believe them. Neither will the police. Er— should you care to have me sum up the incidents?"

Crisply, he told her about the charging roadster on Ward Street, about Cuff and Margie, and the alley cat and the fish balls, about the doctor named Harry, and the theft of Gramma's silver and Harry's best watch.

"Shakespeare!" Miss Tring said. "Shakespeare in a pig's eye! Ananias. Marco Polo. Baron Munchausen—"

"Ah," Leonidas said, "but I'm not through. There was the sedan on the turnpike. That also ran me down, though without malice—"

"I see," Miss Tring said. "Just a friendly little bump, that time. What did that do to you?"

Leonidas shook his head.

"I don't know," he said. "I don't know. It seems to me that I spent the night in this overstuffed chair, right here. All the evidence points to that. At six-fifteen I awaked to find Bennington opposite me. Whether Bennington preceded me or not, I don't know. We may have arrived simultaneously. I—"

"You may," Miss Tring said thoughtfully, "even have thrust that knife into Bennington in your dazed condition. You—"

Leonidas sighed. "That point of view," he said, "is unworthy of you. It is, nevertheless, the opinion I fear the police will prefer to hold. Dear me, the police! We *should* summon the police at once. We really must, you know. Immediately!"

Miss Tring agreed that they should. "Only let's clear up what we can before they plunge into things with both feet. After all, I'm going to be involved in this, too, what with that phone call. I—oh! Oh, I just remembered! Oh, Mr. Witherall, this is simply awful!"

"I've thought so all along," Leonidas said.

"I don't mean this—I mean, yesterday. Mr. Witherall, yesterday in the presence of witnesses, I offered to slice Bennington like an onion, if he didn't stop bothering me. In fact, I said something about cutting his heart out!"

"That is unfortunate," Leonidas said. "Er—Miss Tring, how do you reconcile your general attitude about Bennington with the solicitous manner in which you rush around with emergency funds, and all?"

"But that's my job!" Miss Tring said. "Mr. Brett pays me extra for it! You don't think I'd—I'd—wet-nurse Benny Brett, do you, if I weren't being paid for it? If it didn't more or less mean my job? Don't be silly, Mr. Witherall. My job as August Barker Brett's private secretary depends very largely on how indispensable I am. Jobs these days don't grow on trees. But of course," she surveyed his well-cut dark gray suit, "you wouldn't know that! You—"

"My dear child," Leonidas interrupted feelingly, "I do! I spend three afternoons a week in Bellweather's

Rare Book Store, smoking a pipe which I abhor, just to provide literary atmosphere. And incidentally to pay for my board. Why, in the last six years I've been a janitor, a brush salesman, a floorwalker, a baker's assistant—really, Miss Tring—"

"Call me Dallas, Bill Shakespeare!" she grinned at him. "You might as well. We're going to see this thing through together, apparently, and besides—"

"Really, Dallas," Leonidas said, "I assure you, I understand about Bennington. I used to walk the French poodle of the baker's wife for much the same goal of indispensability. My child, we must call the police!"

"We must," Dallas said, "but I sort of dread the thought. Look, d'you know who that burly gent was, the one prowling around outside just now?"

"He rang the bell," Leonidas told her, "and when I opened the door, he thrust a paper into my hand. Then he whipped it out of my grasp and fled. Really, this is a remarkable town—"

"What's that?" Dallas broke in.

"What is what?"

"Listen, I hear—yes, listen! From the cellar! There's a noise from the cellar— Mr. Witherall, I do believe there's someone down there in the cellar!"

"I shouldn't wonder," Leonidas said. "I shouldn't wonder a bit. There is simply no restraint in this city of Dalton, no limit—"

"Listen, Mr. Witherall! Someone's groaning down there!"

Chapter THREE

LEONIDAS followed her along a hallway into the kitchen, where Dallas nervously pointed to a door.

"That goes to the cellar," she said. "Come on and —oh, *listen* to those awful muffled groans, Shakespeare! They make my blood run cold—why, that's funny! That's odd!"

Leonidas assured her gravely that nothing, at that point, was either odd or funny.

"I don't mean odd, I mean—well, significant—that door isn't bolted. You can't understand how important that is. August Barker Brett has a sort of phobia about unlocked doors. So has Benny. The two of them drive me frantic at the office, always slamming the safe shut, and locking their desk drawers and the clothes closet—this unbolted door *means* something, don't you think?"

"M'yes," Leonidas opened the door, "possibly. At least it means that the general public had an unparalleled opportunity to enter the house at will and roam throughout at random—do you still hear those groans?"

"They've stopped," Dallas said. "Try the game room on the left—"

The cellar of the Brett house startled Leonidas, whose experience as a janitor had included nothing so fancy. The gay scarlet gas furnace that purred so contentedly in the corner contrasted vividly with the sooty object into whose hungry maw he had hurled so many tons of bituminous coal.

Set into the linoleum floor of the game room were a dozen different game markings. A ping-pong table occupied one side; a small but complete bar occupied the other.

Nowhere was there any sight or sound of the groaning person.

"Benny was here last night," Dallas said. "See the glasses? And there's some of his pornographic literature. Positively Victorian, the way that fellow enjoyed pornography and sniggered over it—Shakespeare, where's the groaner?"

As she spoke, the groans began again.

"They sound," Leonidas said, "as though they came from the furnace—"

"From the preserve room—" Dallas corrected him. "That's a sort of storage room," she went on to explain, "for groceries and preserves and things. It's shut off from the cellar to keep it cool. Someone's in there —listen—"

"Brett!" It was a man's voice, and it sounded intensely angry. "Brett, damn your soul!"

Something crashed against the wall and broke.

"He's throwing glass jars!" Dallas said. "We—"

"Brett!" the man was in a fuming, towering rage now. "Brett, damn your dirty hide, come in here and let me out of this hell hole! You let me out, or I'll cut you to ribbons! This time, by God, I'll finish the job, do you hear me?"

Leonidas and the girl exchanged glances.

"Hear that?" Dallas said. "*This* time he's going to finish the job!"

"This," Leonidas said softly, "is Cut-Benny-Brett-into-Small-Pieces Week. Obviously."

"Brett!" the man yelled, "I hear you there! I hear you! You let me out, or I'll start a fire and burn your bloody house around your ears! And when I lay hands on you, I'm going to smash you—like that!"

A series of preserve jars shattered against the wall, forcefully illustrating the man's point.

"If I were Benny Brett," Leonidas observed, "I should not be at all moved to let that wild man out, I'm sure. The very thought of releasing the gentleman would be repugnant."

"Brett, you stinker!"

In something more nearly resembling conversational tones, the man in the preserve closet proceeded to sum up his opinion of Bennington Brett. His conclusions would not have been accepted for transportation by the United States mails. They were slanderous, scurrilous and exceedingly libelous. But without doubt, Leonidas reflected, the man knew Benny.

"Have you got my gun?" Dallas whispered.

Leonidas presented it to her, but she shook her head.

◄§ 45 §►

"Oh, you take it! I don't want it. I'm scared to death of it!"

"So am I," Leonidas said, and returned it to his pocket.

With an amazing display of nonchalance, he turned the spring lock and opened the door to the preserve room.

Within stood a disheveled young man in a mussed dinner jacket. He looked at Leonidas, then he looked quickly away and groaned.

"I will never again mix beer, champagne and whiskey," he said. "I will never again mix beer, champagne and whiskey. I will never again mix beer, champagne and whiskey. I will never again—"

"A laudable decision," Leonidas said. "Very. Er—what exactly do you do here, may I ask?"

The young man opened his mouth and screamed. "My God, it talks!"

"Certainly I talk," Leonidas said. "And may I ask what you are doing in—"

"It talks!" the young man said unhappily. "It clears its throat and talks! I've seen menageries in my day, but never before a Shakespeare. A Shakespeare that talks. With a beautiful girl by his side. If you talk, beautiful, I'm going right straight over to that gas furnace and end it all!"

"You needn't," Dallas said. "And as for talking, you'd better talk yourself. What are you doing in that preserve room?"

"If you think I like it," the young man returned, "you're mistaken. I've been yearning to come out of the place for some time—where is that louse Benny Brett? Benny is the lad I crave to see. I am going to do a job on Benny—"

"Look, Mr. Witherall!" Dallas pointed to the floor. "Look—blood! Blood trickling—"

"It's not blood, beautiful, it's tomato juice," the young man said. "I stabbed a can open with that fork—after all, you certainly can't begrudge a man a snack of tomato juice—what's the matter, Will Shakespeare? What are you two staring at? If a little spilled tomato juice makes you blanch, I'll mop it up—"

Yanking a white silk scarf from his pocket, he mopped away at the tomato juice.

But Leonidas and Dallas continued to stare at the bone handled carving fork on the floor.

Its handle unquestionably matched that of the knife which had been used to stab Bennington Brett. And usually, Leonidas thought, when you had a carving knife and a carving fork belonging to the same identical set, you kept them in a set, in close conjunction.

"That fork! It's—look," Dallas broke off in some irritation, "will you stop ruining that perfectly good scarf with tomato juice? It's so silly of you to mess—"

The young man promptly stuffed the stained and dripping scarf back into his pocket.

"Certainly," he said. "At once. My intentions were sterling. I thought I was removing an ugly and offensive trickle from the sight of your lovely brown eyes—they are lovely, you know, Miss—er—um—" he looked accusingly at Leonidas. "You didn't introduce us, you know, Shakespeare. No dramatis personae. Not even a hint."

"My name is Witherall," Leonidas said. "This is Miss Tring. Now perhaps you will—"

"Tring? Oh, no! Not Tring!"

"Why not?" Dallas demanded with asperity. "What's the matter with Tring?"

"Basically, I suppose it's a fine name. But to foist a surname like that on anyone as seraphic as you! Why, you ought to be called Angela Divine, or something—not Tring! Miss Tring. I suppose everyone calls you Miss String, don't they? Say—say! You're not the Miss String that Charley Hobbs was telling me about last night? The beautiful Miss String who pasted Benny Brett in the eye on Maple Street yesterday, and offered to slice him like an onion? Are you *that* Miss String?"

"It wasn't Maple Street," Dallas told him hotly. "It was at the corner of Oak and Centre, by the drug store. And I didn't paste him, I just slapped his face! And why Charley Hobbs has any reason to bandy my name around—"

"Er—I wonder," Leonidas said, "if we might momentarily shelve that incident, while this gentleman breaks down to the extent of telling us who he is, and exactly what his business here may be?"

"Why, I'm Stanton Kaye."

The young man paused, apparently waiting for recognition. When none was forthcoming, he turned a little pink; it was the first time, Leonidas reflected, that Mr. Kaye's magnificent poise had even so much as wavered.

Hastily, Stanton Kaye enlarged on his statement.

"I'm an awfully nice fellow, really, you know. Charley Hobbs'll vouch for me, Miss Tring. Of course, Benny would too, but that's not much of a vouch. Anyway, us Kayes are a fine old Dalton family, a fine old Dalton name. Brother runs the bank, and Sister runs the Elliott Club and I run the factory—strictly union, strictly union! We—look, something's wrong here. The Kayes are all psychic, you know. We sniff out trouble like a pack of truffle hounds. What's wrong?"

"If you would turn your psychic powers, Mr. Kaye," Leonidas said, "toward telling us how you got here, and what you're doing here? And how long you've been here?"

Something in Leonidas's voice made Stanton Kaye scrutinize his face. Then he sat down on an unopened case of evaporated milk.

"You've touched me," he said, "on my most vulnerable spot. Shall I begin at the beginning—way back there at the beginning, around nine o'clock last night?"

"Please," Leonidas said. "And—er—do be brief, won't you, Mr. Kaye? There is a very vital matter to which Miss Tring and I should attend without delay. We have delayed too long as it is."

The thought that as yet nothing had been done in an official way about Bennington was beginning to haunt Leonidas.

"Last night at nine o'clock," Mr. Kaye began, "I was sitting in my study reading the HYDR to JERE volume of the Encyclopaedia Britannica. Specifically, I was looking up Ischl. That is—"

"A spa in what was formerly Upper Austria," Leonidas said.

Kaye looked mildly surprised. "Yes. Brother and I had quibbled about the spelling—well, to get on, the phone rang, and it was Benny, and he wanted me to dash over here at once on a matter of life and death. He—what did you say?"

"I coughed," Leonidas said.

"I thought you said something. Well, I told Benny to go to hell. He was tight, and once in a big-hearted moment I helped Benny out of a scrape, and I never want to repeat the performance. And then Brother phoned and asked if I'd forgotten Bob Colley's bachelor dinner, and I had, so I got dressed and went. And at intervals, the club bellhops kept tramping in to tell me that Mr. Benny Brett wanted me on the phone on a matter of life and death. Finally I went out and talked to him—"

"Over the phone, of course," Leonidas said.

"Yes. It was—oh, near one o'clock, I guess, by then. Benny said I must come over at once, he positively had to see me on a matter of the greatest importance to me, and of life and death to him. He whimpered so—you know," Kaye said thoughtfully, "Benny usually becomes increasingly blotto as the night wears on, but last night he was more sober around one than when I spoke with him at nine. That, and his whimpering, sort of moved me. I gave in and said I'd drop in on my way home. He said for me to come to the back cellar door. He would be waiting for me in the game room. I was glad enough to use a back door, because—well, that part doesn't matter. I came—"

"You—er—drove, yourself?" Leonidas inquired.

"In my state? No. That dinner had started off calmly enough, but it worked up to a terrific pitch. I paid a bellhop to drive me to the next street and lead me here. He was going to leave the car parked and take a bus home from the pike. I tottered in and yelled for Benny. The game room was empty, and the door to this place was open, so I came in, and the door slammed. Benny's idea of a lovely, lovely joke, that was. And when I find Benny—look, it's Friday morning, isn't it? I mean, I haven't been Rip Van Winkling, have I?"

"It's Friday," Leonidas said. "At least—dear me, it *is* Friday, isn't it, Dallas?"

"Dallas?" Kaye said. "Dallas Tring. Oh, how awful! Well, anyway, I just bowed to the inevitable and went to sleep with my head cradled on a bag of onions. I'm now pretty damn mad about the whole thing. Benny—"

"You saw him, I suppose," Leonidas said.

"Well, no. But the door—oh, you mean it's a spring lock, and I might have locked myself in. Yes, I might have. But knowing Benny, I doubt that very much. Where is the—"

"This fork, here," Leonidas said. "You—er—brought that with you?"

"That? Oh, no. That was here. Benny'd been having a snack—see the sardines and crackers over on the shelf? Gorging himself while he waited to play his perfectly hilarious little joke on old Comrade Kaye."

"So," Leonidas said, "you do not recall actually seeing Benny. M'yes. What, exactly, did you mean, Mr. Kaye, when you yelled things about finishing the job on Benny? You yelled quite a lot about it, if you remember."

"My sister Persis," Kaye said, "is not beautiful, like Dallas. She's quite plain. But she's rather nice. Several months ago I convinced Benny that he would be wise not to repeat a rather foul story he made up about her. I thumped him very thoroughly—"

"Were you the newel post that blacked both his eyes?" Dallas asked. "You were! I forgive you, Mr. Kaye, your cracks about my name. I've wanted to meet the man who gave Benny those shiners."

"I've got a swell left," Kaye said modestly. "If you have anyone you'd like me to demonstrate on, just you point out the lad. Always delighted to be of service, any time. Will Shakespeare, where does all this lead us? You know my story. You know how I landed here. Now—I do hate to bring this up, but what the hell do you and beautiful do here, yourselves? What's the root of all these questions? And these furtive looks? You know, if you both weren't so eminently respectable looking, there'd be something sinister about it all."

"Perhaps," Leonidas said, "you'd best come upstairs, Mr. Kaye. I think that is the simpler way to explain the situation."

Kaye looked steadily at him.

"I have," he said, "a horrid premonition. A horrid, horrid premonition. To quote you, Shakespeare, 'By the pricking of my thumbs, something wicked this way comes—' and my thumbs are pricking. They really are."

Upstairs in the living room, Kaye looked at the body of Bennington Brett for several minutes before he spoke.

"You know," he said at last, "I am responsible for that. The poor devil meant what he said. It really was a matter of life and death. I—I'm sorry. Yes," he turned to Dallas, "you needn't sniff. I mean it. I'm sorry. I can't think, offhand, of any virtues Benny possessed, but at least he had a right to live. I should have known last night from the way he whimpered that he was honestly frightened—Shakespeare, this is —this is bad!"

Leonidas nodded as he put on his pince-nez.

"I was here," Kaye went on. "Everyone at the club and at Colley's dinner knows I was coming here. The bellhop who drove me knows it. Everyone knows. And they all know what I think of Benny. And they all heard me say what I'd do to Benny if this was a false alarm." He made a little gesture toward the figure in the chair. "I didn't kill him. But the police—"

"I share," Leonidas said, "to an even greater extent, the same boat."

Briefly, he summed up his story for Kaye.

"Cool You were here, up here? You!"

"I don't see why you both leave me out of it," Dallas said. "I had as much of an incentive to kill him as either of you. I had the back door key. I was in my apartment from ten-thirty last night until Benny—or somebody—telephoned me this morning. But no one could prove it. And with all I told Benny on the corner of Oak and Centre—well, there we are!"

"M'yes," Leonidas remarked, "here we are indeed." He sighed. "Now, my children, we must summon the police. It occurs to me that the longer we wait, the worse this gets to be. I'll go to the house next door and tele—"

"Wait," Kaye interrupted. "Don't you feel we ought to delve a little first? Shouldn't we—"

"My dear Mr. Kaye," Leonidas said, "we've done nothing but delve for well over an hour. That sort of thing will not appeal to the police. Not at all."

"But these stories of ours! They're so—so—"

"Nebulous?" Leonidas suggested.

"I was thinking," Kaye said, "of ethereal. But nebulous will do. My God, they're haywire! It's all haywire! And look—about the lights in the cellar. Did you turn them out?"

Leonidas shook his head.

"Well," Kaye said, "someone must have. Because the whole cellar was lighted up like a four-alarm fire when I came. That was how the bellhop and I found the place."

"It was dark when I came," Dallas said. "I circled around the house, and it was murky enough then so that I'd have noticed. Well, at least we know that someone left the cellar doors unlocked, and put the cellar lights out. That's something."

Leonidas smiled. "I doubt," he said, "if the police will consider those simple facts to be sufficient justification for our delay in informing them—"

"Wow," Kaye said softly. "Wow!"

"What's the matter?" Dallas demanded.

He pointed at the knife handle.

"That's the other part of the set that the fork downstairs belongs to! No wonder you made gentle inquiries with your eyebrows raised. Oh, that's torn it, Bill Shakespeare. That's done it! I might just as well call Minsky over at the 'Dalton Daily Bugle' and have him bring over his candid camera and start taking shots of the Dalton Blueblood Found with Murder Fork in Preserve Closet after Wild Party. I am—oh, God! Nothing can be any worse than this."

"I don't know," Leonidas said. "I keep pondering. Suppose a policeman were to ring the bell and demand entrance. And find us standing here. Just standing here, having taken no active steps about this situation. I am inclined to believe that would make this seem like—er—"

"Like the good old days," Kaye said.

Dallas shivered. "I—I'm afraid, all of a sudden," she said. "I think I'm just beginning to realize what this all means. If the doorbell should happen to ring, Bill Shakespeare, I should collapse into a dismal heap!"

Almost before she finished speaking, the doorbell pealed.

All three of them jumped at the sound.

"I'll go," Kaye said. "Let me—"

"Perhaps," Leonidas said, "it might be better if I went. Er—it's just possible that your dinner jacket might create a more unfavorable impression than my mussed suit—"

Firmly affixing his pince-nez, Leonidas started for the front hall. But Dallas stopped him.

"As far as impressions go," she said, "I think I'll do better than either of you. I'm the most presentable, even if I did dive into my clothes like a fire horse. Let me—"

"She's right, Bill Shakespeare," Kaye said. "If I was a cop, I'd rather meet her than you or me. Go ahead—"

Dallas stepped into the hall, hesitated a second, and then flung open the door.

Facing her on the top step was the same burly man she had seen prowling around the house on her arrival.

He half thrust a paper at her, then jerked it back, and started down the steps.

"Hey, you!" Dallas said. "Wait—wait! What's the big idea?"

But the burly gent fled down Paddock Street with the same amazing speed Leonidas had told her about.

Dallas stared after him blankly.

Then she went back into the living room and reported.

"It was the doorbell ringer," she announced. "Your doorbell ringer, Bill Shakespeare. He didn't like me either. He gave me one look and then streamed away like a comet. Bill, can you fit him into this picture anywhere?"

"Dear me," Leonidas said, "he is strange, isn't he? I wonder if he's a Dalton custom, perhaps?"

"They only ring bells in Dalton at Christmas," Dallas said. "Except for the children at Halloween. That doesn't help—"

"I mean a custom, like the Daltonville Hospital's endowed geraniums for all patients with broken legs," Leonidas explained. "Professor Otis was telling me about that last night. And about the city caller, who calls on newcomers—perhaps this is the city caller, though I'm sure he looks more like someone from the district attorney's office—"

The bell pealed again.

"The hell with my rumpled shirt front," Kaye said. "This time I go—"

Dallas and Leonidas waited for him.

"Mr. Kaye," Leonidas remarked after several minutes had passed, "seems to be carrying on quite a conversation."

"Mr. Kaye," Dallas returned, "would. He—Bill Shakespeare, he's letting someone in here!"

A middle-aged, motherly looking woman with startling white hair swept into the living room.

Automatically, Dallas noticed the expensive simplicity of her print dress and dark-blue coat. Those weren't any stylish stouts from a department store rack. Dallas knew good clothes when she saw them.

Leonidas, after a puzzled look at her face, noticed the empty cup the woman carried in her left hand, the white tissue paper wrapped package tied with cherry-colored ribbon in her right.

"This is the one," the woman spoke over her shoulder to Kaye. "This is the one, Mr. Kaye. He's the one I ran over. Shakespeare. Good morning, Mr. Shakespeare, how do you feel? This is some calves'-foot jelly for you—oh, no. That's the empty cup, isn't it? How silly of me. That's what I want to borrow a cup of sugar in. This is the calves'-foot—the calves'-foot—"

Her eyes fixed on Bennington Brett.

"I *tried* to tell you, Mrs. Price," Kaye said. "You can't say I didn't try! I told you some fifty thousand times that you'd be sorry if you came in here! I tried to implant the thought, God knows! I said you'd be sorry!"

Mrs. Price sat down very suddenly on the couch.

"Poor Benny," she said at last.

Then she got up and faced Stanton Kaye.

"You told me I'd be sorry," she said, "but you never said a thing about his being killed with my best carving knife!"

Chapter FOUR

IN unison, as though they had been rehearsing for months, Kaye and Dallas gasped.

Only Leonidas retained his composure at Mrs. Price's statement.

"Dalton the jovial, Dalton the hospitable," he murmured appreciatively, quoting the Chamber of Commerce booklet he had read at Professor Otis's. "Dalton the invigorating, whose very atmosphere buoys you up and never lets you down. My, my, how true! Er—Mrs. Price, do I understand that you are one of that vast army who ran over me last night?"

"I didn't really run you *over*," Mrs. Price said. "It was just a bump. The bumper hit your head. You see, the doctor said I had to, I simply *had* to. So—"

"I see," Leonidas said drily. "A pedestrian a day keeps the doctor away. Er—doubtless the doctor had good reasons for such a prescription, but don't you feel it's rather hard on passersby, on the innocent bystanders?"

"Oh, dear, I don't mean that!" Mrs. Price said hastily. "He meant the bifocals. He said I just simply had to gird my loins and wear them, all the time. But every time I do, something happens. Last week, I went right *through* the bakery kitchen display window at Peirce's. Right through! And it was lemon pie day. And then I bumped Sergeant Muir—those white raincoats are so deceptive! And that Italian's pushcart. And—well, you can see why I was so glad to find you so amiable, last night. My brother said, *next* time anything happened, he'd jail me as an example, bifocals or no bifocals! And—"

"Wait!" Kaye said. "Wait—boy, oh, boy, I've just remembered! Mrs. Price, have a seat—oh, you are seated? Well, have a cigar. Take off your hat. Let me get you a footstool—Mrs. Price, isn't your brother, Rutherford B. Carpenter, the chief of police?"

Mrs. Price nodded.

"Yes, he used to be a colonel of marines, and after he left the service, he was so unhappy! And Cabot Martin—he's the mayor, you know—offered him the police, and really, the police has done Rutherford a whole world of good. He—"

"I'm sure," Kaye said, "he just laughs and sings from dawn till night, no lark more blithe than he. Shakespeare, isn't this heartening?"

"More heartening than you imagine," Leonidas said. "Mrs. Price, about that bump last night. I—er —was so amiable?"

"Indeed you were! And you can see, with what Rutherford threatened me, how delighted I was— won't you have some of the calves'-foot jelly, Mr. Shakespeare? It's quite good. I didn't make it, it was given to me when I had the grippe. I can't abide the stuff myself, but I knew that someone would—I wonder," Mrs. Price said thoughtfully, "I wonder what Rutherford will do about that being my knife. He'll be sure to recognize it. He gave it to me last Christmas, and he made such a fuss about the initialing—you can't see the initialing, but he fussed about it, anyway."

"Mrs. Price," Kaye said, "you fill me with new spirit. It's like finding someone who's had appendicitis that you haven't told about your appendix to yet. How did the knife get—"

Leonidas cleared his throat.

"D'you mind, Kaye," he said, "if I find out about myself, first? What happened after the bump, Mrs. Price, and my amiability?"

"Why, you came to—as a matter of fact, I don't really think you were unconscious. And you waved a wallet at me, and the wallet said Bennington Brett on it, and you had a key, too. You said, ever so pleasantly, that you had to see Bennington Brett right away, and for me not to bother a bit about you—oh, yes, you said particularly that you didn't want me to notify the police. Something about leeches and Harry's watch—I didn't quite understand that part. But I was so relieved to find you so amiable and thoughtful—"

"You were out on your feet, Shakespeare," Kaye said. "It happened to me once in football. I answered all the doctor's questions and played like a demon, and I had to read the papers next day to find out what'd happened."

Leonidas nodded. "I feel you're right. And then, Mrs. Price?"

"Why, I brought you here," Mrs. Price said simply. "In the car. I live next door."

"See?" Kaye said. "She lives next door! My God, if I were to wake up under the table with the rest of Bob Colley's friends, I wouldn't be a bit surprised! She lives next door. Just like that!"

"He wanted to come!" Mrs. Price said. "He said, he didn't mind how late it was—"

"D'you recall the time?"

"Around half-past one, I think," Mrs. Price said. "Thursday's pre-view night at the Lyceum—you see that week's two features, and then the next week's two features, and they were all terribly long. That's how I happened to have on the bifocals. I thought I might get used to them if I watched four pictures."

"Mrs. P.," Kaye said, "versus her bifocals, to a decision. How did Bill Shakespeare get in here?"

"Why, with the key he had. He opened the door and went in. I don't understand," Mrs. Price seemed perplexed, "why he doesn't remember. He was so charming! He said good night, and asked if I were sure he couldn't escort me safely home—"

Leonidas sighed.

"You did!" Mrs. Price said.

"What a pity," Leonidas remarked feelingly, "that I didn't. So I came in here. Was the light on?"

"Oh, yes. There was a light here in the living room,

and all the cellar lights were on, too. It was that light there, with the yellow shade. I know, because it went out just before I got to bed."

Kaye went over to the lamp and flicked the chain. "Bulb popped," he said. "Well, Shakespeare, my guess is that you marched in and fell in the nearest chair. If Brett was here, then, it's perfectly possible you wouldn't have seen him, with the only light square in front of you. And my guess is that he was here, then. I wonder if the cellar lights might have popped by themselves, too?"

"Oh, no," Mrs. Price said. "I turned those out."

The sensation she caused bordered on a riot.

"You?" Kaye said. "You—you were here last night? You turned out the cellar lights?"

"I had to," Mrs. Price said. "I simply had to. I couldn't bear seeing all those lights going, with the rest of the house dark. I could see there wasn't anyone down in the cellar, so I just slipped over and turned them out. The back door—the outer storm door—had been banging, so I knew the cellar was unlocked. And I hate to hear a door bang!"

That she might be incriminating herself never seemed to enter Mrs. Price's head.

"We few," Kaye said. "We happy few. We band of brothers. Did you ever threaten Benny's life, Mrs. Price?"

"Of course not! I didn't like him. I never pretended to like the boy. But I never threatened him. That is, except about my Kaiserin August Wilhelm. I told him if he went over my Kaiserin again when he swung into the garage, I should certainly speak to his uncle. He said that the rose garden was in the wrong place, but of course, that was just because he didn't want to admit running over the Kaiserin. It's beautifully placed, my rose garden. The landscape architect said so."

Dallas found herself trying not to meet Kaye's eye. This wasn't, she felt, the time to laugh as whole-heartedly as she would if she ever once got started.

"Er—the knife," Leonidas sounded a little choked. "How did Bennington come to have your carving set?"

"Someone sent him a ham," Mrs. Price said, as though that were all the explanation required.

"Someone knew their Benny Brett," Kaye began, but Leonidas stopped him.

"Didn't Bennington have a carving knife?" he asked.

"No. He said that August had sent all the silver to the bank—he always does when he goes away—and the carving knives and steak sets were included."

"My doing," Dallas said. "I packed the silver up, myself. I just cleaned out everything."

"So Benny said. He said he couldn't carve a ham properly with an apple knife, and would I trade a carving set for some ham. It was simply delicious ham, too. And I sent Mary over, and she took the best cary-ing set, you see. She's new, and she didn't know. That's the way it happened, but—"

"But what?" Leonidas asked.

"But," Mrs. Price said worriedly, "I keep wondering about Rutherford. He likes reasons for things. I'm sure he wouldn't approve of my letting Benny Brett have that carving set that he spent so much time over, just because of some ham."

"There is also," Leonidas pointed out, "the publicity angle. I'm sure Rutherford—that is, your brother —will deeply resent the fact that his easily-identified gift was the immediate cause of Benny Brett's death."

"Oh, dear!" Mrs. Price said. "And he's always so careful about the newspapers, and what they say about him! And if they find out about his knife, I'm afraid they'll say a lot, won't they?"

Stanton Kaye chuckled.

"I don't see anything to laugh about!" Mrs. Price said. "I'm sure!"

"What a field day," Kaye said, "for the 'Dalton Daily Bugle.' Insert. Police Chief's Knife, Weapon Used in Mystery Stabbing Gift of Rutherford B. Carpenter. Prominent Clubwoman and Gardener Involved—"

"At this point," Leonidas said, "I feel we *must* act. Mrs. Price, this telephone has been cut—will you be good enough to telephone your brother and ask him to come here at once?"

"Oh, but I can't!"

"You can," Kaye said. "You've got to. All things being considered, you're both implicated in this, you know. You—"

"But he's away!"

"Where?"

"I don't know," Mrs. Price said. "He just told me

yesterday that he was taking the day off. But he's coming to my house for dinner. At seven. And we—"

"We can not wait till then!" Leonidas said firmly. "We can not! We are not going to delay reporting this another minute!"

"We shouldn't," Kaye said. "On the other hand—wait, Bill Shakespeare, before you start after a phone. Just how far d'you think we're going to get if we try to explain all this to a common prowl-car copper? Cherish that thought in your mind for a minute. Mull it over. Don't forget that—"

"Don't you forget," Dallas interrupted, "that Rutherford B. Carpenter likes reasons. If you ask me, it's six of one and half a dozen of the other."

"Maybe," Kaye said. "But I put all my eggs in the basket named Colonel Carpenter. We shouldn't wait, I admit. But I can't see any other way out. We—"

"We are not going to wait," Leonidas said. "We are not!"

"But really," Mrs. Price put a restraining hand on his arm, "really, Mr. Shakespeare, I do agree with Mr. Kaye! This isn't the sort of thing you can just tell to anyone at random! And Rutherford has—well, I don't know just how to say it, but he's injected a good deal of the service spirit into the Dalton police, you know. They used to be so pleasant, and so easygoing. And now they rush around so, barking out orders, and saluting, and they all wear guns—"

"Oh, let's get it over with!" Dallas said wearily. "Let's call the police and have done with all this beating about the bush! After all, they can't do any more than arrest us, and Rutherford will probably see to it that you, anyway, Mrs. Price, don't mold in jail very long!"

"Exactly," Leonidas said. "Exactly. Now—"

Mrs. Price clapped a hand to her forehead and made strange noises in her throat.

"She's fainting!" Kaye said. "Get some water—"

"No, no!" Mrs. Price said. "The solution! I've got the solution to all this! I knew I'd get the solution if I just thought about it long enough. It's so simple, I can't see why I didn't think of it sooner—you just all come over to my house and have breakfast!"

"On the theory," Leonidas said, "that a good hearty meal will solve everything? I fear, Mrs. Price, that you are over-optimistic—"

"Oh, no! No! You come over, and then *I'll* phone the police, don't you see? I'll tell them that the cellar door is open and that the front door's open—we can leave it that way, you see? And then I'll ask them to investigate. They love to investigate unlocked doors. Rutherford thinks it's awfully good for them. If someone's just been careless, they'll take more care the next time after a visit from the police. And if anything's wrong, why, they find it out."

Mrs. Price sat back, very pleased with herself.

"I think she's got something there," Kaye said. "Definitely, Comrade Price, I think you've got something there!"

"Of course I have! The prowl car will come, the policemen will investigate and find Bennington. Then we won't have to reproach ourselves for being inhuman, and negligent, and illegal, and all that sort of thing. The police will just take care of everything. The proper steps will be taken. But we'll wait right over at my house until Rutherford comes, and then we'll tell him everything. And—why, maybe by then, the police and Sergeant Muir will have found out who—oh, dear!"

She stopped suddenly, and looked very worriedly from Leonidas to Kaye and Dallas.

"What's the matter?" the latter asked.

"Why, I just thought! None of you killed him, did you?"

"No!" Kaye said. "Good God, no!"

Mrs. Price sighed with relief.

"I didn't think that any of you looked like murderers," she said. "Not a bit. But I did have an awfully bad moment! Anyway, who knows. Maybe Sergeant Muir will find the murderer before Rutherford returns. It only took him five hours to find out who shot that barber named Pinanski over at Dalton Falls, last week. Rutherford was awfully pleased. Muir was his sergeant in the marines, and he's been down to the G-man school, and Rutherford says that now Muir can almost find out things before they happen. So maybe he'll find the murderer before seven o'clock. That's—well, it's only around nine, now!"

"M'yes," Leonidas said.

Privately, he thought it would be ample time for the excellent Muir to find either the actual murderer, or them. It occurred to him that there was hardly a doorknob in the house which he had not fingered, so to speak, with his bare hands.

"It's a good idea," Kaye said. "You know damn well it's a good idea, Bill. There's no sense in our making any Roman holiday for Dalton's revivified police force. The earliest Christian, as some sage remarked, gets the hungriest lion. And in the interval before Rutherford B. gets back, we've got some time to delve. There are lots of burning questions we can find answers to. We might even get a little legal advice. After all, we won't be keeping anything back!"

"Just a temporary veiling," Leonidas said. "M'yes. Some might be callous enough to call it the obstruction of evidence—Dallas, what do you think?"

She shrugged.

"Right now, Bill," she said, "I'm remembering the copper who strolled by the corner of Oak and Centre yesterday while I was having my little scene with Benny. He wore sergeant's stripes. That's why I gave him my right name when he asked it. He took Benny's name, too, and wrote them down with a military flourish in a nice little notebook. Yes. Maybe, on the whole, we'd better wait for the Colonel."

As she got up from the couch, where she had been sitting beside Mrs. Price, Dallas reached over to stub out her cigarette in an ash tray. Her sleeve caught in the fringed shade of the table lamp, which promptly crashed to the floor, carrying with it a bookend, three books and an ash tray.

"Ming bites dust," Kaye observed. "No, don't touch 'em—leave 'em—"

But Dallas had already picked up one of the books.

"So this is where Bigelow went!" she said. "I've been hunting Bigelow's 'Real Property' for two solid months. I think—"

"Don't pick that stuff up," Kaye said. "Leave it. Take Bigelow with you. And your cigarette stub, too—"

"What ever for?"

"Well," Kaye said, "if we try to tidy up that broken lamp and put the pieces together, they'll catch Muir's eye right away quick. And if the prints of your dainty fingers are all over everything—well, just leave the mess there. Let's see what G-man Muir makes of it. Don't you agree, Bill?"

"I think," Leonidas said, "the sooner we get over to Mrs. Price's and summon the police, the better. I also think we might exercise some care in the collection of our personal belongings. There's no reason for our giving Mr. Muir too much of a head start."

"Dalton, Dalton, leave no articles in the car," Kaye chanted. "D'you remember that, or didn't you ever happen to ride the old narrow gauge to—. Why d'you stare so at the stuff on the bench, Bill? Isn't that your coat?"

"M'yes," Leonidas said. "That is undeniably my topcoat. I had it on in the doctor's office, but I have absolutely no recollection of pausing in the hallway to gather up my hat and gloves and walking stick when I so hastily departed—how powerful that evil-looking liquid must have been. Didn't you have some outer garments, Kaye?"

"I should have. I remember starting out in a beautiful Chesterfield with a velvet collar, and an Anthony Eden homburg—"

"Find them," Leonidas said. "Rather quickly. And there's your pocketbook, Dallas. And your handkerchief in the chair. And your cigarette case on the table."

It was no wonder, he thought, that murderers were always strewing clews behind them.

Kaye echoed his thoughts.

"This," he said, "is like checking out of a hotel after a convention, isn't it—grab the calves'-foot jelly, Dallas—or shall we leave that and the empty cup behind to confuse Muir?"

"Certainly not!" Mrs. Price said. "That's one of my best Pyrex cups! I—"

"What," Kaye asked curiously, "was the general idea behind that empty cup, anyway?"

"That? Oh, sugar. I was going to borrow some sugar."

"We'll get you some in the kitchen on our way out," Kaye said. "Why not?"

Leonidas sighed.

"Why not," he said, "indeed? A few seconds more one way or another—let us lend her the sugar, by all means!"

"Oh, I don't need it!" Mrs. Price said. "No one ever needs a cup of sugar. That's just an excuse, you know. In case Shakespeare had gone, and only Benny was here. Why, I thought everyone knew that borrowing a cup of sugar was just an excuse—I'll take the cup. Now, don't forget about leaving the front door ajar. You fix that, Mr. Kaye, and then we'll hurry right over and phone—"

But fifteen minutes later they were still frenziedly searching for Kaye's hat and coat.

"Let 'em go!" Kaye said in disgust. "Let 'em go! What the hell!"

"But if you're sure you wore them here," Dallas said, "you—"

"Probably that bellhop liked the velvet collar," Kaye said. "I hope it makes his neck tickle. It tickled mine. Let's go! Let's—Bill, where are your pince-nez?"

Another fifteen minutes passed before the pince-nez were located in Mrs. Price's pocket.

"Now!" Leonidas said.

Stealthily, one by one, they slipped out by the cellar door of ninety-five Paddock Street, and across the rose garden into the cellar garage of ninety-nine.

Mrs. Price paused in the upper hallway at the head of the cellar stairs. Opening the kitchen door a crack, she informed her maid in dulcet tones that there would be three extra for breakfast.

"It may take her a little time," she said, "because she's new. I've only had her since yesterday. But she's a jewel, a perfect treasure. The only honest maid I ever engaged—d'you know, when I asked her for references, she told me candidly she didn't have any, but if I really wanted them, she knew a woman in Boston who wrote peaches at four for a dollar, and if I'd lend her the dollar—"

"The telephone," Leonidas said gently. "Er—the telephone. The police. Remember?"

"Oh, yes. This way—"

She led them into the large living room that stretched across the front of the house. It was a little chintzy and a little cluttered, but the room had a pleasantly lived-in atmosphere which had been entirely lacking, Leonidas thought, in the Brett house. Built-in bookcases lined one side of the room, and a log fire burned cheerfully in the fireplace.

Mrs. Price removed the telephone from a strange box-like disguise and, without apparent emotion, called police headquarters.

After a prolonged chat with the officer who answered, during the course of which the problem of the common cold was thoroughly thrashed out and countless remedies suggested, Mrs. Price got down to business.

"Are the prowl cars busy?" she inquired. "Well, I'll tell you, it's about the Bretts' house, next door. Yes. Ninety-five. Probably Benny's just been careless, but the front door's ajar, and the cellar door's open, and it's made me rather nervous. Oh, will you? Oh, that's so good of you, Feeney. You know how it is, you think about the doors, and you begin to worry —you will, right away! Thank you, Feeney, I shall tell Rutherford how co-operative you are!"

She replaced the telephone in its disguise and then turned around.

"There!" she said brightly. "Feeney says he'll send a car right over, right away. Wasn't I casual? Wasn't

I disarming? He didn't suspect a thing. Not a thing! Why, what's the matter, you're all so silent?"

"It is the silence," Leonidas said, "that follows the extraction of an aching tooth. You are glad to have the tooth out. You are relieved. You know that the tooth will no longer ache. But shortly, the place will where the tooth was— How long does it take Dalton's car to answer a call?"

"Cars," Mrs. Price corrected him with pride. "We have a dozen, you know. Number forty's coming—"

"Number forty?" Leonidas said. "But if there are only a dozen—"

"Rutherford numbered them in tens," Mrs. Price explained. "He thought it might impress criminals, like escaping bank robbers—now, you watch for the car, while I go see Mary."

Leonidas, Kaye and Dallas walked over to the east window and looked, without enthusiasm, at the disconsolate drizzle outside.

"Let's," Kaye said, "talk of graves and worms and epitaphs— Bill, how many useful things your looksake said!"

"M'yes," Leonidas answered absently.

"Well, he did, you know. Many's the useful tidbit that came from his pen. Always a good quip at hand—"

"No one," Leonidas said, "has more admiration for Shakespeare than I. But with the passing of the years, I have become increasingly tired of having him quoted at me—"

"That girl!" Mrs. Price returned from the kitchen, waving a note in her hand. "That girl!"

"What's the matter with the little treasure?" Dallas asked. "Has she left?"

"No, the silly girl's gone to the store—I can't imagine why, there's nothing we need that I know of, and the store's a mile away. Well, at least she wrote me a note—has the car come—oh, there it is! Car forty—why, *there's* Sergeant Muir now!"

"I bet," Kaye's heartiness was forced. "I bet!"

"Muir likes riding in the prowl cars," Mrs. Price went on. "Because of speeders, you know. He likes to stop speeders on the pike. Rutherford says that Muir can pink a gas tank going ninety miles an hour, right in the middle—"

"One word more," Kaye told her grimly, "just one word more about Comrade Muir, and—my God, the man is already coming out! He—says, he's headed here!"

"That horrid appropriations committee." Mrs. Price clucked her tongue.

"That," Leonidas asked courteously, "what?"

"They wouldn't give Rutherford two-way radios. Just one. Muir's coming here to phone back to headquarters about—"

"Dalton, Dalton," Kaye said, "leave no articles in the car—"

"Wait!" Dallas said. "Wait! Oh, Bill Shakespeare, look! Look who's stopped him! It's the burly gent! The bellringer—Bill, he's talking with Muir—oh, Bill!

D'you suppose he'll tell Muir about us, about our being there?"

"I've no doubt in the world," Leonidas said, "that he is busily engaged in doing just that. Somehow I felt that no good would come from that man— Mrs. Price, I think it will be wise if Muir does not find us here when he comes to phone—"

"The back hall," Mrs. Price said. "You three go out there. I'll take care of Muir—here he comes!"

Hastily grabbing their belongings, the trio fled into the back hall, closed the door, and waited.

They marveled at the composure of Mrs. Price's voice as she led Muir in to the telephone.

"Certainly, it's right in that box—here, let me open —there! Oh, did I pinch your thumb in that crack? I'm so sorry— Had Benny Brett forgotten the doors?"

"I got some bad news for you, Mrs. Price," Muir said solemnly. "Bad news."

"I know, burglars!"

"No, ma'am. Not burglars. You better prepare yourself for a shock. Somebody's murdered Benny Brett!"

"Oh!"

Her scream was so effective that Dallas jumped.

"Murdered! Why, Muir! Oh, how fortunate!"

"Huh?"

"I mean, how fortunate I called you! I went over there, you know, and started to ring the bell, and then I didn't."

"Yeah, I know you went over," Muir said.

Kaye punched Leonidas.

"Hear that?" he whispered. "Do you hear that!"

"Why, Muir!" Mrs. Price said, "how did you know that?"

"A man seen you. Well, I'm glad you phoned for us, Mrs. Price, instead of going in and doing any investigating on your own. This is bad business. Hello, operator, Dalton 1000—Emergency."

"Oh, that's the new number!" Mrs. Price said delightedly. "Isn't that a nice number? So easy for people to remem—"

"Feeney? Muir. Give me Mike. Mike? Muir. Listen and take this. General alarm to all Dalton cars and police. Wanted in connection with murder of Bennington Brett. Woman named Dallas—like the city—Tring. Okay. T-r-i-n-g. About twenty-four. Hundred and fifteen. Five feet four. Brown hair. Brown eyes. Wearing dark blue hat. Dark blue knitted suit. Got that? Wanted same. Unknown man. About six-one. One-sixty. Dark gray suit. Wearing a beard. Yeah, I thought so, too. Sounds like the same man for that Dr. Derringer robbery last night. Got that?"

"Wow," Kaye said quietly.

"Wanted, same," Muir continued. "Stanton Kaye. Six-three. Hundred eighty-five. Yeah—that one. Call his home or his factory, will you? How old is he, twenty-eight or so? Okay."

"Wow," Dallas whispered, "yourself!"

"Fix that up and send it out right away, Mike. Give it to Boston. Shoot it to Framingham barracks, tell 'em to send it out on their radio and the teletype. Spread it. Yeah, that'll be the Colonel's Plan Five. We did it last month. Murder layout and how to get suspects for immediate arrest or questioning. That's it. Now, spread that, Mike. Send me car ten and the fingerprint—yeah, follow Plan Five right along. And say. Call the Leicester Arms in Boston and get hold of Captain Hammond from Washington. Yeah. Tell him I got some fun for him."

Leonidas winced.

"That's right, Mike. Just you follow out all the details of Plan Five, step by step. Of course you should notify the colonel! I know he's not, but you notify his house. No, I don't know where, but he'll pick it up on his car radio. He always has it on. Send me anything that you get—that's right."

There was the scraping noise of the telephone being put back into its box.

"Well, well!" Mrs. Price's voice was still bright, but it seemed to have taken on a brittle quality. "So Rutherford has plans for this sort of thing, has he?"

"Oh, yes, ma'am," Muir said. "We have thirty-two Plans. They cover everything. We always know just what to do. This is different from that barber over at the Falls, but I don't think we'll have any trouble picking up those people. From then on, it's just routine."

The trio behind the hall door looked at each other. Their expressions would have been the same had three grand pianos suddenly bounced off their respective heads.

But the real blow came with Muir's next words.

"Now, Mrs. Price," he said briskly, "you don't mind if I search your house?"

Chapter FIVE

TO her everlasting credit, Mrs. Price did not make the fatal error of protesting violently at any such thing, nor did she agree to the sergeant's suggestion with too much alacrity.

Instead she managed somehow to blend entirely genuine amazement with an innocent and guileless acquiescence.

"Search here? Of course, Muir!—But why?"

"There's a man outside," Muir said. "He's the one that saw you going over. He saw the guy with the beard, and the Tring girl, too. He thought he just saw someone sneaking in your house through the garage. He was on the next block, and he couldn't be sure, but we better be on the safe side—"

"The murderer!" Mrs. Price said. "The murderer—sneaking in here! Oh!"

"Don't faint, Mrs. Price!" Muir said anxiously. "Don't faint now—you've taken this swell—don't spoil it now by fainting!"

"No, no, I shan't! I shan't, I promise you. But, Muir, just before I called Feeney, I heard a noise up in the little front room. Maybe it's the heater, as I thought, but suppose—where are you going?"

"I'll just run up and have a look—"

"Wait for me, Muir! Wait till I get my breath. I'm going up too—no, wait! I won't let you go up there alone! Someone might shoot you—"

"But—"

"If a woman is with you," Mrs. Price said, "no one will shoot. Not even a murderer. Oh—my heart is fluttering! Take my arm, Muir. I am going with you!"

The hearts of the three in the hallway also fluttered, but it was the first time in three solid minutes that their hearts had been able to function at all.

Leonidas pointed to the kitchen door.

Silently, they crept through the hallway and into the kitchen.

"Why bother? Let's give in gracefully," Kaye said. "We're licked. We forgot to take the bellringer into consideration. Let's just give up—"

"Now?"

Leonidas's simple monosyllable made Kaye regard him with a respect that bordered on awe.

"You mean you think we—but what can we do, Bill? What can we do?"

Leonidas hesitated only a fraction of a second.

Then he caught up a blue denim butler's apron that hung over a chair back, and thrust it at Kaye.

"Take off your coat and shirt. Put this on. She can stall Muir five minutes at most. Take the silver polish off that shelf. That cloth. Grab that silver pitcher

◆§ 80 §◆

and polish! Muss your hair. Don't wisecrack with him—"

"What *am* I?" Kaye asked, as Dallas took his discarded clothes and tied the apron around him.

"Houseman. Get to work—come, Dallas, here's the maid's room, I hope—ah, it is!"

A new blue maid's uniform lay on the unmade bed.

Leonidas pointed to it.

"Quick, put it on!"

He caught Dallas's sweater and skirt as she peeled them off, and thrust them into a bureau drawer with Kaye's coat and shirt. His own coat and hat went into a laundry hamper, his walking stick went under the bed pillows.

"Now the dust cap, Dallas. Muss your hair, too. Lipstick—on the bureau. A lot. And rouge—quick! Now—"

"But you, Bill! What'll you do?"

"You can't disguise beards," Leonidas said. "I am about to become part and parcel of that unmade bed. See that I'm covered—"

"But, Bill, I looked Muir in the eye yesterday—duck your head more, it sticks up. He'll know me!"

"You're Mary, the new maid. Go in there and fry bacon!"

"But I can't act!"

"Don't try."

"But, Bill—"

"When Muir saw you yesterday, you were mad. Go in there now and fry bacon and see if you can get him to ask you for a date tonight. Make him chuck you under the chin. You're Mary. He's a good-looking cop—what are you stuffing into my ear!"

"Bigelow on 'Real Property.' Bill—"

"Go in there," Leonidas said firmly, "and vamp Muir! Let that be your only thought. Hurry. I hear them—"

When Muir entered the kitchen two minutes later, he saw a neat but rather flushed maid frying bacon at the stove, and a houseman burnishing a silver water pitcher. Both seemed quite at home. The maid looked at him, and Muir suddenly remembered the ticket in his cap. Tomorrow night was the annual spring dance of the Daltonville Athletic and Recreational Club. He hadn't, as yet, found a worthy partner, but perhaps—

"These are the new help the colonel spoke about, I suppose?" he said genially.

He spoke to Mrs. Price, but his eyes never left Dallas's face.

"Yes." Mrs. Price accepted the additions to her household staff without so much as batting an eyelid. "Oh, dear, Rogers, you're using the wrong polish! That's just for the flat silver—didn't I tell you?"

"I'm sorry, ma'am," Kaye said. "This was all there was."

"Wasn't there a glass jar with a blue label—a pink paste? Then we've run out. Be sure to put it on the list, won't you? Muir, this is Rogers, and that is Mary. Rogers is going to drive and help me with the garden

—and we *must* ask the colonel about getting a cot for that attic room for him. He—"

"Oh," Muir said, "they're not a couple?"

"I wanted a couple," Mrs. Price said, "but I've always said, if one's good, the other's bad. Like those awful Finns—or were they Lithuanians? I can't remember, but he was a treasure and a jewel, and she was just drunk all the time. And then I had those Germans—he just never lifted a finger, and she worked like a slave! So this time, I just didn't bother."

Her romancing had the soundest of motives. Muir had seen all the rooms upstairs, Muir knew there was just a single small bed in the maid's room. Mentally, Mrs. Price patted herself on the back. She had, she felt, got out of that very neatly. It occurred to her, as she watched the looks Muir was giving Dallas, that she might have been too neat.

Muir, as Rutherford often sorrowfully remarked, had only one weakness.

"I forgot to tell you," Mrs. Price said. "Muir is Colonel Carpenter's right-hand man on the force, aren't you, sergeant? Don't you want to ask them if they heard anything?"

"Been down cellar lately, Rogers?" Muir asked.

"Yes, sir."

"Hear anything, or see anyone?"

"There was a guy sellin' polish for the car," Kaye said respectfully. "But I told him we didn't want none, and he beat it."

"Okay."

Very deftly, so deftly that Dallas couldn't be sure

that it was not an accident, Muir dropped his visored cap at her feet.

Both of them bent to pick it up, and their heads bumped.

"Smacko!" Muir said. "Didn't hurt you, did I, Mary?"

"Oh, no, sergeant!" Dallas said. "Oh, no!"

She slipped into her apron pocket the ticket which had been thrust into her hand. That ticket gave her courage. She smiled up at Muir, and had the exquisite pleasure of knowing that the smile infuriated Kaye just as much as it pleased the sergeant.

"There's Mary's room," Mrs. Price said hurriedly, "and the laundry—don't you want to see them? I'm sure you do—"

Muir's inspection of both rooms was more than perfunctory. He barely glanced at the bed where Leonidas, feeling very low-comedy indeed, lay huddled under the crumpled green puff.

This Mary, Muir thought, used the nicest smelling perfume he remembered since that little blonde English nurse in Pekin, when he was putting in time with the Horse Marines. And her hands were nicer.

"I guess everything's okay, Mrs. Price," Muir said. "I guess this fellow probably saw the car polish salesman. This fellow was from the sheriff's office, and you know what the colonel thinks of that outfit."

Mrs. Price didn't know what the colonel thought, but she nodded energetically, and wondered how she could pry Muir out of the kitchen. He showed not the slightest inclination to depart, and if he stayed around very much longer, it was just possible that Muir might really look at Stanton Kaye and take to speculating about housemen in expensive silk undershirts.

"I'm so relieved!" she said. "I shall tell the colonel how kind you've been, Muir, to interrupt your Plan —was it Plan Five or Six? Plan Five. Well, I'll tell him that you were so solicitous, you even interrupted Plan Five to make sure that I was not in any danger. I know Rutherford will approve, even though Plan Five is probably very dear to his heart. Very."

"That's right," Muir said. "That's right. I'll drop in later."

Manfully, he wrenched his eyes from Dallas and answered the call of duty and of Plan Five.

At the sound of the front door closing behind the sergeant, Kaye turned on Dallas.

"My God!" he said bitterly. "Another thirty seconds, and you'd have been on that bozo's lap! What an abandoned exhibition, what an utterly uninhibited exhibition of predatory—"

"Bill told me to, you big oaf! And look what Muir gave me! Look!"

Kaye disdainfully inspected the ticket of the Daltonville Athletic and Recreational Club.

"Going, toots?" he inquired acidly.

"Kaye, you lump! I just did what Bill told me to do—and you've got to admit it took his mind off your pretty silken undershirt, and everything else, too— Bill, didn't you tell me to act like that?"

Leonidas, mussed but imperturbable, appeared in the doorway.

"M'yes," he said, swinging his pince-nez on their broad black ribbon, "m'yes. A most efficient job. Er—if that bacon is cooked, don't you feel we might perhaps eat it?"

"You mean you deliberately told her to hurl herself at—"

"My dear boy," Leonidas said, "don't quibble. And d'you mind plugging in that percolator beside you? Thank you. And if that's orange juice in that pitcher—ah, Mrs. Price! May I congratulate you on the masterly way you handled the sergeant? It was superb, dear lady, superb! It—"

"He's gone in," Mrs. Price was too worried to appreciate Leonidas's praise. "In Brett's, I mean. Oh, dear, if only I could have warned you, Mary. I mean, Dallas. Rutherford says that Muir has—that every girl—that is, every good-looking girl he meets—dear me, how can one say that sort of thing nicely?"

"Don't try," Kaye said. "We know what you mean. We get it. That stallion—"

"He's just simply going to *haunt* this house!" Mrs. Price said. "I know he is. It's going to be awful. If you encourage him, you'll—well, if you don't, then he—oh, dear! And if he does—I just don't know which way to turn!"

"I don't just know," Dallas said, "what you mean!"

"I think," Leonidas said quickly before Kaye could speak, "what Mrs. Price means is that if your—er—glamor, let us call it, begins to wear off, then Muir's brain may begin to function and his suspicions will arise and shine. Whereas if your glamor increases—"

"Coo," Kaye said. "Coo, and amen!"

"Now see here!" Dallas said crossly. "I did just what I was told! Can I help it if Muir is like that?"

"No, lovely," Kaye said, "but you can delicately put on the brakes. You can even put him on the skids—"

"And have Muir get perfectly furious, and arrest the lot of us!" Mrs. Price said. "Well, I should say not! She can't put any skids on him now!"

Dallas stalked across the kitchen and paused with her hand on the knob of the hall door.

"I wish," she said, "you'd all go into a nice huddle and get your minds made up. Am I going to be seduced by Muir, or are we all marching off to jail in handcuffs? Figure that one out, and let me know! And—"

"Er—where are you going?" Leonidas inquired.

"I'm going," Dallas said, "to telephone Campbell at St. Petersburg, and have him put August Barker Brett into a chartered plane at once! That's what! It seems pretty clear to me that what we need most of all is August Barker and a good clean breath of sanity!"

In less than a minute she was back in the kitchen.

"I put the call through," she said breathlessly, "but —Bill, that burly gent! The bellringer—he's standing over there on the front steps of ninety-five, peering over here as hard as he can, and he's—I'm afraid of that man! And what did Muir mean, he was from the sheriff's office?"

Kaye sighed.

"I'm beginning to suspect," he said, "that this is all because of me. I'm afraid that your burly gent is a process server, and he's after me—"

"You? What for?" Dallas demanded.

"They must have taken the job from my little Irish pal and given it to this lad. Marty warned me that they might, yesterday—Marty's the little Irishman—and that's why I had the bellhop park my car on the next street—"

"What's a process server after you for?" Dallas insisted.

"Oh, sometimes it's one thing," Kaye said evasively, "sometimes it's another. There was one period of labor problems at the factory when Marty considered his day wasted and withered if he didn't serve from five to ten subpoenas a day on me. Someone must have got wise to Marty's little agreement with me on this, though, and—"

"What are you being subpoenaed for?"

"If you want to know, toots, it's a hundred thousand dollar suit for breaching the promises of a girl named Violet!" Kaye said. "That is why I have been avoiding the subpoenas, and why I shall continue to do so until—"

"And you," Dallas said, "you carp—you stand there and carp about Muir's giving me a ticket for the Daltonville Athletic and Recreational Club's dance! You call him a stallion! You—"

"And so he is," Kaye said promptly. "So he is! And that's got nothing whatever to do with my suit. It's a fake suit, and by Monday we'll have proof it's a fake—"

"Yah!" Dallas said. "Yah!"

"You say another word," Kaye told her, "and I shall turn you over my knee and spank—"

"You will, will you?" Dallas gripped the handle of a frying pan. "You will, will you? Just you try—"

"Both of you," Leonidas said firmly, "stop this nonsense at once! Instantly! Dallas, there's the phone—tell August Barker to fly back like a bird. Mrs. Price, will you watch out for Muir? Kaye, sit down a minute. I've been thinking out some of our problems—what could Benny Brett possibly have had of importance to tell you? Have you any ideas at all?"

Kaye shook his head.

"At intervals," he remarked, "I've been trying to solve that one, myself. To the best of my knowledge, there's not a thing that Benny and I have, or engage in, in common. I never did any business with him. I never did any business with August Barker. Except we're both on a couple of boards together. Even that doesn't come under the head of important business. But, Bill, I do feel that Benny was sober, and serious, when he called me. I think there was something up that was important to me, and if you want to know the truth, I feel pretty wretched about this whole business. Look, Bill—d'you suppose that after he ran you— But that's all messed up, too, his running you down!"

Leonidas nodded.

"M'yes," he said. "Now, Benny started to phone you about this important matter long before I was run down. I was hurrying, at the time, for the midnight bus. That was just a minute or two to twelve—"

"Hey!" Kaye said. "Look—are you sure? Because at twelve o'clock—right on the stroke of twelve, we gave Bob a surprise present. Parade, spotlight, pearl studs on a silver salver—all that. And I had a speech to make, and six times in the two minutes before, I got interrupted by those everlasting phone calls from Benny—Bill, are you sure it was Benny that ran you down?"

"It could, I suppose," Leonidas admitted, "have been a reasonable facsimile. But why should Benny's wallet and key ring have dropped from the facsimile's pocket into the gutter, when he bent to reassure himself of my demise? Of course it could have been planted—"

"That's it!" Kaye said. "That must be it, Bill!"

"But I hate to think so," Leonidas said. "I hate to think so. That offers complications at which my mind rebels. On the other hand, if you are quite certain that Benny was in the process of phoning you at twelve, he could not have been running over me at the same time."

"Unless he had an astral body, maybe," Kaye said, "and somehow I don't think any self-respecting astral body would have attached himself to Benny Brett. The—"

"Muir!" Dallas said, coming in swiftly. "Muir's coming!"

"So soon?" Leonidas said. "Dear me. Did you get through to August?"

"I talked to Campbell. August starts home at once by plane. Be here tonight, they hoped. Kaye, you'd better find something else to do, quick. And put on that white coat I found— Come along, Bill, get back into the bed and I'll cover you up—"

"No," Leonidas said. "This time I am going to retire with dignity to Mary's bath. Muir will undoubtedly come to the kitchen, but if he pursues you further, he deserves to find me. Give me Bigelow on 'Real Property.' I might just as well improve my mind—"

"Bill," Dallas said despairingly as he started through the door, "what are we going to do? We can't keep this sort of thing up, it's worse than a bedroom farce! We've got to get somewhere."

"We have," Leonidas said. "Don't look so surprised. I think we have. Be careful of Muir, Dallas. Try to maintain a—er—discreet balance."

In the living room, Muir made a series of phone calls.

To Mrs. Price, calmly knitting a white jumper by the fire, not one of the calls seemed at all important. Muir was just giving himself a good excuse to see Dallas again.

"How's Plan Five?" she inquired when Muir got through.

"Coming along fine," Muir said. "Working out

great. We haven't located those three people yet, but we got 'em sewed up. They won't never slip out of Dalton. It's just a question of time. Doc says that Brett was killed around one last night—say, was Mary out last night?"

"Oh, yes. Thursday, you know."

The words popped out of her mouth before it occurred to Mrs. Price that while she referred to the real Mary, Muir, of course, meant Dallas. She wondered, in passing, what had become of the real Mary. Enough time had elapsed for the girl to have made half a dozen trips to Dalton Centre and the stores. And if Mary burst in while Muir was there—well, even the most understanding treasure of a maid, Mrs. Price thought, might very possibly resent having her kitchen usurped.

"Mary was out," she added hastily, "but she came home early. Quite early."

"What time?"

"I'm sure she was in when I came home, Muir. I'm sure—"

"I'll find out," Muir said. "You see, if she got home early, she might have heard something next door. Her room's on that side. And if she came in late, she might have seen someone around. You know, somebody or something maybe that she didn't think anything of then, but it would mean something to me. I guess I'll just go and ask her some questions."

"Do," Mrs. Price said. "I'll come along and—"

"I wonder," Muir said easily, "if maybe it wouldn't

be better if I went alone, Mrs. Price? She might talk more free to me, maybe."

"Of course, of course, do go alone—but," she had an inspiration, "you won't be long, will you? Because I simply must find out what we need and get my shopping list made out. Rutherford is coming to dinner, and so I'm going to go to market myself—do you know where he is, Muir?"

"No, Mrs. Price, you know how he always goes off on his own on his day off."

"Yes. Well, run along, Muir. But don't be over five minutes, will you? I must get my dinner thought out—"

That, she thought with satisfaction as Muir departed for the kitchen, wouldn't give him time to bother Dallas and, with luck, she could maneuver him out of the house before the real Mary returned.

In the kitchen, Dallas was washing dishes while Kaye sharpened knives. He happened to know how to sharpen knives, and Mrs. Price's cutlery mercifully needed sharpening. Humming under his breath, he tried to give his undivided attention to the job. The less he allowed himself to think about the problem of Muir and Dallas, the better, Kaye decided.

But Muir, with a time limit of five minutes set on him, had no intention of wasting a second. Rogers, in his estimation, constituted a crowd. Rogers was in the way.

"Feller," Muir's hand landed between Kaye's shoulder blades with a hearty smack, "go get some wood for Mrs. Price's fire. Jump."

The unexpected impact of that ham-like paw did things to Kaye's decision to sharpen knives and keep cool and mind his own business.

"What," he said, "did you say?"

Dallas made signals at him from behind Muir's back.

Kaye ignored them.

"What," he asked again, "did you say?"

"You heard me. Jump!"

Kaye did not move.

"Jump!"

"That," Kaye said, "is just what I thought you said at first."

He started to turn back to his knives, but Muir grabbed his arm.

"I told you to jump!"

"I know you did," Kaye said. "You're a man of few words, and jump is one of them. Take your hand off my arm."

Muir was used to obeying authority, and he instinctively reacted to Kaye's quiet but forceful command. His hand dropped to his side.

And for the first time, he really took a good look at Kaye.

He noticed a number of things, including Kaye's hands and their manicured nails, and the well-cut, well-fitting trousers, and the black patent leather shoes.

"Where did you work last?" he demanded in a voice that was ominously ironic.

"I cleaned spittoons," Kaye said pleasantly, "in the Ritz-Carlton. You want to make anything of it?"

His left, as he had modestly informed Dallas earlier in the morning, was swell. It was also quicker than the sergeant's, and he had been staring for several minutes at the spot he intended to crack.

Dallas waited just long enough for the sergeant's form to hit the linoleum floor. Then she rushed for Leonidas.

"Bill!" she said. "Bill—"

"Ah," Leonidas, comfortably seated on a three-legged stool by the tub, smiled broadly at her and removed his pince-nez. "Ah, Dallas—how fortunate you brought Mr. Bigelow, how very fortunate! The light which Mr. B. has cast on all these proceedings is nothing short of blinding. I can't cry aloud eureka and say that I have found out all, but I have found out—what's happened?"

"Come," Dallas said unhappily, "and see! Come into the kitchen and see!"

Leonidas considered the prostrate figure of Sergeant Muir and nodded slowly.

"Perhaps," he said, "it is for the best. Not, admittedly, the method which I personally should have chosen, but effective none the less. Very effective. Kaye, you'd better take a few precautionary measures, like a gag. Perhaps a little deft binding of the wrists and ankles—"

He stopped short as footsteps sounded on the outside kitchen steps, and someone fumbled at the knob of the back door.

"Lock it, Dallas!" Kaye said.

But before Dallas could cross the room, the door opened.

Leonidas drew his breath in sharply as a girl entered the kitchen.

"Thank heavens!" Dallas said in relief, spotting the blue maid's uniform showing beneath the girl's polo coat. "You're Mary—what's the matter? Who—do you know her, Bill?"

Leonidas was smiling.

"Ah," he said. "Margie."

Chapter **SIX**

"I HAD a curious feeling," Leonidas continued, "that we would meet again, that the octopus of destiny would encircle us with a long and viscid arm—that," he added parenthetically to Kaye, "is one of those things which Shakespeare would have said so much better, and very likely did."

Margie stared down at Sergeant Muir.

Then she looked over at Leonidas and grinned.

"Bill," she said, "I'll tell you what. I'll trade. Last night for this copper."

"What does the woman mean?" Kaye demanded. "What *is* this?"

"She means," Leonidas explained, "that if I agree to forget certain unfortunate incidents of last night, she in return will not call anyone's attention to this fallen hero on the floor. Done, Margie."

Gravely, they shook hands.

"Bill," Margie said, "you'll never know how bad I felt when Cuff snatched those things! Honest, I hated to leave you, but I had to look after him. He's so sort of impulsive."

"M'yes," Leonidas said. "I gathered as much. You got him away safely, of course?"

Margie nodded. "He's a problem, sometimes," she said. "Say, Bill, you'll never know how I felt, either, when I saw you sneaking into the cellar here with Price. I beat it then. I thought you was after me. I wouldn't be back now, but there was so many cops around, and they didn't stop me or say anything—do you know there's been a murder next door? The—"

"Don't tell us," Kaye said. "Don't remind us. We know."

Margie sat down and began to laugh.

"Say! Are you—sure, you must be! You're the three they're combing Dalton for! Boy, that's good! That is—"

"How d'you know we're being combed for?" Leonidas inquired.

"Oh, I heard it over the radio at a corner store in the Centre. They been sending out calls every ten minutes or so, the man said. Honest, Bill, you just never seen so many coppers around! They got riot guns and tear-gas bombs—say, what you going to do about this one?"

She pointed one trim toe towards Muir, who now more nearly resembled a trussed fowl than anything else.

"If you're asking me," Kaye said, "I'm sure I wouldn't know. That's out of my calculations. I produced the body. It's up to someone else to figure out the disposal problems."

"I wonder," Leonidas said thoughtfully, "if there's a preserve room—"

"Say, that's just what I was thinking of!" Margie said. "Just the thing. We got one down cellar—no windows, and a big thick fireproof door, with a lock. Mrs. Price said it was made special for a wine storage, like, for the man who built the house. It's just like a vault. That's the place for him, Bill—say, you better take this—"

She removed Muir's revolver from its holster, and presented it to Leonidas, who thrust it hastily into his coat pocket along with Dallas's small .22.

"And say," Margie went on, "I think he's got—yeah. He's got another in a shoulder holster. I thought he bulged there. And—my God, here's even another rod in his blouse pocket! Here, take 'em. These marines!"

"You—er—know the sergeant?" Leonidas inquired.

There was no more room in his left pocket, so he stuffed the two additional guns in his right pocket.

"Aw, just through Cuff," Margie said casually. "Say, can I swipe his badge, huh? Gee, wouldn't that tickle Cuff! Can I? Do you mind?"

"Oh, by all means!" Leonidas said. "Do. No doubt in the course of time that badge would catch Cuff's acquisitive eye, anyway. Er—Kaye, will you be good enough to remove the sergeant to the preserve room?"

Kaye very deliberately planted his hands on his hips and surveyed Leonidas.

"You don't think," he said at last, "that perhaps—it's just a silly, wild possibility, of course—but perhaps,

Bill, we might be going just a teeny-weeny bit too far, maybe?"

"You should talk!" Dallas said. "The Dalton Bomber. You were the one who started this. You knocked him out! And now you say—"

"I'm not talking about that. I'm—"

"No," Dallas said. "You never do. Muir gives me a ticket, and that's bad, but you're sued for a hundred thousand and that's good. It's bad to stick a cop in a closet, but it's just fine to knock him out—honestly, the limitations of the masculine mind—"

"That's what I mean," Kaye said. "Bill's mind is masculine, but it doesn't seem to have any limitations. Mine does. I don't think it's wise to thrust police sergeants into jam vaults, or to steal their guns—"

"Listen," Margie said, in much the same voice she would have used to Cuff, "if you let him keep the guns, he shoots his way out of the preserve room in half a minute, see?"

"To peel off his badge—"

"Aw, nuts!" Margie said. "He's probably got another!"

"I say," Kaye continued, "this is all going too far! And it is!"

Leonidas swung his pince-nez.

"If you will pause and consider, Kaye," he said, "it may dawn on you that you and Dallas and I are being eagerly sought by the police. For murder. You, in addition, are being pursued by the process server. For the moment, the police have turned their attention from Margie, and her part in last night's incident at Dr. Derringer's—but frankly, Kaye, under the circumstances, can one—er—go too far? I doubt it. Now, put Muir away. There's much to be done—"

Mrs. Price hurriedly entered the kitchen.

"I'm late," she said, "I dropped a stitch and I simply couldn't find—oh."

She looked at Muir, and nodded.

"I was going to suggest," she said, "wouldn't it be better if we just tucked him away somewhere. Mr. Cobble's come, you know, and the minute I saw him, I knew we'd just have to tuck Muir away until Rutherford comes—"

"Break it to us gently," Kaye said. "What is Mr. Cobble?"

"Oh, you're back, Mary? That's good. Mr. Cobble," Mrs. Price said, "is our postman, and he's very pleasant, I'm sure. Always willing to wait while you finish up a letter, and take it back to mail at the office, and all that. But he just talks and talks, and of course he knows everyone's business, and if he started talking with Muir about my maid—because he saw Mary yesterday, and he knows I haven't a houseman, just Mary—"

"Margie," Kaye said. "It transpires that her name is Margie."

"Oh, I knew that!"

"Oh, you did?" Kaye said.

"Oh, yes. I always call all the maids Mary, and the men Rogers. Those were the names of my first couple, and it never seemed worthwhile to make the effort of shifting around all the time—you'd better get Muir tucked away somewhere before someone comes after him, I think."

Kaye fanned himself with a striped duster.

"I suppose," he said, "you'll know just what to tell the officers, when they ask for Muir?"

Mrs. Price thought a moment.

"A good clew—Mary—Margie, I suppose I might as well call you Margie, there's really so little difference—Margie, what was that you said yesterday about the horse race? A sure thing, a—"

"A hot tip?"

"That's it! I'll just say, someone phoned and gave Muir a hot tip, and he said for them to go right ahead on Plan Five while he followed up this hot tip."

"Now, Kaye," Dallas said, "for heaven's sake, stop this glumming around and take Muir downstairs. What, as Bill points out, what have you got to lose?"

Kaye bent over to pick up the sergeant, and then hesitated.

"Bill," he said, "are you the man who kept my elderly cousin, Agatha Jordan, in Boston's headlines for three solid days, while the two of you tracked down the woman who killed John North?"

"M'yes," Leonidas said. "Agatha is an old friend of mine. The rest was all chance, of course. Just chance—"

"Uh-huh. Just that old octopus of destiny," Kaye said. "Waving its viscid arms jauntily in the breeze. I see. I had begun to remember about you. Now, just let me get one more point cleared up. You are definitely not waiting for Colonel Rutherford B. Carpenter, are you?"

"It seems to me," Leonidas said, "that—"

"That we are going to solve this thing ourselves? Yes, I thought so. That has been your intention all along, hasn't it?"

"Oh, yes," Leonidas said. "Quite!"

"Now I think that's a perfectly splendid idea!" Mrs. Price said. "Because if we find Rutherford's murderer —of course, I mean Benny's murderer—why, then Rutherford can't possibly have any reason to be provoked with us, can he? It just won't matter what happens. He can't say a single thing!"

"That, in a general way," Leonidas told her, "is my hope. I can see no other way out."

"Well, it's a perfectly splendid idea!" Mrs. Price said. "And so you know dear Agatha—isn't she a charming woman? So—"

"Cousin Agatha," Kaye said, "combines all the dignity of an archbishop with the unexpected charm of an uncaged leopard. In some ways, Mrs. Price, you remind me of her. Well, now I know the worst. I know what we're in for. 'He,' as Shakespeare said, 'he that outlives this day, and comes home safe, will stand a tip-toe when this day is named'—open the door, Dallas—"

Lugging the still limp body of Muir as though it were a sack of onions, Kaye bore it out of the kitchen.

"Hey, Margie," he said, "come help. Dallas, help her swing his hooves around—oh, my! 'We few, we happy few, we band of brothers. For he today that sheds his blood with me shall be my brother—' "

"A strange boy," Mrs. Price said. "He amazes me with some of the things he says."

Leonidas tactfully restrained himself from suggesting that Kaye might well utter similar sentiments concerning Mrs. Price.

"I only hope," he said sincerely, "that his quotation will not prove apt. I don't mind being his brother, figuratively speaking, but I do dislike bloodshed—there is the doorbell, Mrs. Price. Perhaps you—"

"Hot tip," Mrs. Price said, starting for the hall. "Hot tip—Muir had a hot tip, and has followed it up."

Two minutes later, beaming with pride, she returned to the kitchen.

"I remembered it," she said, "and it worked beautifully. The officer just said he thought it was about time for Philo Vance to get a scent. He didn't seem to think it was at all unusual, Muir's slipping away."

Kaye, Dallas and Margie filed back from the cellar. Margie, Leonidas noticed, carried a neatly folded pair of trousers over her arm.

"They're Muir's," she said in answer to his question. "He's tied up tight, and locked in like he was in jail, but I thought we might as well play safe and take his pants. A guy looks so silly without his pants. Even if he gets himself free, he may kind of think twice about barging out without his pants. So I took them. The rest of his uniform is in the cellar."

"A more abandoned set of females," Kaye said, "I

never laid eye on. Abandoned is not the proper word—"

"Shut up, Kaye," Dallas said. "Bill, you said something about finding something in Bigelow—"

"You mean, we've got something to work on?" Kaye demanded. "Like a rational basis? I can't bear—"

"Will you," Dallas said, "shut up? Or do you really want the dish mop in your mouth? Go on, Bill. What about Bigelow's 'Real Property'?"

"Bigelow is probably the dullest reading," Leonidas told her, "in the world, but I can't begin to thank you for having fingerprinted it into the necessity of bringing it along. I'm sure that Providence had something to do with it—"

"Providence nothing," Kaye said. "It's that fateful octopus, rearing its ugly— Ow!"

"I warned you," Dallas said. "Chew on the dish mop, and like it. Thanks, Margie. Go on, Bill."

"In brief, Dallas," Leonidas continued, "I don't think you could have picked a more significant volume. Thrust inside its pages are several fascinating and thought-provoking items. Here, for example, is an envelope addressed to Bennington. On its back is written a very full list of Meredith Academy affairs, with dates and times—isn't that Benny's scribble?"

Dallas looked, and nodded.

"I thought so," Leonidas said. "Two dates are checked. March fifteenth—"

"The Ides of March," Kaye spoke through the dish mop.

"Yesterday. And March seventh. On March seventh was a reunion of the Academy's former teachers, which I always attend. Yesterday was Speech Day, when I invariably present in person a cup which I donated, myself, many years ago. Following both occasions, I had dinner with Professor Otis and his family. On March seventh, one of the dates Benny has checked, I was driven back to Boston by one of the Otis's friends. Last night, however, I started for the bus as I usually do—"

Kaye pulled the dish mop out of his mouth and whistled.

"You mean, Benny found out for sure just which days you'd be out here, and about your going to the Otis's—I don't suppose that would be hard to discover, if you always dine with them. And probably he was waiting to run over you, on the seventh, and last night, on the other checked date, he pulled it off!"

"That would seem to work out," Leonidas said.

"Yes, except for just one thing—that last night at the time you were being run over, Benny was phoning me!"

"Just so," Leonidas said. "Now, my original thought was that Benny tried to kill me, and that Benny was afterwards killed by—let us call the person X. But that is too involved. Too disjointed. Suppose, now, that Benny and X try to kill me, and that Benny is later killed by X. That provides a certain connection which my original thought lacked entirely."

Kaye and Dallas both seemed to have trouble in

following Leonidas's ideas, but Margie and Mrs. Price nodded simultaneously.

"A double cross!" Mrs. Price said.

"Sure," Margie said. "That sounds okay to me, Bill."

"But why did X and Benny pick you out to kill?" Kaye asked. "Why should you be the victim?"

"At least," Leonidas said, "we have some reason to believe that I was picked, that as I thought at the time, the running over was deliberately planned. Now, I also feel that X did the running over, and then purposely left the wallet—"

"You mean, X disguised himself as Benny," Kaye said.

"I shouldn't go so far as to say disguise," Leonidas answered. "Disguise implies false hair and similar clothing, and that sort of thing. Benny was not of unusual height or breadth or build. A bit of burnt cork would produce a mustache like Benny's, if briefly smeared on the upper lip. And—"

"And if," Dallas said, "you saw someone with a little mustache, and then later picked up a wallet lettered with Benny's name from the spot where the man stood—well, the man would be Benny Brett. Of course."

"I wonder," Kaye said, "if we couldn't work from the car angle. It was a roadster, you said? At least, it's a tangible thing. If it's still there, we might be able to find out who owned it, or—"

"If you mean the roadster that run over Bill," Margie said, "you'll never find out nothing about that car now."

"Cuff?" Leonidas inquired.

Margie nodded.

"We left in it," she said, "and Cuff sold it to a pal of his an hour later. By this time it's two different colors and got new serial numbers and all, and probably already sold to someone else. It was from a U-drive, Cuff said. The guy that hired it probably used a fake license and name, see? That's why he didn't care about leaving it behind."

"So much for that," Kaye said. "But now look, Bill. Why does X kill Benny?"

"Because he comes to the house, to ninety-five, and finds Benny calling you. No, wait before you scoff. Suppose X comes triumphantly to ninety-five, having put old Witherall out of the way, to find Benny whimpering for you—"

"How am I involved, anyway?" Kaye demanded.

"That is one of the things we have yet to find out about. Now, there was another item, in Bigelow, and I will admit that it surprised me. I had not known that Benny had any other relations than August Barker—"

"Oh, yes!" Mrs. Price said. "He has a sister—"

"Zara?"

Mrs. Price sniffed. "She was christened Sarah Ann, but she got to be Zara. You know the sort of woman. She'd have twisted Fanny into Fania and Lorena into Lorna and—"

"By the way," Kaye interrupted, "what's your name,

Mrs. Price? I'm not just curious, I intend to call you by it. I feel we're old, old friends at this point."

"Cassandra—"

Kaye shouted.

"But people usually call me Cassie."

"Cassandra," Kaye said, "I should have guessed. Cassandra, the original advance agent of woe—to know her, as I remember, was to know the worst—"

"Kaye," Dallas said, "either you let Bill go on, or you chew the mop. Take your choice."

"Thank you," Leonidas said. "Mrs. Price, tell me about Zara. Is she like Benny?"

"Oh, no. She doesn't drink. She doesn't have anything much to do with Benny, either. She's older than he is—was—well, she's forty-six, though she pretends she's only forty. But I know better. She was born on my twelfth birthday, because an aunt of mine who was there went rushing off when she heard the news—she was a great friend of Mrs. Brett—and I was terribly hurt that she left. She went in such a hurry, you see, she forgot to give me my present—where was I?"

"Zara," Leonidas said, "is forty-six, officially."

"Well, she's always running clubs—not that she's so popular, because she isn't one bit, but she's willing to spend time, and other women are busy doing other things. Personally," Mrs. Price wound up, "I never could abide the woman. Pushing, I always thought."

"She is pretty Madam-Presidenty," Dallas said, "but what I dislike most about her are those gold turbans. And for all she thinks she's so efficient, I'm always having to straighten out her account with the bank. I say—I forgot. I suppose we ought to phone her, or something? I never even remembered her!"

"If the police haven't told her," Leonidas said, "I've no doubt she's picked up the sad news of Benny by now from the radio—"

"And I'm willing," Mrs. Price said, "to wager she presides at the Friday Morning Club, just the same! In black. Why, when she had appendicitis, she held board meetings all over the hospital! She was awfully disagreeable when the doctor put his foot down and told her she had to rest."

"She can be disagreeable, too," Dallas agreed. "I haven't seen her for a couple of months, but she called last week about her trust fund check—it was a mail late, or something, and she wanted me to rush into Boston and see about it. She had a board meeting."

"So that's where she gets her money," Mrs. Price said. "I've always wondered. She's so extravagant, you know. Always entertaining—she thinks nothing of thirty for luncheon—"

"And a hundred for tea and fifty million for dinner," Margie said. "I worked for that dame for a week, once, and then I quit. And let me tell you, Sister Brett drops plenty on the races, too—"

"Why, Margie!" Mrs. Price said. "She's the president of the League for the Abolition of Horse and Dog Racing!"

"She ought to be," Margie commented succinctly.

"But— oh, I can't believe that, Margie!"

"They cost her plenty, Mrs. Price. Cuff used to work for her bookie. Say, is she mixed up in this, Bill?"

Leonidas produced another sheet of paper from Bigelow.

"Frankly," he said, "I don't know. Here is a note written on the stationery of a hotel in Meldon—"

"That's the state convention," Mrs. Price said promptly. "A week ago. She was a delegate."

" 'Dear Brother,' " Leonidas read, " 'much as I should like the money, I do feel great care should be taken. Whichever way you decide, do be careful. If you can cut him out safely, perhaps that would be better, but I am afraid he will be very angry, and I should make sure first. Let me know about everything. I shall call you at once when I return. Zara.' "

Kaye whistled softly.

"So Benny had some plan afoot," he said, "and he thought of cutting someone out, and Zara thought the someone might be sore. Well, there you are, Bill. Someone got sore enough to kill Benny. I take back some of my ribald laughter, Bill. You've got something there."

"M'yes," Leonidas said. "You could read it that way. On the other hand, this could be about a sweepstakes ticket, or it might be about a dinner invitation. Under the circumstances it has a sinister ring, but if it were a really important note, I do not feel that even as dull a person as Benny would have cherished it. Even Benny would have consigned it to flames."

"Let's go over and see her," Mrs. Price said. "It may be about something unimportant, but—you know, people have always laughed at me when I said she had shifty eyes, but she does. Let's go see."

"You mean, Cassandra," Kaye said, "let's go see, as let's march right out this minute and call on Zara, in person? With radios blaring our description, and the streets bristling with Dalton cops and tear-gas bombs, and riot guns?"

"Well, really," Mrs. Price said, "if you knew Zara Brett as well as I do, you'd know she'd hardly discuss the matter over the telephone! She's very closemouthed. Very. Until Dallas mentioned that trust fund, I never even knew where her income came from! No, Kaye, if you want to find out anything from Zara Brett, you've got to pump! Of course, we'll go right out and find her. Right away!"

"Cassie," Kaye said patiently, "the second we stick an eyelash out of this house, pop we go into your estimable brother's jug or cooler. You don't seem to realize—"

"Tush," Mrs. Price returned. "What I do realize is that we'll never find Benny's murderer before Rutherford comes home if you keep up this silly defeatist attitude. Of course we're going out. What's more, you're going to drive."

"Me?"

"You," Mrs. Price said. "Margie, go find him that chauffeur's outfit we had around somewhere yesterday, when I was hunting clothes for you. Dallas, you and Bill are going to take some thinking—I've got it! Spain!"

"Going to give 'em castanets and a tambourine?" Kaye asked.

"My Spanish refugee bags—don't you think they'll do, Bill, if we use the limousine? They won't arouse a bit of suspicion, you know. Everyone in Dalton has been filling those burlap bags with stuff for weeks. You and Dallas can sit on the floor, and we'll just put the bags on top of you, high enough so they show. And no one'll think a thing. And Kaye can drive."

"I don't want to be accused of cowardice," Kaye said, "but in a quiet way, I'm known in Dalton, Cassandra. I employ six hundred and thirteen people. And I must know a couple of dozen more, easily. And I drive a car quite often."

"One of Jock's noses will fix that part," Mrs. Price said.

"Er—one of which?" Leonidas asked.

"False noses, you know. They come in a box. Putty things. My grandson has such fun with them when he stays here with me. We never bother to tell his mother, because she'd be sure to think they were subversive or something—I sometimes wonder where Dorothy got her ideas on child rearing. Not, I'm sure, from me."

"I bet," Kaye said. "Did Dorothy marry a sort of quiet, mousy soul? I thought so. I felt it. Okay, Margie. Find my outfit—"

Margie hesitated.

"Say, Mrs. Price," she said, "where do I fit in this party?"

"Oh, you want to go, too? Well, I suppose you can—"

"Say, if you think I'm going to stay here, with that cop in the cellar, and do housework—say, you're crazy! I wouldn't miss this!"

"'And gentlemen in England now a-bed,'" Kaye murmured, "'shall think themselves accursed they were not here'—isn't Shakespeare the quotable old thing! You shall sit in front with me, Margie, and heroically grab the wheel from my faltering grip when the tear-gas bombs begin clinging to my putty nose!"

Half an hour later, a handful of Dalton police idly watched Kaye swing Mrs. Price's limousine out of the garage and up the driveway to the front of the house.

One of the group noticed the red-tagged burlap bags and commented, not without bitterness, on the ease with which a bunch of Spigs got stuff as compared to the Policemen's Mutual Aid.

Followed by Margie, Mrs. Price came down the front walk and got into the car.

"Where to, ma'am?" Kaye draped the lap robe over her knees.

"That nose is marvelous," Mrs. Price said. "I hardly know you. You look just like that nice Mr. Weintraub who fixes the vacuum cleaner. To her apartment first, Rogers, three hundred Wellington Road. Just off the Park in West Dalton. If she's not there, we'll just have to go to the Friday Morning Club. They meet at the auditorium."

Two motorcycle policemen, ominously waiting beside their machines at the corner, waved in a friendly fashion at Mrs. Price as Kaye stopped for the red light.

Mrs. Price waved back and opened the window.

"I've got a chauffeur, Morgan!" she called out cheerily. "See? Now you won't have to worry any more about my bifocals!"

Both officers laughed, and Morgan sauntered over to the car.

"Want an escort?"

"Oh, how simply wonderful—should you, Morgan?"

"It's to celebrate your chauffeur," Morgan said. "Where you going? Where? Okay, buddy, never mind the lights. Follow me."

To the accompaniment of a shrieking siren, the limousine shot through the streets of Dalton Hills, past the business sections of Dalton Centre and Daltonville, to West Dalton.

Mrs. Brett, the doorman told them, had just left a minute before for the Friday Morning Club.

"Want to catch her, Mrs. Price?" Morgan asked. "Aw, no, it's no trouble. I'm glad to have something to do. I been sitting around all morning—come on, bud, let's go."

There was nothing for Kaye to do but follow.

"I'm beginning," Leonidas told Dallas as the two of them bounced under the burlap bags, "not to like this much. Had I known that the police intended escorting us instead of pursuing us, I should have been tempted to sit with decorum on the car seat—"

"There she is!" Mrs. Price said, "just going in—in black! I knew it, I _knew_ she'd be draped in black. Just bearing up nobly, that's what she wants people to think. Now I'll run get her and make her get into the car, and we'll drive somewhere and have her explain—"

The plan was simple and direct and logical, and that it failed was due to no fault of Mrs. Price. After all, as she said later, it never even occurred to her to take into consideration Margaret de Haviland's deep feeling for Spain.

Mrs. de Haviland, spotting from afar the red-tagged burlap bags, bounded up to the limousine and threw open the door.

"Darling," she said impassionedly, "Cassie lamb, you've brought me a whole car full for my Spaniards! Darling, how sublime—and the truck's here and with your lovely bags we'll go over the top on our quota and beat the Addington clubs to bits, just simply to bits! We've already got seventeen bags more than they have—"

Her hand reached over for the bag immediately on top of Leonidas.

"Dear, it's too heavy!" Mrs. Price hastily inserted herself between the bag and Mrs. de Haviland. "Much too heavy—oh, much. Much, much—"

"Just laden!" Mrs. de Haviland said, "just simply laden—you're so generous, dear! Lady Bountiful. Your man can take them— Oh, never mind! Here's this marvelous-looking policeman—your brother has the best-looking force! You'll take the bags out for me," she said brightly to Morgan, "won't you, officer?"

Chapter SEVEN

DALLAS found herself giggling uproariously without making the faintest breath of a sound. She couldn't see Bill Shakespeare or hear him, either, but she felt that he was probably giggling too.

After all, it was so silly, so fabulously, incredibly silly! To escape the process server, and all those police, and Muir, and all the rest—and then to be thwarted by Spanish refugees!

"Sure," Morgan said, "I'll take the bags out—if you'll move over, Mrs. Price, I'll have them out for you in a jiffy—"

It was Kaye who temporarily saved the situation. Kaye, and the horn tootings of the impatient Dalton ladies whose cars were being held up by the limousine.

"Maybe, ma'am," he slid open the window, "maybe I better move ahead first. We're blocking that line of cars from getting—"

"Just pull her along past the entrance, bud," Morgan said. "I'll find you a place to park. You go right ahead. It's all full up, but I'll get you a space all right, Mrs. Price—"

"Oh, thank you!" Mrs. Price said politely. "Thank you so much, Morgan, you're so kind— look out for the door closing, Margaret dear!"

Under her breath, as Kaye started the car around, she addressed Leonidas.

"Bill, Bill, Bill—what'll we *do*—that woman's waiting for the bags, and she intends to have them, and Morgan's waiting—everyone's waiting! Bill, *what'll* we do?"

"Get up on the seat with her, Dallas!" Leonidas said. "Quickly. Crawl up—"

"She can't! Margaret and Morgan both have looked inside, and they know I'm alone—"

"Can't help that," Leonidas returned. "Explain her somehow—get up quickly, Dallas!"

Obediently, she pushed her way through the bags and onto the seat. She leaned back swiftly, trying hard to look as though she had been there since the day the car was purchased.

She thanked heaven for the green dress which Margie had provided, and the green hat and coat. Bill's idea about changing clothes had been sound.

"Open the left door," Leonidas said. "Open the left door—"

"Bill, you can't get out! You simply mustn't!"

"I've got to—"

"Hey, bud!" Morgan roared. "Here—over here, see? Pull her in here!"

He had to yell several times more and several degrees louder to compete with Mrs. de Haviland, who was trumpeting at someone up the block.

"Have I—what? Seen who? Who? Oh, Zara lost him, did she? Oh, he hasn't! No, I don't! I haven't seen— No, dear! I don't know him! Doesn't she? No! No! Oh," she marched over to the curbing, "here's a lovely space, Cassie dear! Isn't it marvelous to have policemen do things for you—oh! Oh! I didn't see anyone in here with you!"

"Didn't you, darling? This is my Dorothy's friend, Miss Mappin. The one from Rangoon, you know."

Mrs. Price believed that if one had to tell a lie, it might as well be good.

"From Rangoon? How interesting! But," Mrs. de Haviland continued inexorably, "I didn't see her, you know!"

"Maybe it's your glasses, dear," Mrs. Price said. "You know the trouble I've had with my bifocals! Morgan, you saw my friend, didn't you? Oh, you were in front, weren't you, so you couldn't. Who," Mrs. Price did her best to obstruct Mrs. de Haviland's view of the bags and Leonidas and the interior of the car, "who has Zara lost, dear? Anyone important?"

"Oh, the man. She hasn't exactly lost him. He just hasn't got here—you know, Cassie, I simply can't get over there being someone else with you! I never was so amazed! I—"

"To hear you talk, Margaret," Mrs. Price was beginning to sound a little desperate, "you'd think I was accustomed to wandering around by myself in lonely solitude! I must say, dear, you do exaggerate so!"

Dallas, smiling her most winning smile, leaned forward. It was just about time, she decided, that Mrs. Price got some help.

"You know, Mrs. de Haviland," she said, "we have a saying in India, 'He whose eye is on the tiger sees not the small bird in the tree.' I think you were so interested in your refugee bags that perhaps you did not see the—er—small bird."

She paused for a second and held her breath.

Somehow, Leonidas Witherall had managed to slide out of the limousine, out from under those burlap bags, without being seen either by Morgan or Mrs. de Haviland. A small garter snake could have been no more inconspicuous as far as movements were concerned. Unfortunately, his resemblance to a small garter snake ended there. In the braided cutaway coat and the sponge-bag trousers of the late Bagley Price, with that beard and mustache—Dallas swallowed.

"Not, of course," she said brightly, "that I'm any small bird. But you know what I mean, Mrs. de Haviland. Cassie, I think we'd better get out and let Mrs. de Haviland be convinced that I'm real, don't you?" In Mrs. Price's ear she added, "He's gone!"

"Oh, definitely," Mrs. Price said. "Definitely. Margaret dear—oh. Oh, my!"

Mrs. de Haviland had turned her attention from Dallas.

Pointing a strident forefinger at the figure of Leonidas, Mrs. de Haviland trumpeted to her unknown friend up the block.

"There he is! There he is! Just getting out of the cab. Yoo-hoo! Yoo-hoo!"

Leonidas, who had been desperately attempting to get into the cab, turned and faced the inevitable in the form of the Friday Morning Club's Hospitality and Greeting Committee.

"You must," said the foremost member, puffing slightly, "be Doctor MacNabb!"

Leonidas, affixing his pince-nez, bowed from the waist in a courtly manner.

"If I must, dear lady," he said, "I must."

"We were getting terribly worried about you! We were awfully worried about you!"

"I admit," Leonidas informed her with perfect truth, "that I, myself, have been worried."

Out of the corner of his eye, he watched Morgan.

And there was another officer at the corner. And still another unsnarling traffic at the entrance to the auditorium.

Sooner or later, he thought, one of them would be sure to react to his beard.

"I knew it!" Mrs. de Haviland's friend sighed. "I just knew they'd told you the wrong time—you missed the car we sent, didn't you? That's the second time someone has just got here by the skin of his teeth!"

"That," Leonidas said, "is a very apt phrase. Very. I have, as you see, neither hat nor coat."

"Well, at least you must let us pay the cab!" the woman thrust a bill into the hand of the astonished taxi driver. "And now, doctor, if— well, what I mean is, everyone's waiting, you know. If you're ready, let's go right along in!"

"Ah, yes," Leonidas said, "m'yes. Let us, indeed."

Mrs. Price and Dallas, standing by the limousine, watched dazedly as he strolled along into the auditorium, surrounded by the Hospitality and Greeting Committee.

"He's a hit, all right," Dallas said appreciatively. "They're eating him up."

"Do you realize," Mrs. Price spoke softly to no one in particular, "that *they* think he is Dr. MacNabb? This morning's speaker? And he is going *in* there! Why, he'll have to speak!"

"Don't you worry none!" Margie spoke out of the side of her mouth. "He will!"

Mrs. de Haviland, who had been milling in the wake of the committee, bounded back to where Mrs. Price and Dallas stood.

"My dear," she said, "isn't he simply fascinating! Simply fascinating! I was going in to Stearns's sale, and I'm so glad I didn't! Why, he even looks like Shakespeare, doesn't he? That'll make it so much more interesting and sort of human, don't you think?"

"Make what?" Mrs. Price asked.

"Why, he's talking on Shakespeare, didn't you know?"

Mrs. Price clucked her tongue nervously.

"D'you suppose *he* knows?" she said to Dallas. "Do you suppose he knows!"

Mrs. de Haviland regarded her with curiosity.

"Cassie," she said, "do you feel all right this morning? You're not having that little pain on the right side again, are you?"

"Miss Mappin happens to know Dr. MacNabb," Cassie pulled herself out of the hole, "very well! Really, Margaret, I certainly do hope you get on the president's committee the next time!"

"What?"

"That's why you're so snappish, isn't it? I told Ella she was silly to suggest such a thing, but now I wonder if she wasn't entirely right—where's Morgan, directing traffic? Well, K— Rogers will remove your bags and put them in the truck. D'you mind, Rogers? It's that truck over there—"

Mrs. de Haviland was only momentarily disconcerted.

"Is Dr. MacNabb married?" she asked Dallas.

"He has six children," Dallas said promptly, "and no one ever tried to count his grandchildren. A terribly prolific family."

"His wife," Mrs. Price said firmly, "lectures on birth control. Always being arrested, you know."

"Indeed," Mrs. de Haviland said. "Well, I suppose we might as well go in— Are you coming?"

"You run along, dear," Mrs. Price said, serene in the thought that Margaret was pretty well routed, "I've got to tell Rogers about the car."

Kaye deposited the red-tagged bags in the truck, and then sauntered back to the limousine.

"I still feel," he said, "that it would be right and proper if I waked up under a table at the club—do you know, my own sister just passed by me? And when I winked at her, she looked meaningly toward Morgan— Cassie, don't let's play with Morgan any more. He makes it easier to get places, but look what happens!"

"It's that marvelous nose," Cassie said. "Why your sister didn't recognize you, I mean. You look just exactly like Mr. Weintraub, the vacuum man."

"I feel like a vacuum man," Kaye told her. "Look, what do we do now?"

"I've thought that out," Cassie said. "Dallas and I will have to go in. Then if we have to, we can create a disturbance and give Bill a chance to get out. I can always faint!"

"Considering the membership of the Friday Morning Club," Kaye said, "it would be simpler just to stand up and yell 'Hurray for Roosevelt!' Then everyone would faint and Bill could pick his way out through the inert bodies—okay, Cassie. You and Dallas do what you can, and Margie and I will wait here—"

"Better get nearer the door," Dallas suggested. "If we come out alive, we're going to be in a hurry."

"I don't see what you're all worrying so about," Margie said. "Bill can look out for himself, all right!"

"You seem to have a lot of faith in him," Kaye commented.

"Listen, it don't take me twenty years to make my mind up about anyone," Margie said. "Bill's got those dames eating out of his hand. He'll get whatever he wants from Sister Brett—don't you think he won't!

He may look like something that belongs on a pedestal in a library somewheres, but that guy's got what it takes!"

"Why, I know that!" Cassie said. "I never thought anything different, not for a second! Bill's a terribly capable man—come along, Dallas, or we'll never get a seat. Why, I have the utmost faith in Bill!"

Inside the auditorium, Leonidas sat on a small gilt chair on the platform, hemmed in by a dozen of the Friday Club's more prominent members.

At his elbow sat Miss Zara Brett, obviously delighted at the interest displayed in her by the fascinating guest of honor.

"Watch Bill!" Dallas whispered. "He's cooing at her and she's lapping it up like a kitten!"

"She's positively preening," Cassie said. "I hope he notices her shifty eyes."

"He couldn't help it," Dallas returned. "She hasn't taken them off his face since we came in."

"I wonder if Bill's nervous," Cassie said. "Inwardly, I mean. I do hope someone thinks to tell him what he's got to talk about. Of course, he doesn't look a bit nervous. But then he never does—why, she's putting one of her gardenias in his buttonhole! Now— I call that brash!"

Leonidas, up on the platform, thought that Miss Brett was rather letting herself go, but he accepted the boutonniere gallantly enough.

Mentally he added Miss Brett's nervous hands to his list, which already included shifty eyes, abnormal restlessness, and a curious habit of dabbing at her right temple with a handkerchief.

Her eyes were very like Benny's, and shifty, Leonidas thought, was not quite the proper adjective with which to describe them. There was something strange about the pupils. They reminded him of von Arnheim, the little Austrian who sometimes turned up at book auctions.

Drugs, of course.

That was it.

He bent forward, and then leaned back hastily.

This was, after all, no time for any thorough investigation of Miss Brett's contracted pupils. She had already misinterpreted his gesture.

"Do audiences ever disconcert you, doctor?" Miss Brett asked.

"Oh, no," Leonidas said. "I have faced too many. Far too many."

This was his first experience before a woman's club, but the rows and rows of pink eggs confronting him in the Dalton Auditorium differed very little from the rows of pink eggs in the Meredith Academy Assembly Hall. On the whole, the boys were quieter and they wriggled less. It was quite possible, Leonidas thought, that they might even be more critical than the Friday Morning Club.

He only wished he knew what he was to talk about.

Miss Brett had a program in her hand, but she held it at such an angle that he was able to see only the single word "madrigal."

He knew a number of madrigals, but he hoped

fervently that he was not going to have to sing them.

There was the water pitcher, of course. He could always tip that over, and in the confusion pick up the program and read it.

It seemed simpler just to ask.

"Er—I always like to check," he said blandly, "on the title under which I am to be introduced. And the length of time. And—this is an idiosyncrasy of mine, but may I ask that the doors be closed and that no one be admitted after we have begun?"

While he was at it, he thought, he might as well take a few precautions.

"Oh, certainly," Miss Brett said. "I'll see to the doors right away—thirty minutes will be enough, doctor. That is, thirty minutes is usually the minimum, but we didn't let Mr. Carnegie go for an hour and a half! I'll tell Mrs. West about the doors, right now—"

"Er—the topic?"

"Shakespeare, the Man."

Leonidas smiled.

"The octopus," he murmured, "of destiny. My, my, those viscid arms!"

Cassie Price and Dallas sat like pokers throughout a brief business meeting and the singing of three madrigals by a blonde soprano in a pink taffeta dirndl. They began to relax at the end of Leonidas's opening sentence.

"He's wowing them," Dallas said. "Oh, if Kaye could only hear Bill wow!"

Leonidas, enjoying himself hugely, continued to wow the Friday Club.

Then suddenly a single pink egg lunged up at him from all the rows and rows of beaming pink eggs.

That single face threw Leonidas off his stride.

Clearing his throat apologetically, he inserted a humorous anecdote into his discourse. Eddie Cantor had told the story a month before, but with tailoring it fitted Shakespeare, and the Friday Club thought it was hilariously funny.

While they laughed and laughed, Leonidas poured out a glass of water and drank it.

Then he resumed talking.

But to Cassie and Dallas, it seemed as though some of the fire had gone out of his lecture.

And it had.

The face belonged to Professor Otis's wife. And Estelle Otis was not a resourceful woman. She was an intensely serious-minded individual who, as the saying went, took things hard. She went out of her way to take things hard. No one had ever accused her of seeing a joke. No one expected her to.

Leonidas endured Estelle because she went along with the rest of Charles Otis's possessions. How Charles Otis endured her, Leonidas never understood.

Estelle knew him, all right. And Estelle knew that the Dalton police urgently desired a man with a beard. Estelle had a melancholy fondness for police calls. She listened to them constantly. It seemed to give her a glow of pleasure to know that boys played ball on Sunset Avenue, and that two suspicious cars parked before an untenanted house on Z Street were undergoing an investigation.

Whether or not Estelle's somewhat rigid mind was capable of making the leap of connecting him with the sought-after bearded man, Leonidas did not know.

Hoping for the best, he threw himself into his peroration.

"Is he," Dallas said in admiration, "ever giving! He's knocking them cold!"

He wound up to salvos of deafening applause that shook the auditorium.

"Not since Carnegie!" someone behind him on the platform yelled above the din.

"More than Carnegie!" Miss Brett yelled back loyally. "Heaps louder!"

Leonidas gracefully accepted the plaudits.

The audience was not, as he had suspected, as critical as Meredith's, but they paid far more attention. He had never talked to a more receptive and flattering group.

He had intended to hurry off the platform and talk to Zara Brett, but before he could move, a swarm of women poured up from the first rows below. They encircled him, all chatting lustily at once.

Mrs. Otis was not among them, but Leonidas knew she was on her way. He had seen her start.

He did his best to cope with the throng, but he felt a surge of relief when Zara Brett pounded for order and announced that absolutely not another soul, not another soul, could come up on the platform, the fireman said so. No fireman had said anything, as far as Leonidas knew, but it had the desired effect.

A woman in green tugged gently at his arm.

"Mr.—I mean, Dr. MacNabb—my name is Gettridge."

"Ah, yes. Mrs. Gettridge," Leonidas said mechanically.

"My husband," she said, "had a client who looked like Shakespeare, too. And do you know, you remind me very strongly of an English professor who used to be at Meredith's. I once went to a Speech Day with my nephew—as a matter of fact, I went yesterday."

There was a twinkle in her eye. Leonidas pinned all his hopes on it.

"To think," he said, "that it was Estelle Otis that I was worrying about!"

"I've been watching Estelle," Mrs. Gettridge said. "That's why I've dropped my car keys in your pocket. Number 68807. Parked very near the rear door. Just in case you might—"

"Mustn't monopolize our guest of honor!" Zara Brett took Leonidas by the arm. "I've promised to take him down on the floor—everybody is just clamoring to meet you, doctor, just clamoring! I can't tell you what you've done to Shakespeare for us—why, the man simply lives! Wasn't the doctor marvelous, Mrs. Gettridge?"

"I've seldom heard him in better form," Mrs. Gettridge said. "Good-by, doctor. Those are duplicates, by the way, those—er—books. If you don't need them, don't bother to return them—"

"Wait!" Leonidas said. "Wait—Mrs. Gettridge, your husband is a lawyer, is he not—"

But Mrs. Gettridge had disappeared from the platform.

"He was a lawyer," Zara Brett said, "but he died this winter—doctor, I just don't know how I'm ever going to get you down there through this perfect madhouse! And once I let you down, I'll never see you for hours!"

"I wonder," Leonidas said, "if I might have a few words with you privately, first? It's rather important, or I shouldn't—"

"My dear man, I forgot your check! Of course, come right out to the little dressing room—"

"It's not the check," Leonidas said, and then stopped.

Zara was beginning to get brash ideas again.

Cassie Price, who had been thwarted in her attempt to get up on the platform, instantly noticed it, and whispered a comment in Dallas's ear.

"You're lewd!" Dallas said. "But she did sort of cuddle his arm, didn't she?"

Leonidas put on his pince-nez.

"This is a problem, Miss Brett," he said in what he hoped was a pointedly impersonal tone, "of grave importance. I should not otherwise suggest that you—er—leave your duties and withdraw."

Zara looked puzzled, but she maneuvered Leonidas through the still lustily chatting women and out into a small anteroom.

Leonidas closed the door and stood with his back to it.

"Miss Brett," he said, "just who was planning with your brother Benny to kill me?"

"What!"

"Perhaps I am tardy with the information," Leonidas said blandly, "but my name is Witherall, you know. Not MacNabb."

"You are Leonidas Witherall! You—why, you impostor! You— I'll have you arrested! Get out of the way! Get out—"

"So you know my first name?" Leonidas said. "M'yes. M'yes, indeed. I didn't tell you, but you knew it anyway. Now suppose you answer my question, Miss Brett. Who planned with Benny to kill me?"

"I don't know what you're talking about!"

"Come, come," Leonidas said wearily, "don't waste time."

"I'm going to have you arrested. I—"

"I shouldn't," Leonidas said.

"You're an impostor! You come here claiming to be Dr. MacNabb—and now you threaten me! You—"

Leonidas barred her way to the door.

"I think, if I were you," he added, "I should definitely consider the humorous aspect of this, Miss Brett. The funny side."

"There's no funny side to being an impostor, and holding me prisoner, and—"

"Oh, yes," Leonidas said. "It will be terribly funny when the Friday Club learns that its president has been—shall we say—bilked? And you were so attentive, too. You know, it's quite possible that the Friday Morning Club may bitterly resent the whole episode. They will most certainly discuss it. Ad, I should say, infinitum."

Zara was white with anger.

"Of course," Leonidas continued, "your name will be linked with Shakespeare's, but even so. There are better ways to acquire fame."

"I am going to call the police!"

"There is that old adage," Leonidas said, "about the pot and the kettle. If you talk of turning me over to the police, I can only retaliate by presenting the police with your note to Benny. You might consider that."

Zara sat down on a battered chair and wrung her hands until Leonidas thought they might drop off. Then she began to sob wildly.

Leonidas watched her critically. She was acting, and it was a bad act. Cassie Price would have done better without even stopping to think.

"May I remind you," he said, "that your fellow members are waiting? Champing, by this time, no doubt. Miss Brett, who planned with Benny to kill me?"

Zara continued to sob. She was very near the hair-tearing stage.

"Very well," Leonidas said decisively. "I am going out and tell those women that I am not Dr. Mac-Nabb, that you knew it all the time. Then I am going to the police with that note. I've given you your chance."

She clutched at his arm as he turned to go.

"Benny wasn't going to kill you! He wasn't going

to kill anyone! He was going to make Kaye buy, don't you see? I didn't have anything to do with this—I don't know who he talked with! But they killed him, they killed him—oh, I wish I was dead, I wish I was dead!"

"Were, not was," Leonidas said. "So, Benny and X planned to kill me. X tried, and then killed Benny. M'yes. That part works out as I thought it would. Now, what was Benny going to sell Kaye?"

Almost as he uttered the question, Leonidas knew that he had made a fatal mistake.

He could sense the complete change which came over Zara Brett even before she moved a muscle. He should never have let her guess that he did not know what Benny was going to sell Kaye. He had given away too much of his bluff, and Zara was now no longer afraid.

She lifted her head and looked at him sharply. The pupils of her eyes dilated, and then contracted to pinpoints again.

Then she smiled.

It was one of the most unpleasant smiles Leonidas had ever seen.

"You are an impostor!" she said in her madam-president voice. "You are a blackmailer! I think you may even be a murderer! And, Mr. Leonidas Wither-all, you are going to rue this day—"

Her hand ripped at the front of her dress, and simultaneously Leonidas reached in his pocket and pulled out Muir's smallest gun.

He had not the vaguest idea what he was going to do with it.

He only knew that he was not going to stand idly by while Zara Brett carried out her obvious intention of tearing her clothing to shreds and then screaming for the police.

"Put up your hands!" Leonidas said in tones which he hardly recognized as his own. "You aren't going to get away with—"

Someone knocked in a determined fashion at the door.

"Leonidas! Leonidas Witherall!"

It was the righteous nasal twang of Estelle Otis.

"Leonidas, if you're in there, I think you'd better come right out! Right away! I'm not going to permit this chicanery—"

Zara was on top, in spite of the gun, and she knew it.

Drawing a long breath, she started to scream at the top of her lungs.

"Help! Help! Help—somebody save me! Help—"

Chapter EIGHT

LEONIDAS thrust the gun back into his hip pocket, and bowed.

"Your rubber," he said, "but not your game, Miss Brett! Remember that!"

He pulled open the door so quickly that Estelle Otis tumbled headlong into the room.

Whether she had hurt herself, or whether she was merely frightened, Leonidas did not know. But Estelle's immediate and strident screams were far more vicious than Zara's.

Leonidas darted past her, into the hall.

He did not bother to see if there were hooks or locks or bolts on the door which he slammed behind him. The unearthly din those two women were raising would unmake the stone walls and melt the iron bars of virtually any prison.

At a turn in the corridor, he stumbled into Cassie Price and Dallas.

"For shame, Bill!" Dallas said. "Off twosing with madam pres! The—good God, what did you do to the woman, Bill? Is that noise Zara?"

"Zara," Leonidas said breathlessly, "and Estelle Otis. You two go there quickly. Tell people they saw a rat. Two rats. An army of rats. Explain them as epileptics. As anything. But don't let them talk until I've got out of this place—"

"I'll handle it," Cassie said briskly. "Zara's gone all to pieces. Bearing up after Benny, and all, but now something's snapped. Complete nervous breakdown. They'll believe it, she had one before. I'll handle it—what'll you do, Bill? Where are you going?"

"Anywhere away from here," Leonidas said. "Preferably the Elks Club. Go quickly and quiet them—"

"Kaye's moved the car," Dallas said. "Just slip out into the back alley and you'll land right on top of him—hurry, Cassie, there comes a mob rushing out—"

It was all very well, Leonidas thought as he continued his headlong flight down the corridor, to know that Kaye was waiting near the back alley. It was heartening and encouraging, and it provided a goal. But he wished that Dallas had taken the trouble to tell him how one got to the back alley. As far as he could see, the rear portion of the Dalton Auditorium was a maze of halls and doors and corridors, of stacked scenery, piled-up furniture, and broken gilt chairs.

He couldn't even hazard a guess as to which direction the back alley might be in.

After making two fruitless circuits of the same stack of scenery, Leonidas sat down on the rung of a step ladder to get his breath and consider the situation.

Even if he were caught before he reached Kaye and Mrs. Price's car, he did not feel that his ordeal with the Friday Morning Club had been in vain. On the contrary, he had made some very definite progress.

Zara Brett knew all about her brother Benny's plans with X. That note to Benny which he had found in Bigelow was not just an accident of phrasing. She knew that Benny and X had intended to kill him.

She had provided some light on all of Benny's phone calls to Kaye. Benny had really wanted to see Kaye. Benny wanted to sell Kaye something.

And it seemed quite clear to Leonidas that the something which Benny wanted to sell Kaye played a dual role.

It was also the motive behind the attempt of Benny and his accomplice to kill him, to run him down with the roadster.

And whatever that something might be, Leonidas thought, it did more than serve as a connection between that attempted murder and Benny's calls to Kaye. It narrowed things down. It made things tangible. There were, after all, only so many things for which you could kill a man, and so many things which you could sell.

A distant babble of shrilly excited voices reminded him that this was neither the time nor the place for any prolonged meditation.

As he got up from the step ladder, Leonidas noticed a pair of overalls on the floor beside him.

He surveyed them thoughtfully, and then picked them up. They were baggy things, resembling overgrown rompers, and they said "Eddie's Hamburgers" across the front in red thread. But they seemed to Leonidas to be a very good idea.

Casting off the cutaway of the late Bagley Price, Leonidas climbed into "Eddie's Hamburgers" and zipped himself dressed. In one of the pockets was a red bandanna handkerchief, which he tied around his neck. It smelled remotely of fried onions, but it hid his beard.

A visored cap from a pile of refuse in the corner made him, he hoped, a new man.

As he started along to resume his search for the back alley, a door was flung open almost at his elbow, and a broom was thrust at him.

"Here, you!" said the irate man behind the broom. "Take this goddam thing! I've nearly killed myself on your goddam broom! Whyn't you keep the goddam thing out of the way? Don't you know any better than to leave brooms lying around, for God's sake? Here, take it!"

Leonidas took the broom with considerable pleasure.

The irate man stood in a vestibule. And beyond the vestibule was the back alley.

He had been sitting almost squarely in front of that door all the time.

"Thank you," he said. "Thank you very much—"

"Where's Mrs. Brett? My God, what a hole this is! Where's Mrs. Brett, for God's sake? I never saw such a hole in all my life! I tell you, this place is a hole!"

Leonidas nodded.

"M'yes," he said, "it *is* a hole, isn't it? Er—are you by any chance—could your name be MacNabb?"

"It certainly is! And what do you suppose those fool women did? First they told me the wrong time, and then when I got here, they locked me out! D'you hear that? They locked me out! They wouldn't let me in! Do you know what I think of this club, whatever its name is?"

"What?" Leonidas asked. He was really curious to know.

"I think," Dr. MacNabb pounded a canvas tree so vigorously with his clenched fist that it fell in shreds to the concrete floor, "I think that of all the goddam clubs I ever had the misfortune to meet up with, this is the goddamndest, that's what I think! Are you a married man?"

Leonidas admitted that he was not.

"You thank God," Dr. MacNabb said, "you thank him every night of your life, my good man! That's the way I feel about women, and I wish my wife was here to hear me! Where's that woman named Brett?"

"I haven't seen her for some time," Leonidas said truthfully, "but if you follow the sound of all that noise, you ought to find her."

"Which way?"

Leonidas made a vague gesture.

"There," he said.

"That woman," Dr. MacNabb said, "that woman is going to hear more from me than she ever heard from any man in all the days of her life! And if she thinks she can get out of paying me, she's crazy! Crazy! I'll sue her. I'll sue the whole goddam club, if she dares say one word about not paying me! This way? Good-by. And keep your broom out of that goddam vestibule from now on!"

Dr. MacNabb strode off.

Leonidas smiled, and stepped out to the back alley.

The broom made a nice prop. While he swept off the top step, Leonidas studied the lay of the land. There were streets to his left and to his right, and directly in front of him were the rear entrances of the stores on the next block. A noon hour dullness seemed to hang over everything.

He would try the street to his right, first, Leonidas decided.

Still carrying the broom, he set out.

Almost at once he abandoned the plan.

Two policemen strolled a few feet up the alley entrance and almost surreptitiously lighted cigarettes. It was evident that they were taking advantage of the noonday lull, and that they intended to stay there for some time.

Leonidas turned back to the top step and brushed it off all over again. To run, or hurry, or show any undue haste would, he felt, be a grave error.

After a minute or two, he started for the street on the left. He could see the rear of a car parked just beyond the alley entrance.

He smiled.

It was a limousine.

It was Mrs. Price's car.

Almost at the entrance, Leonidas stopped short in dismay.

It was Mrs. Price's limousine, all right, with Kaye at the wheel and Margie beside him. But, standing and staring at them and the car was the burly gent, the process server!

Leonidas went hurriedly back to his top step.

Perhaps the safest place for him, after all, was the auditorium itself. He would go back inside and wander around among the halls and the corridors and the scenery and the broken gilt chairs. Then, when the coast was less cluttered, he would try again.

As he stepped into the vestibule, he heard the nasal twang of Estelle Otis. She was expostulating with someone just inside.

"I tell you, I knew it was Leonidas! Of course I'm sure! I know! And I'm going to find him, too, and I'm going—"

"Now see here," it was Dallas who was trying to soothe Estelle, "do be reasonable, Mrs. Otis! Even if there was a mistake—didn't you just hear Zara Brett say that there *had* been a mistake, that she was just *so* unstrung, and all that sort of thing? Well, even if there's been a mistake, what *is* the use of bothering about it now? It's all over, isn't it?"

"Why did Zara Brett yell for help?"

"My dear Mrs. Otis," Dallas said wearily, "who am I to interpret the workings of Zara Brett's mind? She's just gone off the handle, if you ask me. Slap-happy. Now, why don't you forget the whole incident—"

"Forget? I'm not going to forget anything! I'm

going straight to the root of this, straight to the very root!"

Leonidas sighed.

If Estelle Otis had made up her mind to uproot the situation, uproot it she would. Dallas was just wasting her breath. For sheer indomitability, Leonidas would back Estelle against anyone.

"He didn't go out the front door," Mrs. Otis continued, "so he went out the back—"

"If he did," Dallas pointed out, "he's over the hills and far away by now."

"Just the same," Mrs. Otis said, "I'm going to take a look around. My mind is made up. Stand aside, please, Miss Mappin. I'm going to take a look out in the back alley and see if he's hiding there—hide! I should think that that man would be so ashamed of himself, he'd want to hide deep in the ground!"

"All right," Dallas said, "I'll go out and take a look around, if that'll make you feel any better. You stay here—"

"I prefer to look myself, if it's all the same to you," Mrs. Otis said coldly. "And if he is not there, I intend to ask if anyone's seen him—if I have to ask the entire population of Dalton! My mind is made up!"

"But—"

"Stand aside—"

Leonidas slipped out to the top step.

The policemen on his right had been joined by a couple of hearty friends, and they were all laughing merrily over something. At the other end of the alley, the burly process server paced back and forth doggedly. Behind in the vestibule, Mrs. Otis and Dallas were still squabbling. Dallas was putting up a noteworthy battle, but her eventual defeat was a foregone conclusion.

There was only one direction left to go, and Leonidas proceeded to go there.

Opening the rear entrance of the nearest store across the alley, Leonidas walked in.

He judged, from the hampers and the piles of dirty clothes, that it was a cleaning establishment.

A massive youth in the corner swung around and faced him truculently.

"Hey, what you—"

"Cuff!" Leonidas said. "Cuff!"

The lettering of "Eddie's Hamburgers" and the visored cap had Cuff puzzled for a second. Then he grinned.

"If it ain't Shakespeare, huh! Hi, pal! Say, I hadn't ought to of left you holding the bag last night! I'm sorry about that. I told Margie if I seen you again I'd—say, did you get away okay?"

"Then," Leonidas said, "but not now—"

He was afraid he would have to go into lengthy explanations, but Cuff's mind reacted instantly. With him, escape was a matter of routine.

"Cops?" he inquired as he shoved Leonidas into the largest of the wheeled hampers and covered him with clothes.

"A woman," Leonidas said. "A horse-faced woman with many teeth. Of course, there are the cops, too. But the woman is the more dangerous right now—"

Mrs. Otis's determined knock sounded at the back door.

"Squelch her if you can, Cuff. Just don't let her find me, that's all."

Offhand, he could think of only one kind thing to say about Estelle Otis.

At least she knocked before entering.

Cuff opened the door.

"Have you seen a man with a beard?" Mrs. Otis demanded.

"So what?" Cuff said.

"Young man, have you seen a man with a beard?"

"Listen, lady," Cuff said, "this is Schlagermann's Cleaning and Dyeing. The barber shop's two doors down."

"There," Dallas said. "You see what I mean, Mrs. Otis? You just can't march around asking about a man with a beard! It's funny!"

"I see nothing funny about it! Young man, have you seen an elderly man with a beard out in the alley?"

"A beard like this?" Cuff pulled at the air beneath his chin.

"That's it! That's it—when did you see him?"

"A week ago. He's the old clothes man. He comes every Friday unless it rains."

"Come on, Sister Otis!" Dallas said.

"I am convinced that this young fellow knows something. Now tell me about this man with the beard—"

"Lady," Cuff said, "if you can't control your husband, why bother me?"

Mrs. Otis snorted and went up the alley.

Cuff came back to the hamper.

"She's gone," he said. "Say, Shakespeare, she ain't your wife, is she?"

"Merciful heavens, no!" Leonidas said explosively. "No! What a repugnant thought! Go see what she's up to, Cuff. Don't think she's given up. She hasn't."

Cuff leaned in the doorway and watched Mrs. Otis stalk up to the policemen and their friends.

"The cops told her," he reported back to Leonidas, "they'd been hunting a guy with a beard for hours. Whoops—she's coming back. Going to Preston Street and look around."

After several unsuccessful interviews with people at that end of the alley, Mrs. Otis marched back and sat on the top step which Leonidas had swept so carefully.

Cuff was chuckling when he reported.

"She says, there she stays. If you didn't go out the front door, and nobody seen you come out here, then you're in the hall, and she's going to stay right there on that step till you come out. That's a lousy break for you, pal, because I can't let you out the front door here for an hour. The girl's gone to lunch, and she takes the key. What a break!"

"What a break for humanity," Leonidas remarked, "if that woman had been Eve. She wouldn't have eaten that apple in the face of starvation. Cuff, let's have a test case. Take one of the other hampers and wheel it out to—is it Preston Street, where the policemen aren't? Well, wheel it out there and see if there's a limousine parked there. You'll know the limousine, because Margie's sitting in the front seat—"

"Gee, is she, huh?"

"Yes. Ask her if the coast is clear—but don't ask her anything if that process server is there—"

"Gee, got one of them, too?"

"I've got everything," Leonidas assured him. "Go ahead, and let's see how that works out. Oh, leave the door open—"

As he suspected, Mrs. Otis instantly demanded to see the contents of the hamper.

"Lady," Cuff said, "I can't let you paw over them clothes. I'll lose my job."

"I demand to see the contents of that hamper, young man!"

Cuff, who could be very self-righteous when the occasion arose, whistled at the policemen.

"Say, sarge," he said plaintively to the officer who strolled over, "this woman—she's hunting a man with a beard, and she wants I should let her paw over these clothes to see if he's in 'em. You know Schlagermann, sarge. You know what he'll say if I let people paw his clothes—look, sarge, you go through this hamper with your comb, will you? Then I can say it was you—"

The officer winked at Cuff and prodded the clothes.

"Nobody there," he said, "but us chickens. Satisfied, lady? And say, you looked up in that drain pipe yet? There's a little hole up there—"

Dallas leaned back against the brick wall of the auditorium and laughed until the tears rolled down her cheeks.

"Sarge," Cuff said, "that's good!"

Inspired by the reception of his witticism, the officer tried again.

"There's that crack in the concrete," he said, "and —say, the coal hole!"

Gravely, he knelt down and removed the coal chute cover.

"Here, beardy," he called enticingly. "Come on up, beardy, your wife wants you! Well, he ain't there, lady. But you can't say that the Dalton police didn't do their best!"

An ordinary woman would have given up, but Estelle Otis was no ordinary woman.

"No," she said to Dallas, "I will not give up! Here I stay!"

"I shall think of you," Dallas said, "on the cold winter nights, with icicles on your nose. In fact, you're going to be pretty damp in another half hour, when this drizzle really gets to rain—"

Cuff wheeled the hamper up to the end of the alley and then returned to Leonidas.

"There ain't no limousine there. There's a guy from the sheriff's office, though, hanging around."

Leonidas sighed.

"Cuff, I suppose you can drive? Well, go out to the other street and see if there's a car with the number plate 68807."

Cuff returned almost at once.

"Yeah, a Ford coupé. There's a lady in a green coat in it. She seems to be waiting, like. Say, this is kind of fun, pal. What's it all about?"

"Margie will tell you all," Leonidas said. "She's

mixed up in it, remotely— Are you—er—quite sure you want to help? You may get involved with the police yourself, you know."

"Any pal of Margie's is a pal of mine," Cuff said. "Besides, I owe you something for last night. What you want done now?"

"Wheel me out in this hamper," Leonidas said, "to the coupé. Say to the woman, Mrs. Gettridge— got that name, Gettridge? Say to her, Mrs. Gettridge, I am returning your keys, if you want to take a chance. Got that?"

Cuff said it over twice.

"Fine," Leonidas said. "If she looks doubtful, wheel me back. If she says yes, put me and the hamper in the car. Now, is that girl still with horse-face on the steps? She is. Now I wonder how we can tell her. Mrs. Otis would see a note. Cuff, can you sing?"

"Say," Cuff said, "I got six thousand eight hundred and sixty-one votes on Major Bowes. Swing Murray, that's me. That's how I met Margie, through my voice!"

"What," Leonidas said, "can you sing as you pass down the alley so that Dallas will understand, and Mrs. Otis won't? Something that will make Dallas grasp who you are—d'you remember—no, that won't do. A Scotch song won't do."

"Can I ever swing 'Loch Lomond'!" Cuff said indignantly. "What do you mean, a Scotch song won't do!"

"Do you know 'I Love a Lassie'? Well, sing 'Margie' for whatever the name is. See? Then a few bars of

'Loch Lomond.' The high road and the low road. Have you got all that?"

"Say, listen, pal," Cuff said, "I know every word of 'All Points West.' You're talking to a guy that can sing!"

"Sing," Leonidas said, "away. Er—swing it, in fact."

Out in the alley, Mrs. Otis interrupted Cuff's song.

"The name of the girl in that piece," she informed him, "is not Margie. It's—"

"Lady," Cuff said, "my girl is named Margie. She's a lassie, and I love her. You want to make anything out of it, huh? Maybe you want I should sing another song? Okay!"

Cuff swung "Loch Lomond" practically out of recognition.

"What an unpleasant fellow!" Mrs. Otis said pettishly as Cuff passed by the policemen and out of the alley. "So stupid—oh, you smoke, do you, Miss Mappin? Now I can't see the slightest pleasure in a woman smoking. For a man, that's different. But I do hate to see young girls blowing that horrid smoke out of their mouths. And their noses. Now, honestly, Miss Mappin, what pleasure do you get out of smoking?"

"Loads," Dallas said.

"But what use is it?"

"You can tell time," Dallas returned, "when you haven't got a watch. I haven't a watch. That is, I have one, but it got left at Mrs. Price's house."

"What a curious reason for smoking!" Mrs. Otis said.

"Not to me."

"I wonder where that stupid young fellow *went?*" Mrs. Otis demanded.

"I think you wrong him," Dallas said.

"Oh, but he's definitely stupid—where did he go?"

Dallas flicked her cigarette into the air and rose from the step.

"'I rather think," she said, "that the stupid youth has taken the high road, as he said, Mrs. Otis—"

"Where are you going?"

"Me? I'm taking the low road. Have fun sitting, Sister Otis. I shall think of you when it really rains —should you like some lunch sent over, or anything? Perhaps an umbrella? No? Not even the name of your nearest relation to notify in case of chilblains? Oh, very well. Have you ever been in Rangoon?"

"Where? Certainly not! Why?"

"In Rangoon," Dallas said, with her hand on the door knob, "we have a saying. I was telling Mrs. de Haviland about it. 'He whose eye is on the tiger sees not the small bird in the tree.' You ought to go to Rangoon, Sister Otis. So long!"

"I'm sure I don't understand you!"

"You will," Dallas said. "Good-by."

Mrs. Gettridge, deftly steering the coupé through Dalton Falls traffic, talked to the hamper jammed in the front seat beside her.

"I'm sure," she said, "you must be terribly uncomfortable—this car is no limousine, anyway. Where shall I take you?"

"In my present cramped state," Leonidas said, "any large open space will do—er—where is Cuff?"

"He's in the rumble. We didn't dare trust the hamper on the seat alone. I'll go as fast as I dare, Mr. Witherall. By the way, shouldn't you like me to stop and get some food for you? You need some, I think."

"Need is a small word," Leonidas said. "Send Cuff in somewhere and tell him to buy food in large quan—ow! Quantities. After food and a good stretch, I may be able to carry on."

Later, on a wood road near the outskirts of the next town of Carnavon, Leonidas sighed with pleasure.

"If anyone had ever told me," he said, "that I could eat five hamburgers— I am worse than that alley cat with the fish cakes, Cuff. Mrs. Gettridge, I can't tell you how grateful I am. I find myself wondering why you should put yourself in such a precarious position for the sake of a complete stranger."

"You're not really a complete stranger," she said. "After all, you were one of Paul's clients. I have written you any number of letters— I did most of his correspondence, you know. I've wondered what you did about your Dalton land."

"That land!" Leonidas said. "You may not believe it, but I'd forgotten that land entirely until I heard your name and asked Miss Brett who your husband was. That land of Uncle Orrin's caused me more pain!"

"I gathered that," Mrs. Gettridge said, "from your rare letters."

"It was a nuisance," Leonidas said. "A millstone. It was not worth writing letters about. The day your husband rid me of that land was one of the happiest in my life—"

"Rid you of it? But Paul never did, Mr. Witherall!"

"Oh, yes," Leonidas said. "Years ago. He sold it, or gave it away, or presented it to the city in lieu of taxes. I was never gladder—"

"But, Mr. Witherall!" Mrs. Gettridge said. "He didn't! Unless you've got rid of the land since Paul died, you still own it! Paul never rid you of it."

Leonidas looked at her.

"Truly, Mr. Witherall! That's one of the reasons I spoke to you today. I wondered what you'd done about it. Because it turned out as Paul said. He said when your uncle Orrin left it to you—how long ago was it?"

"Nineteen twenty-nine," Leonidas said.

"He said then it would be immensely valuable some day. And of course it is, now, with that new development there, and the golf club, and the Kaye estate. It's some of the most valuable land in Dalton— what's the matter, Mr. Witherall, do you feel ill?"

"No," Leonidas said. "No. I feel stupid, Mrs. Gettridge. Very, very stupid. To think that I held the clew in my hand half the morning! I dandled it on my knee. I stared and stared at Bigelow on 'Real Property,' and I couldn't think of land. Because you know, Mrs. Gettridge, this is the answer to all of this. Land."

Chapter NINE

"LAND is the answer to what?" Mrs. Gettridge asked. "I don't understand what—"

"Land," Leonidas went on almost dreamily. "Land, which I had forgotten about, and which now is of some value—"

"Some value? It's immensely valuable! Why, Mr. Witherall, it's worth at least several hundred thousand dollars! Paul told me so the last time I asked him about it, and Paul never overestimated values. But tell me, what is land the answer to?"

"If you and Cuff would like the whole story," Leonidas said, "I will tell you. The first part may seem like repetition, Cuff, but I'm sure you'll bear with me. I'd rather like to go through the whole thing and straighten it out in my own mind."

Mrs. Gettridge listened quietly until he came to his awakening, that morning in the Brett house, and his discovery of Benny's body.

"You—oh! No wonder you had Cuff ask me if I cared to take a chance! You're the man with the beard, the man the police have been hunting!"

"M'yes," Leonidas said. "I—"

"And knowing that the police were after you, you addressed the Friday Morning Club on Shakespeare the Man! You actually got up and faced—"

"It was really through no fault of mine," Leonidas said hastily. "It was forced on me, I assure you. And when I saw Estelle Otis's face in that audience, I— but I mustn't leap ahead of myself—"

Mrs. Gettridge smiled occasionally at the recounting of the morning's events. But as Leonidas talked on, she began to look increasingly worried. A deep furrow appeared between her eyes, and the knuckles of her left hand were white as she gripped the car door handle.

"There," Leonidas said at last. "Now you see how it all goes. Benny and his accomplice wanted to kill me because I owned land, and they knew it was valuable. Benny double-crossed his accomplice and tried to sell the land to Stanton Kaye. I suppose his idea there was to sell it at some fabulous sum, and then give me a few dollars. But the accomplice had already run me down, and when he returned to the Brett house, he confronted Benny whimpering at Kaye over the phone, and killed him. Of course there are many flaws and gaps, but land is without doubt the answer to the whole thing. I'm convinced of it, if it is as valuable as you say your husband thought."

"Gee!" Cuff said wonderingly, "it's like a movie, ain't it? Even the part with Margie and me at first. Gee, it's a movie!"

"M'yes," Leonidas said. "It most certainly moves.

Now, how could Benny Brett possibly have learned about that land, when I myself did not know about it?"

Mrs. Gettridge took a deep breath.

"Because," she said, "August Barker Brett is the executor and administrator of my husband's estate."

Leonidas swung his pince-nez on their broad black ribbon and looked out of the car window at the damp outlines of the Carnavon Hills.

"That," he said at last, "is most interesting. Most interesting."

"August had pneumonia this winter," Mrs. Gettridge said. "That's why he's taking such a long vacation in Florida, to recuperate. My share of the estate really didn't need much settling. Paul had settled most of his personal affairs several years ago after a previous illness. But August Barker has really done very little about the rest. I spoke to him about it before he left, and suggested that he have someone help him, but he said that Benny and his office could handle everything. He seemed rather to resent my bringing the matter up. There wasn't anything more I could do, you see. He is—"

"The boss," Leonidas said. "I see. M'yes, I see. August is ill, and leaves things to Benny and the office. And Benny searches among the various items he finds in your husband's safe, and finds that I am the owner of this very valuable land. I begin to see."

"What I don't see, Shakespeare—I mean, Mr. Witherall—"

"Just call me Bill," Leonidas interrupted. "It's getting to be a universal habit, and it's much shorter—"

"Well, Bill, I simply don't see how you possibly could have forgotten about that land! I certainly should not have, in your position. How on earth could you have forgotten?"

"Er—I didn't actually forget it," Leonidas told her. "I excluded it from my thoughts, which is not quite the same thing."

"But why did you? Why?"

"Uncle Orrin," Leonidas said, "willed me that land in nineteen twenty-nine. Your husband wrote me about it. I was delighted, not so much because I had been given something, but because it seemed a very gracious gesture on the part of Uncle Orrin, who never held me in much esteem. I wrote your husband and told him I was delighted, but that I was retiring from Meredith's, and starting out around the world that very week, and please to cherish the land until my return. I thought to myself, how pleasant to have land in the country. I even went so far as to build—mentally, of course—a white cottage with green shutters, in which to spend my old age. I think I planted a yew hedge—and—but those details won't interest you—"

"They do," Mrs. Gettridge said. "Very much. But I still don't begin to understand how you could have forgotten about it—"

"About two minutes before I left for the train to take my boat in New York," Leonidas said, "your husband arrived at my apartment, laden with papers. I hastily signed them and departed. And the next

I heard about the land was a much-forwarded letter from the City of Dalton, containing a tax bill. Then I began to think less kindly of Orrin. The tax bill was almost twice my yearly salary, and four times the size of my pension. It seemed clear to me that Orrin's bequest was not as gracious a gesture as I had at first thought. I cabled your husband to sell the land."

"Paul thought you were raving crazy," Mrs. Gettridge said. "Why, that was just after the market—"

Leonidas winced.

"Please," he said, "don't let's go into that! The memory still rankles. That erased, as I discovered upon my return home, all my investments and savings. And there was a duplicate tax bill from Dalton. With what amounted to my last nickel, I rushed to a telephone and told your husband again to sell. He said he couldn't, no one could sell that land then—"

"Of course not! Sacrifice that land then! It was absurd—"

"But, dear lady," Leonidas said, "for me to keep it was out of the question, and far more of a sacrifice. I had no money. As I informed your husband at the time, I could practically hear Orrin, on high, screaming with laughter as he plucked his harp. Er— your husband was a very literal man."

Leonidas's actual opinion of the late Paul Gettridge was that the man very much resembled Estelle Otis. Like her, he combined an utter lack of humor with a dogged sense of duty.

Mrs. Gettridge nodded.

"Yes," she said, "Paul was literal. And he was

terribly annoyed with you. He couldn't get over your lack of interest and your never even coming to Dalton to see the land—you never *did* see it, did you?"

"To me," Leonidas said, "one plot of land in the country is very like another plot of land in the country. Besides, I felt too bitterly about it to care what it looked like. Mr. Gettridge kept urging me to come and see the spot, and the more he urged, the more stubbornly I refused. That land, as I pointed out constantly, was a millstone which I could not afford to hang around my neck. Those tax bills haunted me. They gave me insomnia. Oh, your husband and I, Mrs. Gettridge, exchanged some very heated words!"

"I know. I typed some of them for Paul. He was disgusted with you. He thought you took the whole affair too lightly—"

"Lightly?" Leonidas said. "He thought I took it lightly? My dear Mrs. Gettridge, during that period there was more than one occasion when my sole possessions consisted of a toothbrush and those tax bills! At last I telephoned your husband and said that if he couldn't sell the land, he was to give it away. I told him I washed my hands of the whole affair, and never, never, to let me hear a single word concerning Orrin Witherall's bequest again. Then I hung up the receiver and thrust the whole affair out of my mind."

"You don't mean to tell me you thought that would solve everything?"

"It seemed to," Leonidas said. "I never heard another word about it, not even from the City of Dalton.

And that, I can assure you, was a distinct relief. I went happily to work being a janitor, and a brush salesman and a floorwalker, and my eyes were clear and my heart light. I thought I'd been rather silly not to have washed my hands of the land long before."

Mrs. Gettridge looked at him and shook her head.

"You know what happened?"

"No," Leonidas said. "I haven't the remotest idea."

"To begin with, you dropped completely out of sight. The letters Paul wrote you were returned, with 'Address Unknown' stamps all over them. No one seemed to know where you were or where you worked or what you did. Paul put notices in the papers, but nothing came of them, either."

Leonidas was silent for a moment.

"It was rather a grim period," he said at last. "I preferred not to advertise my—er—depressed state. I was definitely one of the underprivileged third. What did your husband do?"

"One of your letters was the equivalent of a power of attorney," Mrs. Gettridge said. "So, with many misgivings, Paul took matters into his own hands, and acted. He rented the land to a farmer, who paid the taxes in return."

"What a perfectly splendid solution!" Leonidas said sincerely. "Splendid! I never should have thought of that."

"I'm glad you feel that way. It always bothered Paul. He said the land would eventually be very valuable, and some day he hoped you'd come to your senses about it. If it made no money for you, he said, at least it would make money for your heirs. And then there was all that litigation about Orrin Witherall's estate, but you know all about your cousins and that."

"I'm afraid I don't," Leonidas said. "My cousins are very tiresome people, and I haven't seen them for twenty years. I've taken great pains not to. They—er—litigated?"

"As far as I know, they still do. Oh, I've wondered about this, Bill Shakespeare, every now and then. And yesterday, when the headmaster introduced you at Meredith's, I determined to speak to you, but I missed you in all the crush at the end. One of the reasons I went to the club today was to ask Estelle if her husband knew your address."

"If Stanton Kaye were here," Leonidas said, "he would murmur brightly about the octopus of fate. Now, this land of mine—it does seem incredible, doesn't it? But you think that it's still farmed by someone who pays the taxes in lieu of rent?"

Mrs. Gettridge nodded. "If you've done nothing about it since Paul died, I know it is."

"I wonder if we could go there, now," Leonidas said.

"Certainly—but do you think it's safe for you to venture back to Dalton?"

"There's always the hamper," Leonidas said. "It's not pleasant, but it's an effective disguise."

"Why do you want to see the land?" Mrs. Gettridge asked.

"The land does not interest me as much as the

person who farms it," Leonidas said. "If the land is now so valuable, I don't understand why someone has not ferreted me out as the real owner. That they have not done so seems to indicate that there has been—er—"

"Dirty work," Cuff said. "Foul play. Gee, ain't this like a movie, Bill?"

"M'yes," Leonidas said. "Rather. Of the vintage of Pearl White, with smacks of Mack Sennett. Yes, I wonder if there may not be some tie-up between the farmer and Benny, or something of that sort. I feel, at any rate, that it is worth looking into. Mrs. Gettridge, why Benny? I mean, why does August Barker Brett allow Benny to handle any of his affairs? Why did he? I should not have."

"Neither would I," she said. "Benny Brett would be the last person I should ever choose to help me in my business. But maybe Benny was clever in business matters, in spite of all his nasty ways."

"Benny," Leonidas said, "couldn't be clever in business matters. He couldn't. He wasn't clever at anything. How he graduated from Meredith's will always be a mystery to me. Of course, Atchison was the head in those days, and Atchison was a very dear friend of August Barker's, and he may have been overflowing with gratitude at the new gymnasium which August gave the school during Benny's first-form year. August Barker was most benevolent towards Meredith's during Benny's school days. But employing Benny in later life seems a tremendous strain on anyone's benevolence. You might almost say that it carried benevolence too far."

"I agree with you," Mrs. Gettridge said. "Once I asked Paul why August Barker endured Benny. He thought the reason was obvious. In August's office, and under August's eye, Benny was less of a threat to the Brett name than if he were loose and on his own. August feels very strongly about the Brett name. He always had. I suppose he looked on Benny as a sort of cross."

"Anyone," Leonidas said, "would look on Benny as a sort of cross, but I still see no reason for bearing him any distance. I wonder—no matter. Get the hamper out of the rumble seat, Cuff, and maneuver me back—you'll have to sit out there in the rain, I'm afraid."

"Gee, I don't care about the rain," Cuff said. "I'm having a swell time—"

"What about your job?" Leonidas asked. "I forgot completely about your job!"

"So've I," Cuff returned, "but it don't matter, Bill. I just got it this morning. You see, I reformed last night. I promised Margie I'd get me a job right away, and I did. She wouldn't even let me spend the money from the car last night or anything, Bill, what do you know? She said I had to put it in a bank!"

"That shouldn't thwart you," Leonidas said. "What, after all, is a bank? But I'm sorry to make you lose your job—"

"It don't matter," Cuff assured him. "I wasn't going to like it anyway. Okay, now, let me fit you in good, and then you won't bounce so—"

Finally the hamper, with Leonidas inside, was arranged and Cuff got into the rumble seat.

As she swung off the wooded lane and back onto the tarred road, Mrs. Gettridge paused.

"What will we do if—but I suppose we can cross that bridge when we come to it."

"If you're thinking about the police," Leonidas said, "don't give them a moment's further thought. If worse comes to worse, you can always say I kidnaped you. They'll believe you. They'll believe anything of me at this point. And don't try to save Cuff. Eluding the law is his particular specialty."

A minute later, Mrs. Gettridge spoke in a strained voice.

"There's a motorcycle cop," she said. "I can see him in the rear view mirror. About two hills back. He—"

Cuff rapped on the window.

"Copper!" Mrs. Gettridge couldn't hear him, but she could see his lips form the words. "Copper!"

"Tell Cuff," Leonidas said firmly, "to keep cool if he stops us. You just act—well, just cope with the situation."

He rather wished Cassie Price were there. She would need no cues.

But Mrs. Gettridge behaved admirably when the motorcycle cop pulled up ahead of the coupé and motioned for her to stop.

"Dear me," she said, "what have I done?"

"You lost your front license plate, lady," the officer said. "I found it up by the lane back there—say, was you up that lane?"

"Yes, I pulled in there to eat some lunch," Mrs. Gettridge said. "This road's so narrow, I didn't want to park on it."

"You want to be careful, lady, where you park!"

"Oh, was I trespassing, officer? I didn't see any signs—"

"It ain't that. But there's a posse out after a bank robber—"

"What! A bank robber? Oh, my! Is he around here?"

"Somebody seen him around this way. He's a guy with a beard. He took fifty thousand cash out of the Carnavon Trust this morning. They think he's the same guy with a beard they want for that murder in Dalton. And they think he's probably an escaped lunatic, too, so just you watch your step where you park, lady!"

"Watch my step?" Mrs. Gettridge said. "I'm going home! Thank you, officer, for warning me. Wouldn't it have been perfectly awful if I'd met him! He—why, he might have killed me—"

"It wouldn't have been any fun, lady," the officer said. "He probably would just take your car to get away in, but of course you can't tell anything about what those crazy guys will take it into their heads to do. We got our orders to shoot him down on sight."

Leonidas sighed quietly. That, he thought, was adding injury to insult.

"On sight!" Mrs. Gettridge said. "Oh, dear! Did you hear that, Cuff?"

"Yeah, I heard," Cuff said. "Gee, it's all like a movie, ain't it? Just like a movie. A—"

"It certainly is," Mrs. Gettridge said hastily, "and it isn't a movie that I care to see! I'm going right straight home—but, officer, are they quite sure that it's the same man they want for the Dalton murder?"

"Well, he's got a beard," the officer said. "It must be the same guy."

"But isn't that being rather hard on men who happen to wear beards?"

Mrs. Gettridge echoed Leonidas's own opinion.

"There ain't many men with beards around," the officer returned.

"But suppose you got the wrong one!"

"Oh, we did. We winged a guy about an hour ago. He was a piano teacher at that girls' school in East Carnavon. But he wasn't hurt much. Just winged. And someone told me that they got another guy in Dalton. But he didn't get hurt much. Well, I got to go scour the woods. Be careful, lady, and don't stop for nobody that waves at you for a ride. Not unless it's one of our posse. If you don't stop for them, they'll most likely shoot at you—"

"But how can I tell which is the posse and which is the bank robber lunatic?"

"The bank robber's got a beard," the officer said. "He—"

"But suppose he's shaved it off?" Mrs. Gettridge said. "Suppose it was a false beard anyway?"

"Say, that's a thought, lady!"

"It certainly is," Mrs. Gettridge said. "You'd better think twice before you go winging any more poor old men with beards— Cuff, before I forget, will you put on the license plate? There are tools on the rumble floor somewhere."

"Sure," Cuff said, "sure thing."

"You need a screw, buddy," the officer said. "You need a nut, too. Wait—I think I got a screw and a nut in my tool kit. I think it's the right size—"

A good quarter of an hour passed before Cuff and the officer managed to combine screw, nut and license plate in a fashion of which they both approved. By that time, they were fast friends. They had even decided to go bowling some time together.

Leonidas, in the hamper, was literally chafing with impatience. Cuff should have known that this was no time to become the soul mate of a motorcycle cop. Mrs. Gettridge should have known better than to let things stall so. Cassie Price never would have permitted it. Never.

"Well, so long, pal," Cuff said. "I'll see you over the Dalton alleys next Monday night at eight, huh?"

"That's right, pal," the officer said. "Well, so long, pal."

"So long, pal," Cuff said.

"So long. Be seeing you, pal."

Before the motorcycle roared away, Leonidas had almost chewed a hole through the hamper.

"Posse or no posse," he said, "let me out of this —this thing! Cuff, what do you mean by—"

"Cuff, what have you got!" Mrs. Gettridge demanded in horror-stricken tones. "What—where did you get those papers?"

"Wait'll I let Bill come up for air—say, Bill, I know what you want to say, but that took time. They was sticking out of his inside pocket, see? I seen what they said and I thought to myself, Bill better have them. So that's what took me so long. Lemme fix that —there, now we can cover you up if we see anybody coming—look what I got you, Bill!"

He passed over a sheaf of papers.

Leonidas took them, glanced at them, and then smiled.

"Cuff," he said, "I forgive you, very thoroughly. Very—"

"What are they?" Mrs. Gettridge demanded. "What did he steal from that cop?"

"Plan Five," Leonidas said. "Orders for the mobilization of the Dalton police in case of murder. Courtesy copy to the police of Carnavon, for purposes of co-operation between the two. Steps to be taken —let me peruse this with care. I'd been rather wishing for a look at Plan Five to see just how much we should be curtailed by it."

"Is it bad?" Cuff asked sympathetically when Leonidas finished reading.

"M'yes," Leonidas said, "it is. It's worse than I thought it would be. There's no sense becoming involved with Colonel Carpenter's service language, but what it means is that among the other places to be guarded is Zara Brett's apartment. And I have got to see her this afternoon! I must! And they will have Kaye's home and office under surveillance, and Dallas's apartment, and August Barker's office—in fact, practically every place that is even remotely connected with this will have a police officer lurking about. I retract some of the things I thought about Colonel Carpenter. He is a most efficient man. Most."

"Where is he, I wonder?"

"Mercifully," Leonidas said, "this is his day off, and he apparently goes into hiding on his day off. That suits me. I trust he remains in hiding. Somehow I have a vision of him leading this man hunt on a white charger, with plumes— Cuff, I'm very grateful to you for procuring Plan Five for me."

"Aw, that wasn't nothing, Bill," Cuff said. "Anybody could of done it—"

"It was the gesture," Leonidas said, "of a true friend. A real—er—pal. Because I had intended to go to Zara Brett's after investigating this land and its farmer, and I even had some notion of poking into August Barker's office, with particular reference to Benny's desk. In other words, I should have been arrested half a dozen times—ah, well, possibly I can achieve my purpose some other way. Let's get on to this land."

"Suppose we meet the posse, or the bank robber— that was clever of the bank robber, to take advantage of your beard, wasn't it?"

"M'yes," Leonidas said. "Very clever. I've no doubt

he writes false ransom demands in kidnaping cases during his spare moments. Pray that we do not meet either him or the posse—"

Their prayers were answered, for the road from Carnavon to Dalton was empty and clear.

Once Leonidas heard Mrs. Gettridge comment under her breath.

"Oh, it wasn't anything," she said in response to his question. "We're just passing by the Dalton Country Club, and I was laughing at the man over on the fourteenth hole. Yes, he's playing, and it's raining buckets, too. Anyway, he just hurled two golf clubs into the lily pond, like Jove hurling thunderbolts—we're very near the land, Bill. How do you want to manage this? Shall I drive right up?"

"Up to what?"

"Oh, there's quite an outfit, you know. Enormous barns, and an office—this is the largest farm in Dalton. The largest for miles around. The—"

"You can't mean that this farmer actually makes enough money over those taxes to build barns and offices? Over those incredible taxes? Do you mean that a man in blue overalls with a straw hat and a pitchfork—he actually makes money?"

"I'm afraid," Mrs. Gettridge said, "that you've got a picture of the wrong farmer. Because this one has a dozen tractors, and any number of hands— Cuff, will you go see if there's anyone at the office over there?"

Cuff pounded at the door, and then wandered around the barns.

"There's a sign," he said when he returned, "that says they're closed Friday afternoons, but they're open all day Saturday and every other day, and after April first they are never closed. Gee, these guys believe in signs all right! There's one over there that says— can you beat this? It says that the land isn't for sale!"

"Blow your horn lustily," Leonidas told Mrs. Gettridge, "and make sure there's no one around. I want to emerge from this hamper and look at that sign."

It was a large sign, and as Leonidas read it a few minutes later, he nodded his approval. Like Colonel Carpenter, this farmer seemed to be a most efficient man. He was a pretty clever man, too.

He read the sign again out loud.

" 'This land is NOT for sale. Please do not annoy us by attempted discussions on the subject. This land is NOT for sale. The Owner.' "

"Well?" Mrs. Gettridge said.

"I think that answers the question," Leonidas told her. "The farmer—somehow that doesn't do him justice, calling him a farmer. Anyway, the gentleman who pays the taxes in return for the use of my land has obviously a brain which he uses. The longer he discourages any potential purchasers, the longer he has the land. I think he's very smart. That would never have occurred to me."

"What are you going to do about it?"

"Nothing, now. Nothing much, later. After all, it is entirely because of this farmer that I own the property— Think of all those taxes!"

"You don't think he had anything to do with Benny, or the murder?"

"Oh, no, he's far too smart. He—"

"Don't you think that the murderer was smart?" Mrs. Gettridge interrupted.

"Oh, yes. Yes, indeed. But this man is too openly and engagingly smart to have anything to do with Benny Brett. He has some sort of lease, I suppose, or agreement? Well, he has a very good thing, and he knows it. If he had wanted to engage in any—er—foul play, he'd have engaged in it long ago. I feel sure, quite sure, that the genius who thought up that sign would never clutter himself up with a weakling like Benny. Don't you happen to know, Mrs. Gettridge, who this farmer is?"

"Paul was close-mouthed," she said. "He never mentioned the man's name, and it never occurred to me to ask. I've often bought vegetables from some of the stands, but I've never seen the man himself."

"By the same token," Leonidas said thoughtfully, "it's possible that the man himself doesn't even know who owns the land. There seems to be a lot of land, by the way—"

"Over a hundred and fifty acres. See, there's the club over there, and there's the new development, Country Club Acres, and over there is Kaye's place —you can just see the chimneys. Do you understand now why this land is so valuable?"

"M'yes, indeed," Leonidas said. "But with this downpour and the mud and the farming debris, I still think it is an unattractive piece of property. Mrs.

Gettridge, how can I get hold of Zara Brett? I've got to see her and find out things that she knows. This time I can bluff her. I know that Benny, while he was going through your husband's papers, found proof that I owned this place. I know that Benny originally planned to kill me for it. His plans, I suppose, included some forging to make the land his own—but that part doesn't matter now. I know enough to bluff her, and I must see her. But I fear that going to her apartment is out of the question—"

"I'm sure it is," Mrs. Gettridge said. "I think that even seeing her is out of the question. People were talking about her outside the Friday Morning Club— they said she'd had a complete breakdown and was a nervous wreck, and they'd called a doctor, and he was sending her home with a trained nurse—"

"That," Leonidas said, "is fiddlesticks, of course. I wonder—no, I couldn't lure her to Cassie Price's. Nor—dear me, the problems that Plan Five creates by curtailing all the available places to go—"

He paused, rather expectantly. Cassie would have had the cue.

"My house!" Mrs. Gettridge said. "That's just the place! No one will be watching that, and Cuff can carry you in, in the hamper. Then you can relax, and plan."

"That's awfully good of you," Leonidas said. "I really shouldn't jeopardize you— Cuff, will you fit me into the hamper again?"

Cuff fitted him in, and they set off in the coupé through the pouring rain.

"I live in the Dalton Farms section," Mrs. Gettridge said. "It's not new and shiny like Cassie Price's street, it's the older part of town. But it's always very quiet there. It's just the place for you! I'm so glad I thought of it."

"M'yes," Leonidas said. "It was indeed an inspiration. Er—is it far?"

The hamper, as the afternoon wore on, was becoming increasingly uncomfortable.

"Just half a block."

Leonidas felt the car swing around a corner and start to slow down.

Then Mrs. Gettridge's foot slammed down on the accelerator and the car picked up speed with a jerk that sent the hamper pitching forward.

"What's—wrong?" Leonidas said breathlessly as the hamper continued to bounce and pitch. "Fire?"

"On my front porch—Estelle Otis! She's sitting on my front porch with two policemen!"

Cuff's voice rose behind them, drowning out the sound of the rain and the noise of the engine.

"Hey, they're chasing us!"

Chapter TEN

LEONIDAS closed his eyes.

It was a futile reaction and he knew it, but it was the only reaction he was capable of making. If Cuff had added that the policemen were accompanied by Gargantua the Great and a herd of wild elephants, Leonidas still would have met the situation by closing his eyes.

"But they're on foot!" Cuff yelled exultantly.

The coupé swerved around half a dozen corners and then came to a stop.

"Okay!" Cuff jumped out of the rumble and opened the car door. "Okay—they only ran a few steps. Then they went back. We're okay!"

"You," Leonidas said, "may be okay. I am not."

"Got bounced some, huh, Bill?"

"Balls bounce," Leonidas said. "What has just happened to me is what happens to flotsam and jetsam in the teeth of a typhoon."

"You got chewed?" Cuff demanded. "How?"

"That settles it!" Leonidas said. "Beard or no beard, I emerge from this hamper. Typhoon, Cuff.

Not tycoon. Typhoons blow— Did you say, Mrs. Gettridge, that Estelle Otis and two policemen were sitting on your front porch?"

Mrs. Gettridge merely nodded. She seemed beyond speech.

"That's right, Bill," Cuff said, "but, say, you know what I think?"

He waited until Leonidas asked what.

"Well, Bill, I don't think them cops wanted us. I think if they knew anything, there'd been a lot more of 'em. And they'd of had cars and all. And they'd been hiding, like. They wouldn't be sitting on the porch like that. Say, what's the—what do you call it when they count you, Bill?"

"If you refer to the police," Leonidas said wearily, "they have never counted me, yet."

"I mean, like every year in Dalton they count everybody—"

"The census!" Mrs. Gettridge said. "The police listings. Cuff, I think you're right. They left blanks to be filled out, yesterday—but that wouldn't explain their running after us, even for a few steps!"

"That was horse-face, I bet," Cuff said. "Maybe she said something like, 'There she goes!' Or something. Then they run after you, and when you didn't stop, they guessed it wasn't you. There's a lot of cars like this. Say, Bill, you want to get out, still? There's quite a few people around."

"I yearn to get out," Leonidas said, "but perhaps, having endured this long, I can endure more. Mrs. Gettridge, can you think of any valid reason for Estelle Otis's coming to call on you? I'd feel happier if you could, because that would mean that Estelle's mind has not yet bridged the gap between me and the bearded man the police are seeking—"

"The Foreign Relations Committee—that's it!" Mrs. Gettridge said. "We were supposed to meet at my house this afternoon, and I forgot all about it. I suppose the rest of the women left when they found I wasn't home—"

"But not Estelle," Leonidas said. "Not Estelle. No. A meeting was scheduled, and Estelle intends to meet if she has to meet alone on your porch with the rain beating down in torrents. D'you mean she's really on a Foreign Relations Committee?"

"She's chairman."

Leonidas laughed. "No wonder," he said, "that foreign relations are strained— Cuff, what do you do when you hide from the cops?"

"I don't usually hide," Cuff said. "I run."

"But if you had to hide, where would you?"

"Gee, I don't know, Bill! I'll have to think."

"Think, then. Think hard. Ponder. This is your department."

"Well," Cuff said at last, "Dillinger used to go to the movies."

"But consider, Cuff, what happened to him when he came out!"

"Yeah, but I hid in the movies once, and it worked out all right. Except the pictures. They were lousy. And I had to stay in there till it got dark out, too. Was I ever sick of that place! Say, I couldn't go to another movie for almost a week. The feature was about this gangster, see, and this blonde moll, and this other gang—"

"M'yes," Leonidas said. "How would you like to while away the remainder of the afternoon at a movie, Mrs. Gettridge? Does the idea appeal to you?"

"No," she said. "Frankly, it doesn't."

"Meaning that you don't care for the cinema, or that you feel it's no place to hide?"

"Well, neither, exactly. You see, the 'Gem' is the only continuous show," Mrs. Gettridge said, "and there's absolutely no place to park, ever. I've had more trouble there. And if we stop in front, how can you get in without being seen by the cop at the corner? And if you have to walk from where I park the car, somebody will be sure to spot you. I do think you'd be wise to wait somewhere until after dark before doing anything else, but—well, there you are. You'll be all right once you're inside, if you can get inside."

"Say!" Cuff said. "I got a new room this morning, Bill, and I moved my clothes over from my old room —that landlady I used to have got too nosey. How's for this lady driving us to my new room, and I can get you some clothes, huh? Maybe we can dress you up, like. Then I'll drive, and I'll let you and her off at the entrance to the movies, and you can hurry inside quick, and I'll park the car, see? And meet you inside. How's that, Bill? Okay? Okay!"

Cuff's room was in Daltonville, and they reached it without difficulty, without seeing a single policeman.

"Without," Leonidas said as they climbed up the stairs to Cuff's hall bedroom, "without even a glimpse of Estelle. I consider that a good omen. A good sign," he added, as Cuff looked puzzled.

"Sure, not seeing cops is always good," Cuff said. "Say, Bill, do you like brown suits?"

"Personally," Leonidas said, "I'm rather partial to gray."

"Well, then, you won't mind if I wear my brown suit, huh? Margie likes my brown suit, and I sort of got a date with her later. But you can have anything else I got. Is that okay by you?"

While Cuff changed his dungarees and sweat shirt for the brown suit that Margie liked, Leonidas searched through the remainder of Cuff's wardrobe for something which might possibly fit him and still not look too bizarre. Cuff had any number of clothes, but he leaned heavily towards plaids and stripes and checks, the sort of thing which Leonidas had learned to refer to during his floorwalking days as Gents Novelty Suitings. The tailoring, Leonidas decided, could best be summed up as Gents Snappy Cut.

Finally he picked out a worn blue serge suit, and a dark overcoat and hat.

Cuff was disappointed at the choice, but he accepted it philosophically.

"I guess maybe it's better you wear something kind of quiet, huh, Bill?"

"I think so," Leonidas said. "It will be safer, I think. Less—er—conspicuous. D'you have a large muffler, Cuff?"

When they returned to the car, Mrs. Gettridge nodded approvingly.

"You look quite well, Bill," she said. "Rather as though you were recovering from tonsillitis, but the scarf is a good idea just the same. The coat fits beautifully. Far better than the suit— Bill, do you see this rain? *Isn't* it torrential?"

"M'yes," Leonidas said, "but none the less I welcome it. If it will only keep up, no one will see anything untoward in our dashing madly from the car into the movies."

No one did.

After hastily parking the coupé, Cuff joined Leonidas and Mrs. Gettridge.

"Got the tickets? Swell. Let's go in—"

It was with a feeling of relief that Leonidas sat down on the hard, leather-covered seat.

That seat, he thought, represented what he wanted most in the world, what he desired even more than the discovery of Benny Brett's murderer. It represented the opportunity of remaining in one place for a period of over thirty seconds, without an interruption of one sort or another. And in comfort.

At least, in comparative comfort.

The air in the theater was hot and stale. It was fetid. It set Leonidas to thinking unkindly of peanuts and humanity and disinfectants. But after his intimate contact with the contents of Schlagermann's Cleaning and Dyeing hamper, it was positively refreshing. After that hamper, when you came right down to it, the Black Hole of Calcutta would have seemed refreshing.

And there was room to stretch.

Leonidas stretched, and leaned back comfortably against the seat.

He would relax completely and take a brief nap, he decided. Then, with renewed vigor, he would set out again and get hold of Zara Brett. Zara Brett knew who killed Benny. He did not think she had committed the murder. She was not capable of that. But she most certainly knew. And Leonidas intended to make her tell, no matter what turned up, no matter what chances he had to take.

And then there was the fantastic notion—in fact, there were two fantastic notions which kept flitting through his head. They were so fantastic that they rather frightened him, but he couldn't seem to get rid of them.

There was one tremendous difficulty, Leonidas felt, in this situation.

Once you admitted the impossible into your calculations, its possibilities became boundless.

A good nap was what he needed.

And he would have had his good nap, if it had not been for the couple sitting directly behind him.

Their whispered conversation was not, in a sense, loud.

It was not loud enough to interfere with the picture's sound track. It was not loud enough for Leonidas to guess what topic held them so enthralled.

He could not, actually, catch one single word.

Neither, with that constant sibilant buzzing in his ears, could he sleep.

Ordinarily, Leonidas would have risen and changed his seat, or have sat still and resigned himself to the inevitable. At that moment, however, while he lacked the spirit to move, he had too much spirit to be resigned. He began to seethe with wrathful indignation.

When caramels began to be unwrapped, Leonidas stopped seething and began to ferment.

Something of the way he felt must have communicated itself to the couple behind.

They stopped buzzing, and with infinite care they unwrapped the caramels more slowly.

Leonidas could have screamed. If there was anything worse than the swishing crackle of cellophaned caramels being unwrapped quickly, it was the swish-crackle, swish-crackle of cellophaned caramels being unwrapped in slow motion. It simply prolonged the agony.

When the cellophane bag at last disgorged its swish-crackling contents all over the floor, Leonidas achieved the boiling point.

With a fine disregard for possible consequences, he swung around.

"My good women," he said in a tautly controlled voice, "will you stop! Will you cease that hideous, disgusting din! Will you—"

"Bill!" cried Cassie Price in delight. "It's Bill—it really is!"

"Bill!" Dallas said. "It really— Bill, what are you doing here? Did you really mean—"

"Do we scram, Bill?" Cuff demanded hastily.

"What's the matter?" Mrs. Gettridge leaned past Cuff. "Who—who is it?"

Leonidas reassured them as well as he could, with Cassie and Dallas both talking at once into his ears.

"Bill!" Dallas said. "Did you really mean— What are you doing here?"

People began to shush them roundly.

"I *was* trying to sleep," Leonidas whispered. "I'm being shot at on sight through three counties, and I thought it would be well to wait somewhere until after dark—"

"You *did* mean for us to meet you here, didn't you, Bill?" Cassie asked. "Dallas laughed at me, but of course I was right—that's why you had the boy sing it, isn't it?"

"Ssh!" Leonidas said, as an usher strolled down the aisle, paused, and coughed.

"Isn't it?" Cassie persisted. "Didn't you mean this picture?"

"What picture?" Leonidas whispered desperately.

"This one. The feature. 'The High Road'—that's what you meant, when you had—"

"Ssh!" Leonidas said.

"We've got so many things to tell you about Zara," Dallas said. "Cassie and I took her home in an ambulance with a trained nurse—"

"And I told everybody—you know, the doorman and people like that—that she was delirious," Cassie said with pride. "And that they mustn't let her out. And there was a—"

"Ssh!" Leonidas said. "Or we'll all—"

"A policeman," Cassie went on, "and he promised he would see she didn't slip out. So Zara's right there where you can see her, Bill, and talk with her. And I told everybody she mustn't see a soul unless it was someone I called up about. So she can't run away, or get to talk with anyone—"

"No talking!" the usher said severely. "No talking!"

Cassie subsided.

But the instant the usher disappeared, she leaned forward and started up again.

"Bill, she knows just everything! I'm convinced. Who killed Benny. And she's scared to death—"

"Cassie," Leonidas said, "you must be still! Or we'll have to go, and—"

"And, Bill, a note had come for her, when she got back to the apartment. And she grabbed it and read it, and then tried to burn it, but—"

"Did you—"

"Oh, yes, I got it. I've got it right here in my bag. Oh, that loathsome youth, he's going to shush me again!"

While the usher was still pacing up and down the aisle in a menacing fashion, the travel short ended and the lights went on.

Leonidas ducked down into his muffler.

"It's all right, Bill," Cassie said, taking advantage of the noise made by the theater's departing clients and by the groups who scurried around into other seats. "The lights'll go right off. It's just for a second, and then they sing. With the organ and those colored slide things, you know. They— What did you say?"

"The note—what was in it?"

"Oh, for Zara to keep quiet. It wasn't signed. But it was written by the murderer, I'm sure. Bill, did you see that process server outside the theater when you came in? Well, he was there, wandering around. I gave Dallas my glasses, though, and so he didn't recognize her. But I had a bad moment when she fell down—those old bifocals, you know. Oh, here go the lights—"

The Naborhood Sing, so-called, was meat to Cuff, who had been deeply bored with the travel short. If there had to be travel shorts, Cuff definitely preferred the South Seas or Bali to a lot of polar bears.

The first song was a particular favorite of his, so he sat up and let himself go.

"Your singing pal, Bill?" Dallas inquired in his ear.

"Margie's singing pal— Where are Margie and Kaye, by the way?"

"My God, Bill—don't you know? Cassie, did you hear that? Bill doesn't know where Margie and Kaye are!"

"What?" Cassie said. "What's that? With all this clamor—my, my. *Listen* to that boy swing the 'Robert E. Lee'! He's *rocking* it! It's simply incredible— Dallas, it sounded just as though you said that Bill didn't know where Margie and Kaye are."

"That's *just* what I said!"

"Well, where are they? Goodness me, where are they?" Cassie demanded anxiously. "Where can they be? Why, I felt sure they were with you, or that you'd sent them off on some errand, Bill! Where are they? How did you get away, Bill, didn't you get away with them? How awful! Where can they—"

She had to stop for a "Hum Lightly Now, Folks" slide that quieted the audience and provided Cuff with a chance to get his breath.

"Where are they— Oh, is that a 'Women Only' slide, now? Sing, Dallas, we'll have to help the girls out—"

While Cassie and Dallas helped the girls out, Leonidas wondered what could have happened to Margie and Kaye. If the process server was outside the theater, wandering around, then at least he had not yet caught Kaye. But with all those policemen—

"Now, Bill," Cuff said, "you listen to this! Listen to me give out on the 'Men Only'—"

Cuff gave until Mrs. Gettridge, who sat on the other side of him, put her hands over her ears.

"There," Cuff said, glowing at the applause he received, "there! How was that, pal?"

"Words," Leonidas said with perfect honesty, "fail me, Cuff—who—"

Two figures appeared on the aisle beside him.

"Cuff? That you— Why, Bill!" Margie said. "Move over, Bill. Where'd you pick up my fog horn? Move over—"

"Shove along, Blondel," Kaye chimed in. "Shove

over, Butch— Where's Cassie and Dallas? Why—
Cassie and Dallas! Old Home Week! And we thought
you'd all been pinched! Old Home Week!"

Three ushers appeared, but Cassie ignored their
requests for quiet.

"How wonderful," she said. "You'll never believe
it, but we were just talking about you! What are you
doing here, did he sing 'The High Road' for you,
too?"

"Quiet!" one of the ushers said. "Quiet, please, or
I shall have to request—"

"Hadn't we better go?" Mrs. Gettridge asked Leonidas nervously. "I think— I'm afraid they're about
to put us out—"

"Margie and I had a choice, Cassie," Kaye said
cheerfully, "and we chose this— What? What are
you talking about, you three gadflies? What?"

"Sorry to request, sir, that you continue your conversation outside the theater—"

"Flying wedge, huh?" Kaye said. "All right, all
right, we'll go— Come on, let's go, Bill. Come on,
Cassie and Dallas—if I'd known you were all still
free, Bill, Margie and I would have left this pest hole
hours ago in spite of gumshoe. Every time we tried
to leave, there he was. You won't believe how many
times we've seen this show— And if I'd had to wait
on that levee just once more for the 'Robert E.
Lee'—"

Mrs. Gettridge walked slowly up the aisle beside
Leonidas.

"What—what do you do now?" she asked.

Leonidas sighed.

"Clearly," he said, "I shall not nap. The Wit's End Club."

"I think I'd better leave you," Mrs. Gettridge said hesitantly, "now that you have your cohorts back. I'm sure that Cassie Price and the rest—"

"You mustn't leave," Leonidas seemed disturbed at the thought. "You mustn't—unless you—but I understand. There *is* a certain reckless abandon about this expedition, and I can't blame you for not wanting to get into any difficulties—"

"It's not that," she said. "But I've more or less served my purpose, and if you haven't any definite plans, I can't see how I'd be of any help—"

"But you will," Leonidas said. "And we do have plans, of a sort. We have Zara. She is going to require a lot of planning—"

The group paused in the dimly lighted foyer of the theater.

For the first time, Cassie Price became aware of Mrs. Gettridge.

"Oh!" she said. "Oh— I didn't know that you— How do you do?"

"Mrs. Gettridge," Leonidas told Cassie hurriedly, "has done yeoman service. She saved me from the toils of Estelle Otis and innumerable police, and with her aid I've found out the basis of all of this— But possibly we'd better find a less public place to discuss all that. Oh—you've changed your nose again, Kaye!"

"It seemed like a good idea," Kaye said. "My

brother took to pacing past the car. And Margie and I got new spring outfits, too. We bought them in Winnerton Centre, which may explain why they're on the corny side. Seems to me you've changed too, Bill. We all look like different people to me. How do we work this departure? We— But first I'll see about gumshoe. No, he's not. There's nothing but rain out there. Now, how do we go? And where? The limousine's around the corner—"

"Is it?" Cassie said. "I had it all thought out—how to get back to my house, I mean. You see, when we couldn't find the limousine with you two, Dallas and I went over to Rutherford's house and borrowed his sedan. He's got the roadster, but the sedan's got his official insignia, too. So safe and nice. And then I dropped in at Sutter's and bought a folding wheel chair and a cane, in case—"

"I get it," Kaye said. "Old Uncle Bill!"

"Yes, I thought that would work out. Dallas can pretend to be a sort of attendant— Isn't that simple and nice? I don't know why I didn't think of it this morning. Sutter's delivers wheel chairs in emergencies, they said. It just didn't occur to me, and it would have been so much better than those Spanish bags. Now, I was going to use Rutherford's car, but if the limousine's here, we'll take that, and I'll just ask some policeman to take the sedan back for me. And—"

"No," Kaye said. "No. Not a cop— Look, Cassie, don't you think you'd better curb this blithe instinct of yours for calling on the cops for every little task?"

"Why not? Rutherford loves having them useful. He always says they're public servants and— But let's plan. Mrs. Gettridge, you'll come with us—of course?"

Leonidas noticed Cassie's slight pause, and nodded slightly.

"M'yes," he said. "Mrs. Gettridge will come in the car with us—"

"But I've got my car here. I can—"

"M'yes, but I think it will be better if you come with us," Leonidas said. "Er—safety in numbers, you know."

"That's right, Bill," Cassie said. "There's plenty of room. We can all crowd in easily— Oh, those loathsome youths!" she added as the ushers bore down on them. "Let's hurry out of this place!"

At Kaye's suggestion, the group bunched itself around Leonidas as they left the theater.

"Like a bodyguard, Bill!" Cuff said. "Like Dillinger, huh, Bill?"

Leonidas winced. He had been thinking of Dillinger. He had been thinking of many things, including the danger and the rashness of this carefree departure.

As they passed under the marquee of the theater, a policeman strode up to them.

Leonidas was not surprised. He was getting to a point where he could feel policemen at a distance.

"Hey! I want you!"

The whole group stood like statues, but it was at Mrs. Gettridge that the policeman wagged his finger.

"I want you!" he continued. "This time I— Oh, hello, Mrs. Price. How are you? This time you're smack on the hydrant. Smack on it! And you know what I told you the *last* time, don't you?"

Mrs. Gettridge stared down the cross street. Her little coupé *was* smack up against the hydrant. Cuff, in his haste to get back to the theater, had not bothered with items like hydrants.

"But," Mrs. Gettridge began nervously, "I didn't—"

"No excuses this trip, lady! There's plenty places to park without parking on hydrants—"

"Do something!" Leonidas, who was holding his breath, formed the words with his lips in Cassie's general direction.

Cassie leapt into action.

"Now, officer," she said winningly, "you wouldn't arrest a friend of mine, or anything! You wouldn't, would you? Just for parking near an old hydrant—"

"Sorry, Mrs. Price, but your brother'd back me up. This ain't the first time I've had trouble with this woman. She's been warned enough times before. Parking on hydrants. Parking on yellow curbings. Overtime parking. Parking on corners. Parking across alleys— She can park anywhere but the right place. That is, she *thinks* she can. This time she's going to learn different. This time you come along to the station. I'll trail you down in my car—"

"It seems," Mrs. Gettridge said to Leonidas, "that I leave you after all— No, of course there's nothing you can do. If you remember, I said there was always a parking problem here—"

"It's too bad," Cassie said, "but I suppose it can't be helped. If you've been warned— Well, you go pay your fine, and get your scolding, and then you drive over—"

"Oh, no, she don't!" the officer said. "She don't drive anywhere, Mrs. Price! She don't get out of it this time with a fine and a few words. This time she gets her license taken away—"

"Then Cuff can go," Kaye said, "and drive—"

"Oh, no! She gets her registration suspended, too. She can turn in her plates right away. We got enough traffic violations against her to get the registry's okay on that, all right. And they got this new drive on parking, anyway. After that school fire last week when the hydrants was blocked— Well, come on, lady. So long, Mrs. Price, sorry to bust up your party, but it can't be helped."

"You did your duty," Cassie said, "and I think you did it very well. I shall tell Rutherford as much. Good-by—"

The six of them watched Mrs. Gettridge, followed by the officer, across the street.

"Gee," Cuff said, "I never even seen the hydrant. But can you beat that, taking her for—"

"No," Kaye said, "you can't beat it. They want the bunch of us for every charge on the books including murder, mayhem, assault and battery of an officer—and then they pass us by to arrest her for parking beside a hydrant. Oh, well. 'There are more things in heaven and earth, Horatio—' "

"If you feel it necessary to quote Shakespeare,"

Leonidas said, "consider the line about 'Three misbegotten knaves in Kendal green'— Those ushers, you know, are about to shoo us forcibly off their sidewalk. Let us get to the car. I have what amounts to a burning passion to see that note you got from Zara's apartment."

"Yes, do let's get along," Cassie said, "only can't you wait until we get home for the note, Bill? I just remembered Jock in the movies, and he always comes on the four-forty train. Do you mind?"

"I don't mind," Leonidas said, "nor do I quite understand. What Jock did you remember in the movies, that comes on the four-forty train?"

"Oh, my grandson. You know, the putty-nose one. That Kaye put on—"

"I think I get the drift," Kaye said. "You mean, Cassie, you have a grandson named Jock, and he stores putty noses at your house, and he's coming to Dalton on the four-forty, and you just remembered it."

"Well, I said it in fewer words," Cassie said. "I am trying to hurry, and you do explain things so— because it would be tragic if Muir was let out now, wouldn't it?"

"Don't *think* of things like that, Cassie!" Kaye said. "It does things to my spine. Let Muir out now? Oh, Cassie, what a thought!"

"But Jock will," Cassie said patiently, "if we don't get there first, don't you see? You can be so stupid, Kaye! Jock always goes right straight to the preserve room—"

Kaye looked up at the clock on the top of the Chamber of Commerce building.

"Does he walk from the station?"

"On rainy days he takes a taxi," Cassie said, "if I'm not there to meet him, and— Oh, is it quarter to five already? Dear me—how time flies!"

"You fly," Kaye grabbed her by the elbow. "You fly, Cassie. Run, sheep, run—there's the car—"

"Does Jock," Leonidas asked as they bundled into the limousine, "have a key?"

"No," Cassie said, "I've only got one latchkey— I keep meaning to get some others made, but I never seem to— Now don't get caught speeding, Kaye! Remember Mrs. Gettridge! But Jock always gets in. Usually up the Van Fleet trellis. He's very agile. And of course he's terribly bright, but you'd never guess it. I do think bright children are so tiresome— How in the world did you ever pick her up, Bill?"

"Who?"

"Lila Gettridge. I was flabbergasted, simply flabbergasted to see her with you. Of all people! Of course—"

Cassie broke off suddenly.

"Of course what?" Dallas asked.

"Of course," Cassie said, "there's always the chance that Jock may take the five-eighteen. Sometimes he waits over to watch the streamliner go out at five. It's nice about streamlining things, isn't it? Jock never took the slightest interest in trains until they were streamlined and chromiumed and all. I was so worried. It didn't seem natural for a boy not to be interested in trains— Aren't you awfully quiet, Bill?"

"I'm thinking," Leonidas said. "Pondering on possibility. Once you take the impossible into your calculations, Mrs. Price, its possibilities are boundless."

"Why, of course they are!" Cassie said. "I knew that. You'd better get that chair fixed, Dallas—"

In spite of the rain, a sizable group of morbid curiosity seekers overran the section of Paddock Street near the Brett house. But their interest in the limousine, and the man in the wheel chair, and the people who assisted him into the house next door was only transitory. They were far more absorbed in the police and the police cars.

Cassie Price glanced around the living room and sighed with relief.

"He's taking the five-eighteen," she said. "Oh, I am glad! And didn't that chair work nicely—"

"What's that noise down cellar?" Dallas demanded.

"Kaye's shutting the garage doors," Cassie said. "They always sound like that. You'd better pull down those shades, Dallas, before we put on the lights. And, Margie—see if the groceries have come. I ordered them by phone while I was at Zara's. And someone ought to see to Muir. And somebody put up the thermostat. It's chilly in here— Kaye, will you? It's in the dining room—*that* way, Kaye—"

But Kaye continued to stand in the doorway and stare at the overcoat which Leonidas had just removed.

"William," he said, "father wants to know where the hell you got his coat."

Leonidas looked at him for a moment, and then put on his pince-nez.

"Your coat?" he asked politely. "This coat?"

"Yes, son. My coat. Father's nice new Chesterfield that he wore last night. See father's name and date on the nice label? William, you're a good lad, and popsie would hate like hell to think you'd been lying—"

"Wait," Dallas said hastily. "Wait—whatever's wrong, Bill can explain—"

Kaye's jaw was beginning to jut out, just as it had before he demonstrated his left on Muir.

"He better," Kaye said. "Bill better explain, quick. And it better be good, or popsie will knock Bill three blocks from next Michaelmas—"

"Says who?" Cuff elbowed Kaye out of the doorway. "Who'll knock Bill, huh? Say, who do you think you are, huh? Who—"

"Cuff!" Margie said. "Snap out of it! You—"

"Stop it, Kaye," Dallas said. "Go sit down and let Bill explain—"

"Bill," Cuff said, "is a pal of mine, see? And any punk who says he's knocking Bill around—"

"What about the coat, Bill?" Kaye said.

"Oh, dear!" Cassie said. "I do wish you'd stop all this nonsense about coats! Who cares about your old coat! What difference does it make if—"

"Whoever took my coat from Brett's cellar last night," Kaye said, "makes a lot of difference! The coat—"

"Will you stop this foolishness about coats," Cassie said hotly, "and tell me about the note! Who took the note? Because I don't think it's very funny, to steal that note from my pocketbook!"

"But nobody stole the note, Cassie," Dallas said. "Nobody stole—"

"They certainly did! The note is gone!"

Chapter ELEVEN

"BOUNDLESS," Leonidas said, sitting down on the couch. "Simply boundless possibilities. M'yes, indeed. Boundless—"

"What are you parroting about, Bill?" Kaye demanded wrathfully. "Who stole what note, Cassie? Oh, you mean *that?*"

"Yes, *that!*" Cassie was angry. "And I repeat, Stanton Kaye, who stole that note is a lot more important than your old coat— I simply hate men with those velvet collars, anyway. They look so sissy. I repeat, somebody has taken that note from my pocketbook, and I want it returned to me this instant!"

"When did you have it last, dear?" Dallas asked soothingly, having decided that the thankless role of oil-pourer had fallen to her. "When did you have—"

"Don't say that again!" Cassie said. "I don't know anything in the world that infuriates me more than being asked when I had things last! What has the time element got to do with—"

"Where, then?" Dallas said. "Where did you have it last?"

"That's just as silly, Dallas! I had it in my pocket-book, of course! My pocketbook! Haven't I made it clear that this was the note I had in my pocketbook? In my pocketbook. I wasn't carrying it in any forked stick. I wasn't wearing it thrust through my upper lip like an Ubangi! It was in my pocketbook—"

"I wonder," Leonidas began tentatively, "if—"

"What do you wonder if?" Cassie retorted.

He smiled blandly at her.

"Really, Cassie," he said, "really— I may call you Cassie? Thank you. But is this any time to quibble over the niceties of the language? Is this any time to be—er—meticulous? In short, Cassie, at what point in the events of the afternoon do you recall having definite proof that the note was in your pocketbook?"

"In the theater—"

"I suppose," Kaye said, "you opened your bag?"

"How else would I know?" Cassie said. "While the lights were on, just before the singing, I opened my bag to see, and the note was there then! So there!"

"Well," Kaye said, "that's a cinch. While you pawed around, the note fell out—"

"It did not fall out!"

"Now, how can you tell it didn't?" Kaye asked. "Of course that's what happened—it fell out in the theater."

"It did not, Stanton Kaye! And don't ask me how I know, as if you thought I didn't. Of course I know I had it, and I know it simply could not have fallen out! Because I did what I always do with tickets and things. I took a piece of Scotch tape—"

"You mean that self-gummed sticky stuff," Dallas asked, "like adhesive tape?"

"Yes, only it's cellophane. Well, there was a roll on Zara's desk, and I took a piece and stuck it across the note's envelope so that there were ends. Like apron strings. And then I stuck the ends against the lining of my bag. So that note was as good as glued in there. It couldn't have fallen out. It couldn't even dangle. The only way that note could have left my pocketbook was in someone's fingers! And," Cassie said, "I want it back!"

"Come on, Cuff," Margie said. "Come on. Did you—"

"Did I what?"

"Did you take the note, dope, from Mrs. Price's pocketbook? Hand it over!"

"Honest to God, Margie, I never!" Cuff appealed to Leonidas. "You tell her, Bill! I never took no note from out her bag! So help me!"

"Cuff, I know you!" Margie said. "And after what you promised me! You—"

"Truly, Margie," Leonidas said, "I don't think that Cuff did. I'm quite sure he did not. Er—Cassie, tell me. Why did you change your mind and discuss streamlined trains and their effect on the young instead of continuing on the topic of Mrs. Gettridge?"

"Oh," Cassie said, "I didn't want you— Why, Bill! What do you mean, I changed my mind?"

"Cassie," Leonidas said, "I will admit that your thought processes occasionally baffle me, but when one woman abruptly drops the subject of another woman for a discourse on streamlined trains— What were you going to say about her, Cassie?"

"Oh, dear," Cassie said. "I thought I'd done that so nicely. Really it was just that I didn't want you to think I was being catty. I knew Dallas would understand, but men always think you're being catty when you ask them questions like that. So I didn't ask you. I just talked about trains. Trains are—"

"Always a good, safe subject," Leonidas said. "M'yes. You were going to ask me, what in the world was I doing with Lila Gettridge, weren't you? I thought so. Because Mrs. Gettridge is such a dear friend of Zara Brett's. Is that right?"

"Why, you knew, Bill!" Cassie said. "You knew it all the time! I needn't have worried a bit about what you might have told her! Because the Gettridges have always been awfully good friends of all the Brett family—except Benny, of course. She couldn't get on with Benny any more than anyone else could— So you knew it all the time, Bill!"

"Unfortunately," Leonidas said, "I didn't. I'm afraid I guessed—"

"You mean it just sort of dawned on you?"

"M'yes. A belated dawning. It didn't come until long after I'd told her everything. But perhaps, on the other hand, it's just as well that it happened that way. I—"

"Well, under the circumstances," Cassie said, "a belated dawn is better than none— What made you guess?"

"Experience," Leonidas said, "has proved to me that

interest, beyond a certain point, ceases to be motivated by purely humanitarian instincts. And Mrs. Gettridge was so interested in me and my general safety and well-being, and my Uncle Orrin— You know, the boys at Meredith's invariably took a similar interest in me just before the final examinations. Particularly the members of the baseball team and the crew. M'yes. I was wondering, back there in the movies, whether it would be better to leave suddenly, or to adhere to Mrs. Gettridge with all my might and main, but—"

"Fate," Dallas said, "solved it for you. That old octopus—"

"I was seriously considering telling her the story of my life," Leonidas ignored the interruption. "At least I will say for her, Cassie, she listened very well."

Cassie nodded her head vigorously.

"Those mousy women," she said, "they're all alike. Great listeners. Always hanging on every word a man says. And getting their husbands hot lunches—not that Lila had husbands. Just one, poor man. You know, always baking potatoes and making chowders and Brown Bettys. I always told Bagley, if he'd been the sort of man who came home for lunch and wanted it hot, I'd have divorced him. Bill, did you tell her every single thing?"

"I'm sorry," Leonidas said. "But I learned a great deal, which I've yet to tell you about—and really, Cassie, I doubt if Mrs. Gettridge's knowledge will be so disastrous to us—"

"Not unless she tells Rutherford."

Cassie had the satisfaction of seeing Leonidas actually look taken aback. His pince-nez dropped from his nose.

"She is—she is a great friend of Rutherford's, too?" he asked.

"Oh, yes. Couldn't you guess, the way she'd got away with all that parking? I never realized until then how well she must know him— Rutherford's very strict, you know, about traffic. Yes, indeed, these mousy women! Practically the minute Paul Gettridge died, there were whispers— Dear me, if I go on, you'll say I'm catty! But she might very well tell Rutherford."

"And if you should ask me," Dallas said, "Rutherford would forgive and forget a couple of head-on collisions with a hydrant if she told him where to find us!"

"I'm afraid so," Cassie said. "And of course she'll tell Zara Brett everything. Simply everything. That's why she took the note out of my pocketbook, I suppose. Don't you think so, Bill?"

"M'yes," Leonidas said. "I think—"

"Wait!" Dallas said. "Cassie, you mean that this Mrs. Gettridge, who saved Bill from the clutches of Sister Otis and cops too numerous to mention—Gettridge swiped that note from you?"

"M'yes," Leonidas said. "She must have. She had every chance. She was directly behind Cassie when we left the theater, and she stood very close to her out on the sidewalk. And of course she heard Cassie tell me that it was right in her bag—"

"Say," Cuff said. "Say!"

"Yes?" Leonidas said encouragingly. "What?"

"Say, I'm mixed up, like, Bill."

Leonidas nodded. He had noticed the confused expression which appeared on Cuff's face practically every time Cassie Price opened her mouth.

"Say, Bill, tell it to me slow, will you?"

"Let me," Margie said. "Listen, Cuff. Mrs. Price has a note in her pocketbook. See? The lady with Bill swipes it from Mrs. Price on our way out of the movies. Get it?"

"Sure, I got it," Cuff said. "Wait a minute. It's out in my coat."

Margie grabbed him by the shoulders.

"Cuff Murray! You have the— But you told me you didn't take that note!"

"Aw, Margie, I didn't! I told you the truth!" Cuff said unhappily. "I didn't take no note! But I got the other dame's bag, don't you see? And most likely, if she took the note from Mrs. Price's bag, she put it into hers, see? Gee, sometimes you're dumb! Wait, and I'll go get it—"

Margie tried to say something, but the words stuck in her throat.

"Don't take it so hard, dear," Cassie said. "And don't tug at your hair that way. Cuff means well—"

"So does a doctor," Margie said, "when he lances a boil. Honest, sometimes I wonder if it's worth the effort, Mrs. Price! I wonder if any guy— No, I don't want the note, Cuff. Give it to Bill. He's that man over there with the beard. That's the boy!"

It was a simple note, printed in pencil on a cheap sheet of notepaper.

" 'Zara,' " Leonidas read it aloud, " 'be careful. Don't talk.' "

"It's awfully childish printing," Cassie said, "but of course no child wrote it. The murderer wrote it, don't you think so, Bill?"

Leonidas looked curiously at Cuff.

"Why did you take her bag, Cuff?" he asked.

"Aw, I was kind of sore at her," Cuff said. "She got me sore, the way she looked at me when the cop fussed about the hydrant— Gee, with all that rain, I never seen no hydrant! And I wanted to get your gun back, too, and that was the easiest way—"

Leonidas clapped a hand against the coat pocket of Cuff's blue serge suit. The gun he had waved at Zara was gone.

"Sure, she took it off you," Cuff said. "Didn't you know, Bill?"

"No," Leonidas said, feeling that he had lost face. "No, Cuff, I didn't."

"I guess you was busy thinking," Cuff said, "that— Say, Bill, I didn't know you packed a rod. Not till I seen you stick it into the pocket when you was changing your clothes in my room. That overall thing hid it before. But in the blue coat, it bulged. I guess she didn't know, either, till she seen that bulge. She took it off you during the polar bears. I was going to take it back, but then Margie come, and I sort of forgot."

He looked at Margie and grinned, and she grinned back at him.

"And then," Cuff said, "I remembered it again when she got me sore, and it seemed like it was easiest just to take her bag, see? So I did. But I didn't know I had the note till you put me wise."

"I think you're perfectly marvelous!" Cassie said. "I really do— How'd you take the bag without her guessing?"

"Aw," Cuff said modestly, "it wasn't nothing. She had that sort of cloth knitting bag thing, and she had this pocketbook inside of that, see? And she took out the pocketbook to get at her car keys, and she thought she put the pocketbook back into the big bag. Only she didn't. She—"

"What's all that noise next door?" Dallas demanded.

With Margie and Cuff, she rushed over to the window and peeked out.

Kaye watched them go, and then he watched Leonidas and Cassie as they investigated the contents of Mrs. Gettridge's pocketbook.

His jaw was still jutting out, although no one had taken the trouble to notice it.

"There's just the usual junk," Cassie said, surveying the miscellany which erupted from the pocketbook. "Key ring, comb, nail file, pencil, compact, lipstick, handkerchiefs, theater stubs, grocery lists, driving license and registration— Hm. Not having *those*'ll make trouble for her! Change purse, billfold, glasses— I didn't know *she* wore glasses! I suppose she's too vain to wear 'em in public. Cigarettes— She would smoke mentholated cigarettes, wouldn't she? Matches. No mirror—those always get lost, always. What's that list? Ten best books—how enlightened of her. Well, there's really nothing at all, Bill. Just the usual junk. Except for your gun, of course. Who d'you suppose wrote the note?"

Kaye spoke up before Leonidas had a chance to reply.

"This group," he announced in a grim monotone, "is unfair to Stanton Kaye. This group is unfair toward organized minorities. This group is unfair to Stanton Kaye. This group is misled by pocketbooks. This group tends toward capitalism. This group is unfair toward—"

Cassie, who had been listening to his monologue while she watched Leonidas toy with Mrs. Gettridge's purse, squealed suddenly.

"Why, that's another compartment!" she said interestedly. "Isn't that clever—that must be a Marjory Cutliffe bag, they always have such tricky compartments. I don't like them, myself. I always lose things and forget about—why—"

Kaye sighed and stretched himself out on the floor.

"Roll on, Niagara," he said, "and when you freeze up, and when you get through with the pretty bag and your pretty fancies, let me know. Maybe it doesn't matter who stole my coat from Brett's—"

"Why, Bill!" Cassie said. "She did! She wrote it! She wrote that note herself!"

"M'yes," Leonidas said, looking thoughtfully at the cheap small packet of notepaper that had come from the tricky compartment. "I thought she had—that pencil's the right shade of lead. M'yes, indeed. After seeing me, after I finished my contribution on Shakespeare to the club, she rushed to the corner drug store—"

"There's one right next the auditorium," Cassie said.

"To the drug store next door," Leonidas amended, "and bought a ten-cent packet of paper and envelopes. Then she printed this note— Did you say it had been delivered at Zara's apartment?"

Cassie nodded. "I asked the doorman, and he said it was brought by a ragged boy. Isn't it amazing, Bill, the way some people always find a ragged boy to run their errands? I never can, and I've looked for years. Once I found a sort of ragged one and offered him a dime to carry my bundles, but he told me to go to hell. So she's the murderer! Now, that does startle me!"

"The cops have all left Brett's," Dallas reported, coming back from the windows at the other side of the room. "They— Did you say, she's the murderer? My God—"

"They just thought that one up," Kaye said languidly from the floor.

"Gettridge? She's the murderer? I don't believe it— Kaye, what are you doing on the floor?"

"It's a lie-down," Kaye said. "So, Gettridge is your murderer, is she, Bill? I think that's such a peachy notion. Now tell me, just for fun—how did Gett-ridge swipe my coat and hat from Brett's cellar last night, and how come you wear them now? It's too bad you didn't get my suit too—that serge is substantial, but my coat fit you much better. That suit—"

"So what's the matter with that suit?" Cuff demanded. "What's the matter with that blue serge suit of mine? That suit's just as good as—"

"Oh, dear!" Cassie said. "What *is* all this argument about clothes and suits and coats? Here we've got the murderer, and you argue about clothes like—like a lot of women! Of course, Bill, that's why. Clothes. I mean, Lila Gettridge is always wishing she had nice clothes and a bigger car and a nice house on a nice street—"

Leonidas nodded. Mrs. Gettridge had brought up the subject of her small car, he remembered. She had mentioned that her house was elderly and in the older section of town.

"She's one of those 'You-can-afford-it-but-I-couldn't-possibly' women," Cassie continued. "She could, of course, but she doesn't. She's always wishing she could afford a new awning or a new ice box— Why, she got misty-eyed about my electric garbage chopper! She— But that won't work out, will it?"

"This whole damn outfit is unfair to Stanton Kaye!" Kaye said in a loud voice. "This whole damn outfit is unfair to sanity. This whole damn outfit is unfair to Stanton Kaye—"

"Shut up!" Dallas said, "or I'll ask Cuff to— Well,

maybe I hadn't better. What won't work out, Cassie?"

"I was assuming that if Lila killed Benny, she did it for money. I worked at it from the wrong angle, didn't I? I mean, I know she always wants things, but we don't know that Benny was killed for money. But if he was, she's certainly—"

The doorbell pealed out.

"Two long and two short—that's Jock!" Cassie said. "He must have taken the five— No, I'll go—"

"How conventional of the lad, ringing doorbells!" Kaye said. "I fully expected him to canter up a trellis. Or scorch in through a steam pipe— Jock is definitely not a chip off Cassie's block. And the dear boy's alone? He hasn't even brought a cop or two along? Or the scout troop? I feel depressed. Cassie's grandson has already let me down. Thud, thud—"

Cuff was not at all sure what Kaye was talking about, but he understood the acrid sarcasm in Kaye's voice, and he actively resented it. Bill's pals, Cuff felt, were his pals. And Margie thought Mrs. Price was fine.

"Say!" Cuff said belligerently, towering over Kaye. "Say, what are you talking about, huh? You want to thud, do you? Well, you—"

Jock and Cassie entered just in time to avert the incipient bloodshed.

Leonidas, who rightfully considered himself a connoisseur of boys, liked the looks of Jock. He was twelve or thirteen, but he had the self-assurance and self-possession of a seasoned concertmaster.

His large black eyes examined Kaye on the floor, flashed over Cuff, appraised Dallas and Margie, and lingered for several seconds on Leonidas. He was obviously thinking of Shakespeare, and his restraint in commenting on the resemblance further endeared him to Leonidas.

"How do you do?" Jock said, matter-of-factly accepting the group en masse. "Gran, I've got a new—"

"Darling, there's been a murder, next door at the Brett's—"

"I read about it in the papers," Jock said. "It wasn't very exciting. Just a stabbing. Gran, I've got—"

"Well, darling," Cassie said, "all these people are the ones the police are after. Uncle's police. They're terribly nice people—these people, I mean. And I'm helping them. They didn't do it, of course. We're keeping it from Uncle Root—that they're here, and I'm mixed up in it. You'll remember that, won't you?"

"Yes," Jock said. "I will—look, Gran, I've got a brand-new Lieutenant Hazeltine for us to read—brand-new! I saw it at the station and bought it, and that's why I'm so late. It took all my train money, and I had to come out on the street cars, and walk over from Daltondale car barn—"

"A new one!" Cassie said. "Oh, that's splendid—but, darling, if you walked over from Daltondale, you must be—why, you are! You're sloshing wet. You'd better change, I think. Your shoes and everything—did they go to Pinkham Notch?"

His grandmother's mental leaps did not appear to disconcert Jock at all.

"Yes, Father and Mother decided on Pinkham after all. There were two more inches of snow there, and the Vails were going, so they went together. Father lost his new wax—"

"His family ski, you know," Cassie said. "They just ski all the time—if there isn't snow, they ski on pine needles. They used to make Jock go along, and he had to break his legs any number of times before they decided he was better off here with me. That was what we wanted, of course—Jock, where's Lieutenant Hazeltine this time? I do hope it's Deepest Africa again!"

"He's come home most unexpectedly," Jock said, "to save the United States Army from utter destruction at the hands of Prince Casimir Vassily—remember Casimir?"

"That lovely one with the mustaches and the nitroglycerin!" Cassie said delightedly. "Oh, I love Casimir—Jock, you didn't begin, did you?"

"Listen!" Kaye sat up "I am a reasonable man. I can take it. Even the C.I.O. organizer admitted that Stanton Kaye could take it. But if you're going to ring in nitroglycerin and—what is Lieutenant Hazeltine? One of Rutherford's cops?"

"Oh, you don't know Lieutenant Hazeltine? Oh, they're marvelous books," Cassie said. "Never a dull moment. Hazeltine gets into more trouble—you know him, don't you, Bill?"

"Intimately," Leonidas said, polishing his pince-nez

carefully. "M'yes. I am intimately acquainted with the excellent lieutenant. A bright man if ever there was one—"

"He certainly is!" Cassie said. "And he's almost indestructible, too. For two hundred and twenty-five pages out of every book, that man is buffeted around by fate—more buffets and more fate than you'd believe possible. And then he thinks of Cannae—"

"He thinks," Kaye said, "of what?"

"Cannae," Leonidas said. "M'yes, indeed. Cannae. That historic battle between the Romans and the Carthaginians, fought in Apulia in the year 216 B.C., in which the small, weak army of Hannibal cut the incomparable forces of eighty-five thousand proud Roman legionaries to pieces—"

"To shreds," Jock said.

"To shreds. In that," Leonidas continued, "by means of an ingenious strategical concentration, it caught the enemy from the flank with cavalry, and surrounded him. Clausewitz and Schlieffen, of the Prussian General Staff, elaborated the idea of Cannae into a general theoretical doctrine, and then compressed the doctrine into an exact strategical system. That, in brief, is Cannae."

"Well, you've certainly read Lieutenant Hazeltine!" Cassie said. "That's word for word, isn't it, Jock?"

"Except pieces for shreds," Jock said.

He looked on Leonidas with new interest.

"To think," Leonidas said, "that at this point I could have forgotten Cannae. Thank you, Jock. Thank you—"

"Thanks," Kaye said, "for the memory. And now, what about my coat? And when I say, what about my coat, I mean that full explanations are going to be forthcoming, practically at once!"

"You'll get it," Margie said, turning ominously to Cuff. "Don't worry, you'll get—"

"Before you start any more bickering about your clothes," Cassie said, "I must tell Jock—darling, you'd really better change. They may decide it's better for you to break legs than catch colds. And I bought you one of those unspeakably hideous shirts. It's on your bed—"

"Oh, Gran! Barber pole stripes? In blue?"

"Barber poles in blue," Cassie said. "I'm sure your mother'll think it's subversive, but you can wear it here—yes, tonight, if you must. You can stun Uncle Root with it—and, darling, you won't forget about not telling him about all these people, will you, dear?"

"No, Gran, you're tops!" Jock said in one breath as he raced up the stairs.

"Are you quite through?" Kaye inquired. "You're sure, Cassie? I wouldn't want to think that I interrupted anything—all right! What about that coat, Margie?"

"Cuff, you took it, didn't you? Yes, I thought so. You see, Kaye," Margie said, "he came home with me last night, and all the lights were on in the cellar next door, and of course he had to peek in. And he saw that coat, and he said he always wanted a coat like that. But he'd promised me to reform, so I—but you wandered right in and took the coat, didn't you,

Cuff Murray! The minute you left me! The minute my back was turned! Didn't you, Cuff?"

"Aw!" Cuff said. "Aw—"

"Did you take my car, too?" Kaye inquired. "I noticed when I drove out today that my favorite convertible sedan was missing from the next street where the boy left it—"

"Aw!" Cuff said, "was that yours? I didn't know."

"Cuff Murray!" Margie said. "You took that! You —and you promised me—"

"Aw, I said, tomorrow I'd get a job and all," Cuff said. "But then I thought—you see, that wasn't tomorrow, then, see? And I got me a job today. That's how I met Bill again. Didn't I have a job, Bill? Wasn't I working? Didn't I reform, and all?"

"Reform!" Margie said. "Say, from what I can make out, you helped Bill get away from the cops, and parked in front of a hydrant and got a dame arrested by the cops, and stole a handbag—"

"And if that's not reform," Kaye said, "I don't know what the term means. He's sprouting wings, Margie. So the coat is just a side issue, is it? Just fate? I see. It's nothing to get worked up over. And Mrs. Gettridge—Comrade Gettridge killed Benny because she likes nice clothes. Only of course we don't know Benny was killed for money. That's the sum total of this day's work—my God, you need a battle of Cannae! You need—"

Jock, resplendent in the barber pole striped shirt, bounded down the stairs.

"It's keen, Gran," he said. "Thanks. You're tops.

And look, maybe you'd better tell me their names, Gran. All these people, I mean. If I have names, then I can act better in front of uncle. And can we go to the farm tomorrow?"

"Oh, Jock!" Cassie said. "I completely forgot—I ought to have gone there this morning. I forgot all about it—"

"You've forgotten about Rutherford B., too, haven't you?" Kaye asked. "Wasn't he coming to dinner here?"

"Yes, but he's so punctual, he won't be here till the stroke of seven. He learned that in the service, to be on the dot. I told him seven, and he'll be here at seven. We don't need to worry about him for an hour. But I should have gone to the farm—we'll run up first thing in the morning, Jock."

"Will they have the tractors out, do you think, Gran?"

"Ah," Leonidas said interestedly. "Tractors—you have a farm, with tractors?"

"It's all Rutherford's fault," Cassie said. "He always wanted to be a gentleman farmer when he retired. It was all he dreamed about when he was in Haiti and Guam and Nicaragua, and places like that. He thought that all he wanted was to sit on a New England hillside and count sheep, and prune trees, and grow things. Especially asparagus. He never had enough asparagus. Except canned, and he doesn't count that. So he got this farm—of course it bored him to extinction in six months, but he kept the place because it made so much money. You know the place, don't you, Kaye? It's near your—"

"Is it," Leonidas said, "that very large farm between the Country Club and that new development? Could it be *that* farm?"

"That's the place," Kaye said. "I tried to talk to Rutherford once about selling it to me—"

"He doesn't own it, you know," Cassie said. "He has some sort of funny lease from the owner that Paul Gettridge got. That was the most amazing thing. Rutherford wanted a place to farm, when he retired, and he told his caddie at the club, and the caddie told Paul, and it seemed Paul was trying to get someone to farm that land. It worked out so nicely. Much cheaper than buying, of course, but Rutherford lives in fear the owner will take the land back and sell it, and after all he's put into that farm—"

Leonidas laughed softly.

"So you," he said, "thought up the 'Not for Sale' sign, Cassie? My, my, I should have guessed!"

"Rutherford didn't think it was quite proper," Cassie said, "but I convinced him it would stave off the evil day when someone buys—"

"Who *does* own that land, anyway?" Kaye said. "I made some feeble attempt to find out, but it seems the place is tangled up with some estate that's being fought over. I wanted to buy it before some damn developer did."

"Rutherford's always brooding over that owner, too," Cassie said. "He was always wanting to go and ask Paul Gettridge about him and who he was, but

I wouldn't let him. I said, why not let well enough alone. If he went to Paul and brought the matter up, Paul might come to and remind the owner, and bring the matter up to him, and then he'd sell. We think it belongs to that enormously rich old Vandergriff, the one who lives in Cannes. He owns miles of Dalton—"

"Yes, I wondered if he didn't," Kaye said. "The estate talk was probably a blind. Well, some fine day he'll need a new yacht—say, Cassie, if Paul Gettridge managed that land, something may come out in the wash when someone else takes over—"

"August Barker Brett's taking over Gettridge's affairs," Dallas said. "That is, he will if he ever gets around to it. Benny's done what little has been done. He's been terribly lax. I didn't even know anything about that particular land—"

"Wouldn't that be a simply lovely motive, now!" Cassie said dreamily. "Land. An unknown owner. Benny finds out. Lila kills him for it—land is a much nicer motive than money—"

"Yes," Kaye said. "Less sordid. Cassie, what are you jabbering about? Let's get going on this murder business and stop all this fantasy—"

"But it would be such a nice motive," Cassie said. "You see, Lila could have killed Benny for the land—what a pity you don't own the land, Bill. Wouldn't that straighten it all out?"

"M'yes, indeed," Leonidas said. "It—er—it has, you know. That's what Mrs. Gettridge and I spent the afternoon discussing. That land—"

"*That* land? But, Bill!" Cassie said, "you never told us a thing! Not a thing! You—"

"I really haven't had the opportunity," Leonidas said. "But I do remember telling you that I had got down to the basis of the matter. And now we've cleared up a few points that were bothering me—"

"Who owns the land?" Kaye said. "Who—"

"Why, I thought you understood," Leonidas said. "I do."

In the outburst that followed, they did not hear the front door open, nor the footsteps in the hall.

They did not even notice the man who stood framed in the doorway.

Chapter TWELVE

LEONIDAS caught sight of the man just a split second before Jock spoke and confirmed his guess.

After all, it was not a very difficult guess.

Even Jock added the tall erect figure to the military bearing and got four.

"Uncle Rutherford!" Jock said. "Why, Uncle Root —we didn't expect you until seven! You're awfully early—"

"Been golfing all day long." Rutherford's voice, Leonidas decided, was one of the few he had ever heard which he could honestly describe as a boom. "In the rain. Trying out a new mashie."

He paused, ostensibly waiting for introductions and for an explanation of all the noise that had been going on.

So the colonel, Leonidas thought, was going to play them like a fish on a line. He didn't blame the colonel. In his position, Leonidas would have done the same thing.

"What do you do, Uncle," Jock beat Cassie to the breach, "when someone loses his voice?"

"Someone lost his voice, hah?"

Jock pointed at Kaye, still on the floor.

"He was talking perfectly all right, and then his voice just dried right up—he can't say a word!"

Leonidas nodded as he calmly polished his pince-nez.

He had not been mistaken in Jock. The boy could apply what he had learned. Lieutenant Hazeltine had once saved the life of a brother officer, captured by the enemy as a spy, by a similar ruse. Jock had just heard Kaye say that he had once talked with Rutherford about the farm, and Jock had sense enough to know that the colonel would probably recognize Kaye's clear and rather distinctive voice.

"Damn nuisance," Rutherford boomed sympathetically. "Lost my voice once. In Vera Cruz. Remember it well. I had to write orders for two days. You never know how much you talk until you have to write it down. You'll just have to wait. It'll come back. Fellow explained it all to me—vocal cords and so forth. Cassie, I didn't know you were having a party. My car broke down, and I walked all the way from the club—"

"Rutherford," Cassie said in strained tones, "have you been up at the club all day long, in the wet?"

"Yes, all day long. Went up at seven this morning, took a few sandwiches along. Wanted to try out this new mashie a fellow sold me while I had plenty of elbow room. And I did, you know. Wasn't a soul around up there all day. I walked all the way here. Didn't know you'd have company, y'see, Cassie.

Thought I wouldn't bother changing. But if you've got company—"

He paused again.

Leonidas swallowed slowly.

Either the colonel was a magnificent actor, or— Leonidas began to swing his pince-nez from their black ribbon. Or—it seemed incredible. It was not possible. It couldn't be possible that the colonel didn't know what had happened!

On the other hand, Mrs. Gettridge had mentioned that golfer in the rain.

Leonidas tried not to let himself smile.

"Your car is out of order again?" Cassie said. "What's the matter with it now, Rutherford?"

"Ignition, I think. From the radio. The radio wouldn't work this morning again. Probably a short circuit somewhere. I'm going to speak sharply to that battery fellow, Cassie. He's not competent. That's the second time that battery's gone to pieces. Didn't matter so much today, but I like to keep in touch with the department—"

"Haven't you," Cassie paused and moistened her lips, "haven't you been in touch with the department today? Not at all?"

"Not at all," Rutherford said cheerfully. "Had a fine day's rest. Not going to think about the department till I drop by headquarters tonight—don't want to hear a word about the department. Cassie, you still haven't said if I've got to go home and change, or if I can stay like this. Perfectly willing to go home and change, if one of your friends'll drive me over."

Cassie let out her breath slowly, and her face wreathed itself in smiles.

The incredible had happened. Rutherford did not know. He didn't know!

The atmosphere relaxed.

"Darling," Cassie said, walking over and taking his arm affectionately, "don't you even think of changing. Why, I shouldn't dream of having you go to all that work. We hadn't intended to dress, or even change. You can just run up and take a tub, and there's that old tweed suit of yours in the closet. It's so lucky that people leave things here. Jock was drenched, too, when he came— Oh, Dorothy and Edgar went to Pinkham Notch again."

"Did, hah?" Rutherford cleared his throat with a rumbling sound that fascinated Kaye. Dallas's warning look reminded him in the nick of time that he must not speak, even though he yearned to take a crack at that rumble.

Cassie explained at length that Jock had come by street car, after spending all his money on a new Lieutenant Hazeltine.

"New one out?" Rutherford said. "Be sure to let me have it when you're through. Marvelous fellow, Hazeltine—Cassie, you haven't—that is, I haven't met your friends, you know—"

"How rude of me!" Cassie said. "I forgot—but you've heard me speak of them. Mr. and Mrs. Mappin, Mr. and Mrs. Cuff, and—and Mr. Mappin, senior, with the beard."

Rutherford was not satisfied with her all-inclusive gesture.

"Hah!" he said. "Want to know which is which, Cassie. Have a bad enough time remembering names —which is which?"

"The Mappins," Cassie pointed to Dallas and Kaye, who both grinned broadly. "The Cuffs," she indicated Cuff and Margie. "Mr. Mappin, with the beard—who does he remind you of, Rutherford?"

"Thought of it the very minute I laid my eyes on him," the colonel said. "Right away, I said to myself, by George, how much that fellow looks like Shakespeare! Served with a man on the old 'Utah' once that looked just like Kipling. Perfectly amazing— Jock, there's a new boat out in the hall I brought with me. Just remembered."

"A boat?" Jock said. "Oh, that's swell—what boat, Uncle?"

"That thing you wanted. Spanish galleon. Looks hard to me, Jock. Awful lot of rigging. Lugged it down with my clubs all the way—"

"Uncle, you're tops!" Jock said. "Will we start right in on it?"

"Of course you can!" Cassie said heartily. "You can make it tonight, can't you, Rutherford? Jock wants to start in right away—"

"But," Rutherford insisted, "you've got—that is, with Mr. and Mrs. Ma—er—Macklin, and all—"

"They won't mind!" Cassie said. "Will you? Of course they won't mind a bit if you build boats! Hear, dear? They shan't mind a bit!"

They shouldn't have minded a bit, Leonidas thought, if Rutherford had shown any inclination to knit a necktie of live cobras. What Rutherford did, didn't matter. The only thing that mattered was that Rutherford should do it, that he should wallow in it raptly, wholeheartedly and to the complete exclusion of anything else.

"Well," Rutherford said.

"As a matter of fact," Cassie said, "our plans are awfully unsettled. I was—that is, we were rather wondering if perhaps you mightn't have some plans— Oh, you know what I mean!"

Somehow, with some deft eyebrow work, she managed to convey to Rutherford the impression that these unexpected guests had thrown everything into a hideous turmoil, and that the only possible salvation lay in Rutherford's building boats with Jock.

That suited the colonel, who had only been trying to be polite to his sister's guests. His fingers were itching to start on the galleon.

"Matter of fact," he said, "it's a very interesting model, y'know. Got real sails, real anchor— Tell you what, Jock, I'll change, and then we'll go down cellar—"

Leonidas prodded Cassie.

The cellar, with Muir still in the preserve room, was no place for Rutherford.

"Darling," Cassie said, "you can't use the cellar. Because of—of the curtains. They were washed today, and they're all over the place on those stretcher things. Mrs. O'Malley left them to dry."

"Hah, spring cleaning!" said the colonel. "Well, we can't work here—there's nothing left but the little front room, Cassie!"

Obviously the use of the little front room was a moot point.

"All right," Cassie said. "The little front room, then. But just this once! All those chips, and that messy cement— Rutherford, you go dry out, and we'll go get some dinner—"

"We? Where's your new maid? Thought you had a jewel of a new maid."

"It's—it's almost too awful to speak about," Cassie said. "You tell him, Dallas—"

Cassie's bump of invention had taken a terrible paring, and she felt that it needed a good rest.

"That maid!" Dallas said promptly. "She didn't get in until four this morning, Colonel. Dead drunk. Cassie couldn't do a thing with her. Couldn't even move her. She slept it off, finally, and Richard," she nodded toward Kaye, "packed her off this afternoon. After we came. It was too bad. She was such a nice-looking girl."

Margie ground her heel down on Cuff's foot just as he was about to rise and demand an explanation.

"You can't ever tell about maids," she said demurely. "I always say, it just seems as though you couldn't get a decent maid any more."

"Seems so, Mrs.—er—Duff, seems so," the colonel said. "Cassie, in a situation like that, you should have called Muir, without any hesitation. Can't tell what you might have run into. And, by the way, your front door was open. You *must* be more careful about that latch. Better call that locksmith fellow and get a new one. Why, anyone could have walked in here! Well, I'll go up and change—"

"Do, dear," Cassie said. "Oh— Jock, just a minute. I want to tell you about next Friday, while I think about it—"

She waited until she heard the splash of the colonel's bath water running into the tub upstairs.

"Jock," she said solemnly, "whatever else you do, keep him out of the cellar! I forgot to tell you, but Muir's in the preserve room. All bound up and gagged and everything—"

"Are you sure he is?" Dallas asked. "Did anyone make sure?"

"Yes," Kaye said. "I heard a slight ruffle of indignation when I came through the cellar after putting the car up. And the key's in place, and all the stuff we stuck in front of the door. He's there. My, he must be mad!"

"Jock, darling," Cassie said, "if you love your feeble old gran, don't let Uncle Root guess a thing. Make him build boats—"

"He will, Gran," Jock assured her. "He's been crazy to do the 'Santa Maria' for months. You just leave him to me. You know, we worked on the 'Flying Cloud' till three in the morning, and he wouldn't have stopped then if you hadn't threatened to turn off the electricity!"

Kaye got up from the floor.

"Jock," he said, holding out his hand, "I take back

what I said. You're two chips off the old block— Cup Cake, do you think you can hold him for us? Oh, of course you can. I know you can. You're a bulwark, like your grandmother. And that voice business was superb—wasn't it, Bill?"

"Hazeltine himself," Leonidas said, "could have done no better. Mind the doorbell and the phone, won't you, Jock? Don't let anyone see the colonel, or talk with him. If we can keep Uncle Root in blissful ignorance for a few hours more, possibly we may yet—er—pull through."

"Got any ideas, Bill?" Kaye demanded.

"M'yes," Leonidas said. "Many. Dinner, first. We must get through with that, before we really set to work. You'd better not find your voice, Kaye. And, Margie, keep a firm hold on Cuff. No matter what you don't understand, Cuff, don't comment on anything. Agree with Rutherford— You know who he is? Perhaps it's better that you don't. And, Cassie—"

"Don't count on me, Bill!" Cassie said. "I warn you, I've just about reached the end of my tether. And don't think that Rutherford is dull, just because he booms around that way."

"Any man who could think up Plan Five," Leonidas said, "is very far from dull. Plan Five, Cuff, is going to prove of inestimable value. It is going to come into its own, now. Er—someone said that the police have left the Brett house? That's fine. Have you an extension telephone, Cassie, in some remote corner? I want you to call police headquarters for me—"

"There's the phone in the laundry," Cassie said, "but I—"

"Now, look here, Bill," Kaye said, "don't you catch this cop-calling disease! Let's not play that game. Let's not call any more cops, please!"

"But this is very necessary," Leonidas said. "Cassie, call and ask for Rutherford, and see if you can find out the name of the officer at the desk. Jock, you might get the ship model and wave it in front of your uncle— He mustn't lose sight of that model—"

"Scrub his back for him," Kaye said. "Tell him what you did in arithmetic class today. Tell him what Adams said to Swett Minor. Discuss the situation in the American League. Get his opinion on the Swiss Navy. You don't know, Cup Cake, how we count on you!"

"Oh, I think so," Jock said confidently. "It's like Lieutenant Hazeltine that time in London, when he so captivated the blonde duchess that Meribel—she's his girl, you know, who helps him—she actually crept into the very room, and stole the treaty unobserved. It's the same— Mr. Mappin, your nose is coming off!"

"Get him a new nose, Dallas," Leonidas said briskly. "Or vulcanize him—fix him, some way. From the sounds, I should say that Rutherford was a very speedy bather. Hurry—Margie, do something about dinner. Help her, Cuff. Cassie, we must do our phoning at once—"

Cassie sighed as she called police headquarters.

"The thing that bothers me most," she said, "is that we'll need cooking sherry, and I don't see how we can get it without rousing Muir— Hello, head-quarters— Oh, Feeney! This is Mrs. Price. Has anyone seen my brother? Oh. I see. He hasn't. You think he and Muir are solving— I see. Thank you. If he should call, Feeney, won't you have him call me? Thank you —don't you have long hours! Feeney! Oh, is he sick? I see. Thank you so much."

"I gather," Leonidas said, "that Feeney is still at the desk."

"He says that Conry's sick, that's why. Bill, they think that Rutherford and Muir are scurrying around solving this thing by themselves!"

"A splendid thought," Leonidas said, taking the sheaf of Plan Five papers from his pocket. "I see they have vast confidence in their leader. A commendable thing. I am glad of it— M'yes, here it is."

Cassie watched him curiously as he studied Plan Five.

"What are you going to do, Bill?" she asked.

"I should long ago have grasped the resemblance," he said, "between our adventures and those of the excellent Hazeltine. I should have remembered Cannae. That I didn't is almost unforgivable. After all the time I have spent with Cannae! We have been waging, Cassie, a war of positions. When pressure has been exerted on us, we have moved. When pressure was exerted again, we moved again. If you recall your Hazeltine, you will remember that he often refers to deadlocks. We have been rushing from one deadlock to another."

"Well," Cassie said, "that's one way of putting it, I suppose. But—"

"So," Leonidas said, "we are going to take a leaf out of Hazeltine, and play Cannae. We will concentrate our somewhat meager forces and attack on the flank. What was that code word—ah, yes."

He cleared his throat and reached for the phone.

"Dalton one thousand," he boomed. "Hah. That's right. Emergency. Hah!"

He sounded so much like Rutherford that Cassie blinked.

"Feeney, hah?" Leonidas said. "Hah! Feeney. Yes, yes. That's right. Hah, yes. Muir and I have been active. Very active. Want you to listen carefully, Feeney. And haven't you forgotten to ask me something?"

Cassie could hear the agitated squeaks on the other end as Feeney explained why he had forgotten to ask the code word that was to proceed any change of Plan Five orders that were given by phone.

"Don't forget again, Feeney!" Leonidas said. "Very important! 'Remember the Maine.' Hah! Now, want you to listen carefully, Feeney. Want you to cancel the hunt for those three—Kaye, Tring, and the man with the beard. That's right. Send that out at once. Want you to remove all officers from the vicinity of the Brett house. That's right. Want you to send a car to Mrs. Price's. Driver can go. Needn't wait. Twenty will do, yes. Hah! Got that?"

Cassie sat down heavily on the laundry stool.

"Now," Leonidas continued, "want you to cancel

items two, nine, twelve, sixteen and sixteen A. Got those numbers? Repeat them."

"Bill!" Cassie said. "Bill Shakespeare! Why, aren't you— Isn't this— Why, why!"

"Correct," Leonidas said. "Want you to be careful about this, Feeney. Very important. Muir and I are at a very important point. Crucial. Got a most important clew. Mustn't be any slip-ups. What's that?"

Feeney squeaked for several minutes.

"So they got the Carnavon bank robber, hah?" Leonidas said. "And he's got a cast-iron alibi for the Brett case. Hah. Thought so. Knew it. Never thought he was our man. What? Speak up, man, I can't hear you. And hurry—haven't got all night!"

"Ask him about Lila Gettridge!" Cassie whispered. "Ask him what—"

Leonidas motioned for her to be quiet.

"What friend?" he asked. "What woman, Feeney? Who? Oh. Did, did she? Again? And she hit a car on the way to the station? That's bad. Very bad. Hah! Anybody hurt? I see. No, I don't suppose so."

"Did she hit a car?" Cassie whispered. "She did? On her way? Is she hurt? No?"

"No," Leonidas said. "Can't see how we can. Tell you what, Feeney. We'll teach her a lesson. Hah. That's right. Teach her a lesson. You keep her right there until I come for her. Mind, now. Don't do anything till I come. Hold her. That's right. What, call my sister? All right, all right! I will. Now you be careful, Feeney, and have no slip-ups on those changes. Hah. Good-by!"

"Bill," Cassie said as he replaced the receiver, "you are a genius. Hazeltine never thought of anything like that!"

"No, but he will—" Leonidas coughed. "Cassie, your brother's voice must be under a constant strain. That boom is wearing. I feel as though I had been broadcasting a salvo by salvo report of target practice—"

"It's perfectly marvelous," Cassie said happily. "We can have dinner, and then go get Lila Gettridge, and everything will be all right—Bill, I do think you're clever!"

"I am afraid," Leonidas said, "that things are not going to be that simple— Cassie, do you know Zara Brett's telephone number? Will you get it?"

"Right away," Cassie said.

Leonidas leaned against the wash tubs and waited. Zara was the next step. He wished that he could get to her at once, but they would have to wait until after Colonel Carpenter had his dinner and was safely at work on the "Santa Maria" up in the little front room. The colonel, as Cassie said, was not to be underestimated. After perusing Plan Five, Leonidas had no doubt that the colonel could outdo both Jock and Cassie, if aroused and given the opportunity.

Cassie bustled back.

"I had to find Rutherford's shirt," she said. "Sometimes it seems to me that my life has been one long shirt hunt. My father, my brothers, Bagley, Jock— It's so strange. I never knew a woman to lose a shirt—

here's the number, Bill. Why are you going to call her?"

"Zara," Leonidas said, "expects us to call on her in person, and so we are not. We are going to invite her to call on us—"

"But she won't come, Bill!"

"I think she will," Leonidas said, clearing his throat. "Stand by the door, Cassie. If Rutherford is at the shirt stage, we must watch out. Would Zara recognize his voice?"

"Oh, I think so, if— Oh, I sée!" Cassie said. "You're going to boom at her and be Rutherford again! Oh, Bill, you're just so smart!"

Zara answered the phone herself, and from the speed of her response, Leonidas judged that she had been sitting by the telephone.

"Miss Brett, hah?" he said. "Colonel Carpenter speaking. Hah. Meant to call you sooner. Sorry about all this. Wonder if I could see you—know you're all broken up, and so forth, but wonder if I could?"

Leonidas held the receiver so that Cassie could hear Zara explain how broken up she was, how the whole sad affair had simply shattered her nervous system, how she had grieved and brooded and worried about poor dear Benny.

It was very likely, Leonidas thought, that she had brooded and worried, but he felt quite sure that her brooding and worrying had not concerned poor dear Benny.

Cassie's curt, descriptive monosyllable echoed his thoughts.

"Frightful, Miss Brett," he said. "Now, could you manage to— Hah, that's fine, that's very co-operative of you. Now, I'll send a car for you— Best thing, dear lady, best thing. I know what's best. Hah, what? That's right. Send it right to your door. At nine o'clock. Where? Want you over at your brother's house. Hah! Need you. That's fine. Appreciate it, you know. Greatly appreciate this sacrifice of yours. Good-by."

"Bill," Cassie said as he hung up, "words just fail me. That's what Rutherford would have said, just exactly. But why do you want her at Brett's? And how— I don't understand this part."

"Kaye," Leonidas said, swinging his pince-nez, "is to don Muir's uniform, and take car twenty— Feeney's sending car twenty over here for us, you know. Kaye will call for Zara Brett at nine this evening. He will bring her over to ninety-five Paddock Street—"

"But how can you get in there? How can you get in next door?"

"Cuff," Leonidas said easily. "Cuff can manage that without effort, I feel sure. That is the sort of undertaking which Cuff seems instinctively to understand. To me, the breaking and entering of a house would loom as a major problem. To Cuff, it will be child's play. A cinch. A snap. Now—"

"But why Zara, anyway? What do you want with her, Bill? What about Lila Gettridge?"

"Mrs. Gettridge is safe," Leonidas said, "in Rutherford's jail. They're quite annoyed with her for having a slight accident with another car en route to the station, and they resent her not having her license and registration. But Feeney assured me that she is being treated with every consideration, as befits a friend of the chief. We shall let her stay there. As for Zara, she has had the whole day in which to worry. I like to think that she may have worried herself into something which might be described as a state. Once we have her over at Brett's, we shall proceed to worry her to a point where she breaks down completely. That, at least, is my hope. I feel—"

"There's Rutherford booming!" Cassie said. "We'd better go out—"

"He's coming here," Leonidas said. "Don't get jumpy. So you really feel that the monel metal boiler is worth the money?"

"Definitely," Cassie said. "The Dalton water's so odd, you know. People always said that copper was the only thing, but now there's some new little bug in the water, and copper won't— Oh, Rutherford! All ready, dear? I was showing Bill the boiler. He wondered about the monel."

"Boiler, hah? Fine thing. Fine. Er—Cassie. Just a minute—"

The colonel drew her into the entry.

His anxious, throaty whisper was just barely audible to Leonidas.

"Cassie, that Matton fellow—the young one. What's the matter with his nose?"

"Oh! Oh, you noticed that? I hadn't a chance to warn you, and I was so afraid you'd speak of it," Cassie said. "Accident, you know. This perfectly hideous auto accident in the Alps. They're rebuilding his nose, and in between operations they sort of have his nose filled out and the scars hidden with some sort of stuff. For the love of heaven, Rutherford, keep your eyes off it, and don't mention it! He's terribly sensitive about it, naturally. And of course it's so painful. And so hard for him, never knowing if it's all right—if it should look funny, tell his wife. Don't tell him. Just pass it off. Like your friend Youngman and his glass eye."

"Had an awful start," Rutherford said. "Just saw it under the reading light, you know. Looked just like putty. Hah! Poor fellow. Who are these Mappits—these Moppets? Never heard of them."

"Mappin, darling. Mappin and Cuff. I met them on that North Cape cruise. They were terribly nice to me, but of course you know what you always say about people you knew on boats when you get them ashore! And think of their landing here today, of all days, with that wretched maid! So help me, darling. Be charming. Tell them all your best stories. They have a really remarkable sense of humor. And then do amuse Jock for me— I couldn't take him to the farm, because they were here, and he's just been wishing for you!"

"Seem like nice people," Rutherford said. "Better than those what's-their-names you met going to Mexico. They were terrible. All right, I'll take care of Jock. That's quite a boat, that galleon—"

"Why don't you show Bill and Richard how it works?" Cassie asked. "The parts, I mean. You could do that while we women finish getting dinner together— Do be charming, now, darling, because I've talked you up so! Bill—oh, Bill! Rutherford is going to show you how that model works—"

The colonel needed no further encouragement to display the model kit to Leonidas and Kaye.

During his lengthy explanation, and later during dinner, Rutherford obeyed Cassie's orders and studiously refrained from looking at Kaye's nose.

And he was charming, too. Once he got going on his stories of life in the corps, his boom became infectious. By the end of dinner, they were all booming with laughter, even Cuff.

"I hate to leave the old boy," Kaye said, after Rutherford had departed with Jock and the galleon to the little front room. "I never laughed so— Oh, dear! That story of the mess sergeant and the bromo-seltzer is going to liven the Kaye family for years! Bill, what do we do now?"

Leonidas looked at his watch.

"You," he said, "get into Muir's uniform, take the police car outside the house, and go get Zara Brett. Quickly. Don't make me explain. We've got no time to lose. It's quarter to nine. Get Zara, and bring her over to the Brett house. D'you understand? Well, never mind if you don't understand. Do it. Hurry. Cuff, can you get into that house next door?"

"Aw, sure," Cuff said, getting up from the kitchen chair. "Got a screwdriver anywheres, Margie? Okay, Bill. Come to the front door in about five minutes and I'll let you in."

"I told you," Leonidas said to Cassie, "that was his department. Don't put on a light, Cuff, until we get in and get the shades pulled down—"

"Okay," Cuff said, departing with the screwdriver.

Five minutes later he let Bill, Cassie, Dallas and Margie in through the front door of ninety-five Paddock Street.

"This," Leonidas said, "is an achievement, Cuff, an exploit of which Lieutenant Hazeltine would be proud. I personally look on you with admiration. We —er—didn't hurry you?"

"Gee, no," Cuff said. "I had time to pull down the shades. It wasn't nothing to get in. Shall I put on the lights now, Bill?"

The click of the light switch under his finger was the last sound made by any of the group for several minutes.

They were too dumbfounded even to gasp.

In front of the couch, on the floor, lay Zara Brett. She had been stabbed.

"Oh!" Cassie said in anguish. "Oh! Oh, how awful! Oh, please, please tell me it's my bifocals! Oh, I hope it's the bifocals!"

Leonidas was not quite sure whether she referred to Zara, or to her own carving knife.

For without question, Cassie's carving knife, the same knife which had killed Benny, had also killed his sister Zara.

Chapter THIRTEEN

LEONIDAS put on his pince-nez and crossed over to the couch.

"She's dead." Dallas did not make a question of it, but her voice rose slightly, as though she hoped that someone would contradict her.

"M'yes," Leonidas said.

"Oh, I never pretended to like Benny—but this is terrible!" Cassie took hold of Margie's hand and gripped it. "It's terrible! Zara—why should anyone do this to her? It's— Why, nothing like this ever happened in Hazeltine, Bill! Not even that Casimir was as brutal! As— Oh, I'm sorry for her, and I'm so—so furious that anyone could have done such a terrible thing! So—why, if Lila Gettridge were to walk into this room, I really think I'd fly at her!"

"It's awful," Dallas said. "Awful!"

Even Margie was blinking to keep back her tears. "It's tough," she said.

Only Cuff seemed to be able to accept the fact, and proceed on to the inevitable conclusion.

"Gee, yes," he said. "Tough for us, too. Gee, this

is a spot, Bill. This is plenty tough. We better get going—"

"How'd Lila Gettridge get out of jail?" Cassie demanded. "I thought you told them to hold her there, Bill!"

Leonidas nodded as he turned around. He felt very sure that Mrs. Gettridge was still in the Dalton police headquarters, but this appeared to be an excellent opportunity to get the three women away before they burst into tears and embarked on their individual variations of hysterics. They were very near to it now.

"I wish, Cassie," he said, "that you would go over to your house and telephone—this phone here has been fixed, but I doubt the wisdom of using it. Call Feeney, and find out about Mrs. Gettridge. Perhaps you'd better go the back way—and perhaps you'd like to stay over there—"

"You've got to call the police, haven't you?" Cassie said. "And Rutherford— Oh, dear!"

"Presently," Leonidas said.

"I guess," Cassie said, "that your page out of Hazeltine is a failure, Bill. I'll go phone, but we'll all be back. Yes, I guess we can't depend on Hazeltine, Bill. We'll have to depend on you—"

"Which," Leonidas murmured as they left, "amounts to the same thing."

He turned around and looked again at Zara Brett. He was no judge, but it did not seem to him that she had been dead very long.

"Gee, Bill," Cuff said, "see the tag on the knife, will you? It says 'Exhibit B.' Wonder what 'A' is?"

"Very likely," Leonidas answered, " 'A' is a picture of the body of Benny Brett. I think the police will regret having forgotten to take that knife with them. M'yes, Cuff, you're quite right. This is going to be tough."

"Yeah." Cuff watched for a moment as Leonidas swung his pince-nez. "Say, Bill, what's your racket?" he asked. "I been wondering."

Leonidas smiled grimly. "So have I," he said. "I used to teach, Cuff. Lately, I've lived by what I liked to think of as my wits. It's amazing. I prided myself on my wits. I thought they were quick. I really did. I—"

His irony escaped Cuff.

"Gee, you do think quick," Cuff said. "And I like the way you talk, too. I wish I could talk like that—"

Cassie, followed by Margie and Dallas, returned.

"Bill!" she said. "She's still there! Lila Gettridge, I mean. She hasn't been out of the station since— Oh! You knew that, did you? You guessed it? Well, then, who killed Benny and Zara?"

"Not Mrs. Gettridge," Leonidas said. "I never thought she did. That was entirely your idea, Cassie, if you'll pause and reflect—"

"Then who did? What's Lila got to do with this?"

"She," Leonidas said, "is the person who telephoned Dallas early this morning, saying in a thick voice that she was Benny, and for Dallas to come here at once."

"I never heard of such a— Why? Why'd she do that?"

"It was a very bright move," Leonidas said. "A very

neat way of getting the police here. Rather like your calling about the door being ajar, Cassie. Dallas would come, you see, and summon the police— My, what a magnificent alibi the murderer must have, to bring the murder so boldly to light! Yes, Mrs. Gettridge made that call, I feel sure. And I rather think she may have inspired the whole thing. She knew about me and the land— Don't forget, the original plan was to kill me—"

Kaye, in Muir's uniform, rushed into the room, looked at Zara, and then rushed out into the hallway and shut the front door.

"This," he said when he returned, "is no time to leave that door open! As Rutherford said, you can't tell who might drop in— Bill, my God! Bill, I was just going to break the news to you that Zara had beat it. Bill, who did this? This—this is curtains for us! Oh, Bill, I—I feel sick!"

"I feel," Leonidas said, "rather the same way you felt this morning about Benny. You felt that if you had come to see him, he wouldn't have been killed. I feel, now, that if I had not tried to be so clever, Zara would still be alive."

"Say, Bill," Cuff said, "let's get going—"

"I know what you mean," Kaye said. "It's a terrible feeling. You're shocked and afraid and guilty, all at once. I've kept telling myself all day that if Benny was double-crossing someone he probably would have been killed anyway. But it doesn't alter the way I feel—"

"Bill," Cuff said, "let's scram out of here, and—"

"I've been telling myself," Leonidas said, "that someone almost had to do away with Zara before she talked. She would have talked, of course, sooner or later. But it doesn't alter my feelings, either. And—"

"Kaye," Cassie said, "Lila Gettridge's still in jail— think of it! Bill says she didn't do this. He says she didn't kill Benny, either. All she did was make a phone call, he says!"

"By God!" Kaye said. "But I thought you had it all doped out that she did— Bill, if she didn't who did? And—"

"Bill—" Cuff was clearly losing patience—"let's scram, Bill! Let's get going out of here, huh?"

"I do wish you'd be still!" Cassie said. "How can we think, with you wanting to scram—do be quiet!"

She spoke more harshly than she intended, and Cuff looked very hurt.

"Oh, I didn't mean to crush you!" Cassie said. "I just meant— Look, you're probably bored. Why don't you sit down over in that nice corner chair? Or at the desk. There are magazines and things—"

"Pencils, pen and ink," Kaye said. "You could write a letter, Cuff. There's a good guy! You—"

"Say, Bill!" Cuff was getting angry. "Say—"

"Cuff," Leonidas said, "my admiration for you is undimmed. And, shortly, I'm going to need you to do something else of great importance for me. Will you? Thank you, Cuff. If you would wait, and bear with us just for a few minutes—"

"Come on, Butch, stop pouting," Margie said, patting Cuff's cheek. "Come on over to the desk. There, Cuffy, wait there—"

"Now," Cassie said, after Cuff was thoroughly mollified, "who, Bill? Who?"

Leonidas smiled a rather lopsided smile.

"There's only one answer," he said, "and it's difficult to tell you. You're not going to believe me, and I have what amounts to no proof. That is, I have proof that satisfies me, but nothing which would appeal either to Rutherford or his police."

"Well, break it to us, man!" Kaye said. "Gently— but break it! Is this a new thought of yours, by the way, or have you been cherishing it all day?"

"It's one of the fantastic notions," Leonidas said, "that has been haunting me, particularly since this afternoon. It's so obvious, you know. This murderer feels so very secure! So above suspicion! So far above! Er—does Mrs. Gettridge wear glasses, Cassie?"

"Oh, dear me!" Cassie said. "Are you back to her? Bill, you're such a confusing man! Jumping around so— No, I told you I never saw Lila Gettridge wear glasses. I don't think she does. I'm almost positive, because I called up practically everyone I ever heard of who does, to see what happened when they got bifocals. If they got them of course—"

"M'yes," Leonidas said thoughtfully. "She drives a car without wearing glasses, and she watches movies without them, and she read Plan Five without them—"

"What about sewing?" Kaye inquired. "Or didn't you happen to get that far with her?"

Leonidas ignored him.

"How fortunate, considering her reading of Plan Five," he said, "that she is still in jail. M'yes, I think we may take for granted the fact that Mrs. Gettridge does not wear glasses. And if she does, I rather doubt if she would wear that type."

"What type?" Kaye asked.

Leonidas took from his coat pocket the pair of glasses which he had removed from Mrs. Gettridge's pocketbook.

"These glasses," he said. "This type, with the thin gold rims and bows. I feel sure that my oculist would deplore these gold-rimmed things as vociferously as he deplores my pince-nez. They are both the sort of thing which he views with alarm. Sometimes he even mutters things about horses and buggies. He—"

"Let me see those glasses, Bill," Dallas said. "Oh, that's funny. They're like August Barker Brett's— I thought he was the only one left who ever wore that kind! August's a glasses shedder, you know. Always leaving his glasses in strange places. He has a dozen pairs, but I still have to take a day off once in a while and call around places and collect 'em. Once I picked up four pairs at the Athenaeum. Probably I'll have to write letters when he comes back from Florida—"

"M'yes," Leonidas said. "Just so. Exactly."

"What? Oh, he'll be back tonight some time," Dallas said. "That's what you mean, isn't it? For a second I thought you meant that these were his glasses."

"But I did," Leonidas said. "I did, you know."

"What!"

"M'yes," Leonidas said. "I've seen him at the Athenaeum, too. He is one of many who wear glasses, but he is the only one I can recall who wears this type."

"Pooh!" Dallas said. "Stuff and nonsense! Of course they're not August's! What a silly thought, Bill!"

"It's not at all impossible that they might be his," Cassie said. "He's such a friend of the Gettridges, of course. He may have left them there a long while ago. And Lila put them in her bag— You know how you cart things around in bags! Why, I once carried a boy scout knife, that belonged to a friend of Jock's, for a good six months. And you know what those knives are! Why, you might as well cart around a hardware store—"

"What Bill is driving at, Cassie," Kaye said, "isn't so much the glasses. What he is trying to break gently to us is that August Barker Brett is the lad we're after. The lad we want for these two murders. He's—"

"But that's utterly ridiculous," Dallas said matter-of-factly. "That man a murderer? Why, August is an old dear. And besides, he's in Florida! Cassie, tell Bill how utterly crazy he is!"

"I do think you are, Bill," Cassie said. "Really. It's possible that those glasses may belong to him, but the rest is too bizarre even to consider. Of course."

"Whom was August staying with in Florida?" Leonidas asked.

"With Harvey Campbell— I talked with him this morning. And Harvey Campbell used to be the mayor of Dalton, Bill. Why, he was lieutenant-governor of the state, once. So you see how silly it is to think of August in connection with this—"

"Wait, now," Kaye said. "I don't know—I don't know that it's so silly, Dallas. Did you talk with August this morning?"

"With Campbell. And for heaven's sake, don't ask me if I know, if I'm sure, if I'm positive! Because I've talked with him often, and I know him and his voice, and it was Campbell!"

"Well," Kaye said, "possibly so. But I just saw Campbell over in Dalton Centre. He rushed out into traffic and hailed the cab in front of me, and they tore off lickety-split through a red light—"

"So what?" Dallas said. "It's perfectly possible that he flew with August back from Florida, isn't it?"

"M'yes, indeed," Leonidas said. "I'm sure he did. D'you begin to understand, Kaye? If you go to Florida to visit a prominent citizen, and if you fly home with him, you could not possibly commit a murder—"

The doorbell rang loudly.

"Wouldn't I scream with laughter," Dallas said hotly, "if that was August now!"

"He," Leonidas reminded her, "has a key. Did you find out how Zara left the apartment, Kaye? By car, alone, how?"

"The doorman just said that she hurried out on foot an hour or so ago— She told him she had an appointment with Colonel Carpenter— Aren't we," Kaye said as the bell rang again, "going to answer that? Maybe it's my subpoena— It's about time that lad mooched around again—"

"I'll go," Leonidas said. "I—"

"I'm going with you," Dallas said, "so I can laugh if— Bill, I like you and all that, but this thought of yours about August is too— Really, I shall chortle if this is August. Why, Bill, he's such a dear old lamb—fussy, but a dear!"

She reached the door ahead of him, and flung it open before he could caution her. There was always a chance that some stray policeman might not have heard of the changes in Plan Five.

Dallas pointed to the man standing on the door-step, and crowed.

"It's Mr. Campbell, Bill," she said. "Just as good as— Look, didn't I talk with you over the phone this morning in Florida, Mr. Campbell? Didn't—"

"And where the hell have you been since, Miss Tring?" Campbell yelled at her. "August is nearly crazy, hunting you! Of all the times for you to take a day off! If you were my secretary, I'd—I'd fire you so quick—"

Dallas stared at him as he spluttered wrathfully away.

"Well," she said at last, "if you often boil over like this, thank God I'm not your secretary! What's the matter with you, Mr. Campbell? What—"

"I'm sorry," Campbell said, making an obvious effort to control himself, "but I'm dead tired, and I've had August on my hands— He's been hunting you, and—yes, I talked with you this morning. But I flew back with him. Didn't intend to, but there was a delay in starting because of that fishing trip, and

I had some business to do anyway. And I didn't want August to make the trip alone. He's upset—but you know all that."

"No," Dallas said. "I haven't seen him. He—"

"You didn't get any of his messages or telegrams?" Campbell began to yell again. "You didn't— I don't believe you! Why, August started trying to contact you before we left! And when you weren't there at the airport to meet him—"

"But I didn't get any telegrams!" Dallas raised her voice. "I haven't—"

"Well, even so, couldn't you have made some effort, Miss Tring? Couldn't you have shown some efficiency in dealing with this situation? Some consideration? You might at least have sent a car to the airport for us—for him! A car to meet him wouldn't have taken much intelligence on your part!"

Leonidas put a restraining hand on Dallas's arm.

"Er—Miss Tring," he said, "has had rather a difficult day, Mr. Campbell—"

"She's had a difficult day, has she?" Campbell interrupted. "What kind of a day do you think we had? Those god damned papers, they got August so worked up— Yes, I know she's had a hard day. We read some tosh in the papers about some misunderstanding the police had about her—but what of it? What," he broke off as the cab driver started up the steps, "what do you want? Get back to your car. I'm coming right along—"

"But—"

"For the love of God!" Campbell said, "do what

I tell you! Get back to your cab and wait for me! If you've changed your mind again about the fare—"

"I haven't, I—"

"My God," Campbell said, "I didn't know there were so many dolts in the world! Here, Miss Tring, give August these damned things—"

Leonidas reached out and took the pair of gold-rimmed glasses, and thanked Mr. Campbell politely.

"Mr. Brett's, of course?"

"Whose else? You don't think I'd wear such god damned atrocities, do you? I just found 'em in my bags, and I know they're his last pair. He's strewn the rest around Florida— For God's sake, Miss Tring, get in touch with August at once. He wants you and he needs—"

"We rather expected him here, you know," Leonidas said. "I'm Mappin, by the way. State police. And —er—in view of your rather warm feelings on the subject, I think perhaps you both might have had less difficulty if you'd got in touch with the police, instead of sending futile telegrams to Miss Tring. A knowledge of Mr. Brett's plans would have helped us—er— Didn't you think of that, Mr. Campbell?"

"Well," Campbell said, "no, we didn't. He—that is—"

"M'yes. Where is Mr. Brett now?"

"At his office," Campbell said. "He had a million things to do, so he went there directly from my house. He probably wants his glasses there," he added in a burst of honesty, "but I was too damn tired to go over there— What a day I've had with him!"

"M'yes," Leonidas said. "How has Mr. Brett been—I suppose you've been with him constantly?"

"Oh, he's been fishing and golfing and driving about," Campbell said, looking around at his cab. "He was fine until this fishing trip— A three-day fishing trip can be strenuous, if you're not used to that sort of thing. He had rotten luck he told me this morning when he came back. I think he'd been seasick, too. Looked terribly tired. My God, driver, what do you want? Can't you wait till I—"

"Just a moment, driver!" Leonidas spoke so sharply that Dallas jumped. "You just ran through a red light in Dalton Centre, didn't you?"

"This guy told me to," the driver said. "He says he's in a hurry—"

"Come in here," Leonidas said. "Into the hallway here. I want—"

"Now, see here!" Campbell interrupted. "He just went through a light, that's all! Is that anything to make a fuss over? If it is, fuss tomorrow, and I'll fix it up— My God! I decide to run over here with those damned glasses, and this driver starts off with a bang, and then he runs out of gas— I tell you, let it go! I want to go home to bed! I—"

"You may, at once," Leonidas said. "Miss Tring, tell the sergeant inside to drive Mr. Campbell home in my car. You may go, Mr. Campbell, but your driver stays. I've had enough—"

The completely bewildered driver stood in the hall while Kaye and Campbell drove off in car twenty.

"Say," he said to Leonidas, "was it you in that

prowl car behind me in the Centre? I thought I seen that car, but this guy tells me never mind— Say, he never paid me no fare! All this talk and argue, and the bastard never pays me no fare at all!"

"My dear fellow," Leonidas said cordially, putting on his pince-nez, "think nothing of it. You will be amply paid. You will be rewarded. In fact, all I have is yours, if what you've been brandishing in your hand is what I think— It is a glasses case, is it not?"

The driver looked more bewildered than before.

"Yeah," he said, shrinking into a corner as Cassie and Dallas bustled into the hall. "Yeah. That's what. A glasses case. It's got glasses inside it."

"If I may have them, please," Leonidas said. "Ah. M'yes. M'yes, indeed—"

"Why, they're more of August's!" Cassie said. "And Dallas tells me that Campbell brought another pair— Isn't it simply amazing, the way—"

"Please," Leonidas said. "Just a moment, Cassie— I want to know about these glasses. Will you—er—tell all?"

"Well," the driver said, "this guy just now, he tells me he's returning somebody's glasses, see? And then he argues about the fare, see? And we get that settled, and then we run out of gas, see? And while I get the gas, bang! I think about this guy I had last night. He'd left that case with the glasses in my cab, see?"

"You refer," Leonidas said, "to the—er—guy you drove to the airport last night. That guy?"

"Yeah, that guy. The airport one," the driver said.

Whatever curiosity he may have felt as to how Leonidas knew about the airport was overcome by his
relieved feeling that they were getting somewhere
at last. "That's the guy I mean. He leaves this glasses
case behind. I found it later, and I looks in the case,
see? But then I forget all about it until this guy
just now. This guy just now's got a pair of glasses
in his hands like the glasses in the case, see?"

"I see," Leonidas said. "Clearly. Go on, please."

"So while I'm waiting for this guy now, I thinks
to myself, maybe they're the same guy's glasses, see?
You don't see that kind very often, see? Them glasses
is old-fashioned, like yours, and—"

"Quite so," Leonidas said. "Now, let's get back to
this guy last night. You picked him up in Dalton?"

"Over the Centre, around half-past one or two. I
think he's just going home from the train, see, but
he tells me to drive him to the Boston airport, he's
got to get this chartered plane that's waiting, see?
So I takes him over, and he's in such a hurry he
forgets his glasses in the case, and I don't find 'em
till I get back here to Dalton, see? And then it's too
late to do anything because he's already gone, and
besides, I get four drunks from Mike's Sandwich
Shop—"

A squealing of brakes outside announced the return of car twenty and Kaye.

"For quick service," Kaye said as he entered the
hall, "use a police car. No linger, no dally, no stop.
Boy, does Campbell have a grouch on! August has

led him a life today— Say, still more glasses? How come?"

"Listen to me!" Dallas said. "Something's got to be done about Bill! He says—he insinuates—"

Breathlessly, she repeated their conversation with Campbell, and with the taxi driver, who listened blankly.

"They certainly are the same glasses, aren't they?" Kaye said. "Nice connection, Bill. Hooks him up with Sister G., and a plane last night would have made it, easy."

"Never!" Dallas said. "It would not—"

"Would too," Kaye said. "Special plane, no stops— get there this morning. Says he's been fishing. Hears the news, turns around and flies smack back. I call it solved, Bill."

"M'yes," Leonidas said. "I like to think of him arriving at Campbell's this morning from his presumed fishing trip. So tired, so safe—"

"Listen, mister," the driver said wearily, "if you know the guy that owns those glasses, give 'em to him. I got to go. And about my fare—"

"If you could wait," Leonidas began, "a moment—"

Dallas stamped her foot angrily.

"I suppose you think," she said, "that poor August was the man with the mustache that ran you down last night! The one that looked like Benny because he had a mustache—"

"Come to think of it," Kaye said, "Benny and August are built on the same general family lines.

August with a cork mustache, or a court plaster mustache, or a mustache—"

"Mustache, mustache!" Cassie said. "I don't want to see or hear another mustache! All this, and you pause to discuss mustaches—and— Oh, dear! Something's happening inside. Margie—she's chasing Cuff!" She opened the French door into the living room. "Margie! Cuff! What are you doing! Come here, Cuff. What's the matter?"

"Aw, nothing! I wasn't doing nothing! Just—"

"The big galoot!" Margie said. "He's been drawing mustaches on all those pictures he found on the desk in there. A big book of snapshots. And pictures—look!"

Kaye snatched the picture out of her hand, and whooped.

"Hey, Bill! Look—August with a pencil mustache is Benny. Look, Cassie. Look, Dallas. Here, you," he grabbed the driver, "you look, too—"

"Yeah," the driver said. "That's who I thought he looked like, last night. Benny. I know Benny. I drove Benny lots of times. Like from Mame's to Gert's or maybe Maizie's. Say, does he live here? I didn't know he had a home. Yeah, that's the guy last night that left the glasses, all right. And say, mister, you got my fare?"

"Fare?" Kaye pulled out a wallet and extracted a handful of bills. "Here. I don't know how much it is, but take it and wait outside, will you? Till we want you?"

The driver looked at the bills and smiled.

"Bud," he said, "I'll wait six weeks for that."

"Now, you listen here!" Dallas said as the driver returned happily to his cab. "You come into the living room, all of you, and thresh this matter out! I can't believe this. No one could. I don't care how many mustaches and glasses and cab drivers you find! Or fishing trips!"

"I told you that you wouldn't," Leonidas said calmly. "You're not supposed to believe it. You're not supposed even to consider it. Don't you like to think of August, scanning the newspapers for the news of my death? I'm sure he was just as worked up as Campbell said—"

"It explains the fork," Cassie said.

"What—er—fork?" Leonidas asked politely.

"And the sardines and crackers. I knew there was something wrong about those. *Not* Benny. August."

"Hold on, now!" Kaye said. "Now you've swung over, Cassie, don't jump too far ahead. What fork, what sardines and crackers?"

"Why, those in the preserve room, where you were last night, Kaye. You said Benny'd been having a snack. But he's allergic to fish. So it was August who had the snack before he left— He loves sardines. He buys them by the case from that man on India Street. Doesn't he, Dallas? Yes. Well, there you are. That settles it. Get our coats, Dallas, will you? Very quietly. But you might peek in on Rutherford and Jock— We should get started right away, shouldn't we, Bill?"

"I think so, yes," Leonidas said. "I feel that the sooner we call on August, the better—"

"Listen!" Dallas said. "I work with that man! I know him. I can't believe he's capable of anything like this! In all the months I've worked for him, I never found a trace of anything that wasn't fine and decent— Think how well he's treated Benny! Think—"

"M'yes," Leonidas said. "Mrs. Gettridge and I thought of that this afternoon, at length. I decided then that the most benevolent defender of home charity would never tolerate Benny, unless—"

"Unless he had to," Cassie said. "You mean, Bill, that August had to keep him, just the way Casimir in Lieutenant Hazeltine has to keep that horrid Olga in sables and emeralds, or she'll tell on him. Isn't it amazing that I never thought of that! Of course no sane person would tolerate Benny unless they were afraid to do anything else!"

"Afraid!" Dallas said. "Bill— Kaye! Cassie! What's come over you? Don't you realize what you're doing! You're calling one of Dalton's finest citizens a murderer! You have no real proof! You—"

"Dallas," Leonidas said, "consider the emergency fund for getting Benny out of scrapes. Think what August stood. Think it out—"

"Do, dear," Cassie said. "And get the coats—we've no time to lose. Just you think, Dallas. I know you'll remember all sorts of little things. Just the way I remembered about the sardines. And how he used to play stick knife when he was out gardening. Many's the time I've been out in the rose garden and watched him pin a cut-worm or a slug at twenty feet with his knife, or shears— If you'll just think, dear! He was a great one for handling knives while he talked. Wasn't he, now? And he used to stuff animals and things, when he was younger— He knows all about stabbing, and where, and all that!"

"Yes, I— Oh, dear!" Dallas said. "I hate to give in. But I suppose you— I'll get the coats. Want yours, Bill?"

"Poor girl," Cassie said after Dallas left. "It's hard for her to feel she's worked for such a man. And of course it is hard to change your mind about people. Particularly someone you always thought of as good. But once you change, you think of so many things. I keep remembering the way he used to watch that pretty little maid of the Duncans when she went by. And things Bagley said of him— I always thought Bagley was rather nasty about him, but now I understand. Bill, someone should stay here. With Zara here. Shall I?"

"Let me," Margie said. "You'll do more good going— How you planning to get the old buzzard, Bill?"

Leonidas shook his head.

"I have no plans. But with Cuff's aid, and with Kaye's left, we'll manage somehow. We've got to do it quickly— Kaye! What's that noise!"

"It's that cab!" Kaye said. "If he's beat it— That louse has gone! He's—"

"Cuff!" Leonidas said. "Go see if Dallas is next door—quick!"

Kaye looked at him.

"My God, d'you think the little fool— I thought she changed her mind pretty quickly! And I just told that cab driver to wait until we wanted him, so he'd probably take her! Bill, that little fool's gone to warn August!"

Cuff, returning from his hasty search of Cassie's house, just managed to leap on the running board and grab the door handle of car twenty as it started down Paddock Street.

He did not bother to tell Cassie and Bill and Kaye that Dallas had gone.

It seemed, Cuff decided as he gripped the door, it seemed to be a fact they already knew.

Chapter FOURTEEN

"I KNOW where his office is," Kaye said. "The two hundred block on Oak, near the corner—and if that cab driver's there, I'm going to pound him to pulp—"

"No," Leonidas said meditatively, apparently unaware of the rapidity with which the Dalton landscape was flashing by. "No, I don't think you'd better, Kaye. Not, at least, until he's testified in court. And I don't think you'd better stop directly on the corner, with a great squealing of brakes. Turn the corner. Quietly. M'yes, possibly it might not be amiss to deploy—"

"Hell of a time to deploy!" Kaye said grimly, as he hurled car twenty across the turnpike between two trucks. "Don't be quaint, Bill! This is no time for—"

"Oh, yes, it is," Cassie said. "And that's the second red light you've— Oh, I forgot. We don't have to bother with them in this car, do we? But that second truck skidded up over the sidewalk curb, did you know? It stopped so— Yes, this is the time for strategy, Kaye. Because after Dallas has told him, August won't run— Isn't that what you think, Bill? Because he feels so terribly safe. August isn't stupid. Running away would show guilt. He won't. He'll stay and brazen it out—"

"I think so," Leonidas said. "And if we advertise our arrival, he'll be just that much more prepared, and on guard. But we'll leave Cuff around, just in case he should try to cut and run. And we'll give the cab driver a few instructions—"

"What we want to do," Kaye said, "is to go in and nab—"

"We've got to do more than nab," Leonidas said. "We've got to make him talk. Without a confession from him, all our conjecture is useless and futile—"

"Okay, Bill, you're the boss—"

Kaye turned the corner of Oak and Locust and brought car twenty to a stop."

"Gee!" Cuff said. "Gee, guy, that was driving—"

"Come on!" Kaye said. "Come on, Bill! Don't waste time sneaking around— What are you holding me back for? What's the idea, peeking around the corner like—"

Leonidas motioned for him to be quiet.

"Wait, Kaye. This is going to turn out better than I had hoped. I think I just saw—"

"Yes, I saw her too," Cassie said. "That was Lila hurrying along Oak, back there. I recognized her hat. She swears by some little milliner in Carnavon, and you can always tell Lila by those hats. I suppose she's talked her way out of jail, and now she's rushing to

August—and he's there—see the light up in his offices?"

The four of them stood in the shadow of the corner store and watched Mrs. Gettridge as she half walked, half ran, toward the doorway of the two-story office block across the street.

She paused for a second and looked at the taxi waiting out front, and then hurried through the doorway and disappeared.

"She feels better," Cassie said. "She thinks it's August's cab— Shall we go?"

"M'yes," Leonidas said. "Cuff, you're to linger in that doorway. If that man whose picture you decorated with mustaches should appear, stop him. Stop Mrs. Gettridge, too. By any method you see fit—"

The cab driver, ignorant of the crisis he had helped precipitate, beamed genially at Kaye.

"Bud," he said, "make it ten weeks. I just counted that roll again—"

"Bud," Kaye said, "don't you move from that spot for anybody, no matter what they offer you, until *I* say so! Or you'll spend those ten weeks in plaster— Oh, Bill! Will you hurry!"

Cassie nipped in the bud Kaye's headlong rush through the doorway by the simple expedient of grabbing his coat tails and anchoring herself to him.

"I certainly do wish," she said, "that you'd read Hazeltine! You never ought to rip and tear at a time like this! You've nothing to gain and everything to lose—"

Growling under his breath, Kaye slowly led the way up the worn wooden stairs at the end of the hall.

At the landing, he paused, and then ducked back. Mrs. Gettridge was pounding at a door.

"August! August—open the door—unlock this door!"

Leonidas frowned. So August had locked— But then he remembered that Dallas had spoken of August's habit of locking doors.

"August!"

She pounded again and again.

The three huddled on the landing could hear her heavy, labored breathing.

"August! Open the door! It's Lila—"

Kaye flattened himself against the wall as the door finally opened and a triangle of light jutted out into the hall.

"August! When did you—how are you? Did you—"

"Ah. How do you do?" August said. "How do you do?"

His inquiry was courteous and impersonal, as though Mrs. Gettridge were a stranger whom he had never seen before in his life. He might have used the same tones, Leonidas thought, to someone selling shoe strings or lead pencils.

Mrs. Gettridge caught her breath sharply.

"August! I've just managed to get away from the police— You didn't kill Witherall, did you know? And I'm sure he suspects— What shall we do? I was going to keep him with me till you got back, but—"

"My dear woman," August said solicitously, "you are overwrought! Perhaps you'd better come in and

sit down and calm yourself! I don't understand—
What have you done that the police—"

The three on the landing started to creep up to
the door as August led Mrs. Gettridge inside.

Leonidas heard the click of the key turning in the
lock.

"Get Cuff," he whispered to Kaye. "Quick—"

There was no need for them to glue their ears to
the door crack. Mrs. Gettridge's shrilly frightened
voice was clearly audible in the hall.

"August! What's the matter with you?"

"There's nothing the matter with me," August said,
"but you— Mayn't I get you a drink of water? I do
feel that you need something to quiet your nerves—
What happened to you— The police, did you say?"

"You— What are you trying to— August, I didn't
understand! What's come over you?"

"Drink this water," August said. "I'm sure you'll
feel better—"

Cuff loomed beside Leonidas, who pointed to the
lock and went through a brief pantomime.

Cuff nodded, and pulled something that resembled
a buttonhook from his pocket.

It was amazing, Leonidas thought, the way Cuff understood some things. He even grasped the idea that
the door was only to be unlocked, not opened.

Leonidas gravely nodded his thanks, and Cuff made
the gesture that accompanied his usual aw-it-wasn't-
nothing statement.

"I know!" Mrs. Gettridge's voice was still shrill,
but with anger now, and not fright. "I know— There's

her handkerchief! You're got that girl here! I suspected that. I suspected that you— Where is that girl? Where is that girl?"

"Really, I am quite alone," August said. "And I don't understand you, at all—"

"Yes, you do! You've got that pretty secretary of yours here! I always suspected there was something between you and her— Where is she? If she's here— if you've planned to run away with her and leave me— She is! She *is* here, and you *did* plan to— I know it! I'm going to the— Oh, what are you doing with that knife! Put that knife away! Put it—"

"If you think you're going to ruin my plans," August's voice underwent a sudden change, "by going to the police— Ah, that was your idea! I thought so! Benny tried to ruin my plans. So did Zara. Now—"

"Now," Leonidas said. "M'yes."

He flung open the door.

Somehow, rather to his astonishment, he seemed to have that little gun in his hand again.

He pointed it at August, whose long-bladed pocket knife was very near to Mrs. Gettridge's heart.

"There, see?" Cassie said. "He knows just where to stab—"

Walking across the room, she snatched the knife from August's startled grasp and flung it into a waste basket. Then, bursting with indignation, she slapped August in the face.

"You horrible man!" she said. "You're all that Bagley said! And what Paddock Street will say when they find out about this— Where's Dallas?"

August did not answer.

"Cuff," Leonidas said, "in car twenty there are handcuffs and those ankle things—will you get them? Thank you. August, will you face the wall and raise your hands, please? You, too, Mrs. Gettridge— Frankly, I think you would have shown more wisdom in staying safely at the station with Mr. Feeney," he added as she began to sob. "Although you *have* helped us, in a sense—"

"Where's Dallas?" Kaye grabbed August by the shoulders. "Brett, what have you done with Dallas?"

August gave no indication of having heard the question.

"Don't hurt him," Leonidas said, "yet. She's probably in one of the private offices. Go see—"

"They're locked," Kaye said as he tried the doors. "I'll break them down—"

"August probably has keys," Leonidas said. "Er—frisk him, Kaye."

Kaye found the keys as Cuff returned, jangling the handcuffs.

"Want I should put 'em on, Bill?" he asked eagerly. "I always wanted to put 'em on someone—"

"By all means," Leonidas said. "And then sit and wave the gun—"

August made no sound as Cuff snapped on the handcuffs, but Mrs. Gettridge screamed.

"There," Cuff said with satisfaction. "*That's* what I wanted to know about. They hurt anyways, no matter who puts 'em on. This guy didn't make no noise, but I could see they hurt— Gimme the rod, Bill. I'll watch—"

Leonidas hurried into the office where Kaye and Cassie knelt by Dallas, on the floor.

"I'm all right," she said. "I just can't quite move yet. It's the paralysis of fear. I couldn't even make a sound when Gettridge came in. I just— Really, Rutherford was right. Things happen to the vocal cords, and so forth—"

"Water, Kaye!" Cassie said, putting her arm around Dallas. "Kaye, get her some water, you ninny! And bring in my little purse. I've got some aspirin in it, and eau de cologne— I smacked his face for you, dear. Hard. D'you want to have a good cry, lamb, or will you tell us about things?"

"Probably," Dallas said, "I'll do both at once. You know what? August thought I came to warn him because I was crazy about him! And when he found out he was wrong, he got ugly and pulled out that knife— The man's mad. He's gone off the handle— If Gettridge hadn't come— Oh, my! It took me by surprise so. That dear old man just stark raving mad!"

"Olives," Cassie said. "After you get one out of the bottle, the rest are easy. It's probably the same way with murders. After you've killed one person, you just keep on— How do you feel?"

"Shattered," Dallas said. "But— Well, it's all over and settled. I want to forget this episode— Give me a cigarette, Kaye. Bill, you look worried."

"August," Leonidas said, "is not going to talk. Mrs. Gettridge will, but he won't. And if he does talk, he's going to deny everything. I've no doubt some fishing boat captain in Florida will swear on a stack of bibles that August fished for three seasick days. They will probably describe his brave efforts to snare the denizens of the deep in the face of insurmountable odds—"

"But the cab driver," Cassie said.

"A driver," Leonidas said, "who plies his trade between Mame's, Gert's, Maizie's, and Mike's Sandwich Shop—I rather fear he will be the breath of life to a defense attorney. We are just where we started—"

"But we heard him threaten Lila," Cassie said. "We—"

"But we didn't see him," Leonidas reminded her. "For all you know, August was rehearsing a play. And—"

"Let me tell you," Dallas said, "it was no play he rehearsed with me! It was practically the final touch!"

"To us, yes," Leonidas said. "But his attempts to put you and Mrs. Gettridge out of this life don't prove that he killed Benny and Zara. I wonder, what would Hazeltine do? M'yes— I think perhaps— May I have one of your cigarettes, Kaye?"

Curiously, Cassie and Kaye and Dallas followed him to the outside office.

"August," Leonidas said politely, "are you still quite determined not to talk?"

August said nothing.

"That guy ain't human," Cuff said. "He ain't moved a muscle. But," he added meaningly, "if you give me five minutes alone with him, he'd come clean all right. Got a cigar, Kaye? Gimme that cigarette, Bill. That'll do."

Leonidas looked almost fondly at the cigarette he had just lighted.

"M'yes," he said. "M'yes. You mean to apply this—"

"To the armpits," Cassie said. "Or the soles of the feet. In Hazeltine, they always do that. The villains do. Once Casimir was on the verge of putting Rodney's eyes out, but Lieutenant Hazeltine came just in the nick of time. Why don't you let Cuff try it, Bill? I think August deserves it. Lynching is too good for him, even. Let Cuff, Bill. Go on. Let him."

"I think it's a fine idea," Leonidas said blandly. "I'm just wondering, where should we begin? Soles or armpits? Take off his shoes, Cuff, while we toy with possibilities. And should we let Cuff do it, or shall we let Kaye act on Dallas's behalf? Cuff, of course, is more experienced. Undoubtedly. Cuff would do the—er—the neater job—"

"I resent that, Bill!" Kaye said. "If you'll just allow me the chance, I'll make Cuff look crude. I'll—"

"You've had some experience with a piercing machine, haven't you?" Leonidas asked.

"I invented one," Kaye said, entering into the spirit of the thing. "And of course I spent years and years out on that dude ranch. If you want me to go into the branding angle, that is. Take off his coat, Cuff—

Cassie, perhaps you and Dallas had better go downstairs. There's a horrid odor to burning flesh—"

Leonidas nodded his approval as August's shoulders visibly sagged.

"We can just open up the windows, I suppose," Kaye continued. "Oh, say—I've got a cigar, after all. Tell you what. Cuff can have the cigarettes and one side of August, and I'll take the cigar to the other. Let's have those matches, Cassie, and I'll get this cigar going. One of the cowhands told me about some rustler they branded out in Montana, once, and d'you know, the burns never healed? They—"

"Butt burns don't heal, neither," Cuff said. "I know a guy's got three—"

Before Cuff and Kaye exhausted the topic of burns, Cassie was beginning to feel ill.

Leonidas, looking at her face, decided that they had gone far enough.

"Run along, Cassie," he said. "You, too, Dallas. Leave this to us. All right, Cuff. You can—"

August, his face an unpleasant shade of gray-green, turned suddenly around.

"Don't!" he said. "Oh, don't let him! Don't let them! I—I can't stand it—"

"How perfectly cowardly of you!" Cassie said. "Why, Bill, I do believe he's going to faint!"

"He ain't going to faint!" Cuff said. "I'll fix that—"

August screamed, as Cuff approached with the cigarette in his hand.

"I'll tell you everything!" August cried. "Everything. Anything. Only—don't let him! Don't!"

Leonidas sat down at Dallas's desk and removed the typewriter cover.

"Dictate, August," he said briefly.

Cuff listened for a few minutes to August's dictation, and noted, without emotion, the sobs that racked Mrs. Gettridge's body. Then he got up and paced restlessly around the room.

"Now," Leonidas said when August finished, "Mrs. Gettridge. He's already sufficiently implicated you, but it will be better if we settle everything. Oh, witness August's signature, Cassie. You, too, Kaye. And please, Mrs. Gettridge, don't force us into any unpleasant conversation involving lighted cigarettes. Because we will—"

With many pauses, and with many promptings from Leonidas, Mrs. Gettridge finally complied.

"There!" Cassie said. "That's fine, now we can go and— Cuff, what were you doing in that office? Have you— What've you got in your pocket?"

"He's been opening the safe!" Dallas said. "See! He's been into August's private wall safe! And I was wishing we could get into it! Cuff, come here. Give me those things you've got in your pocket. At once!"

"Aw," Cuff said, "I din't take nothing. Just some envelopes. I—I wanted the stamps for my kid brother. He likes stamps. He's crazy about stamps. He collects 'em—"

"Those aren't even stamped!" Dallas said. "They— Oh, look, Bill! Here's one with your name on it. 'For my nephew, Leonidas Witherall, when he comes to inspect his Dalton property. Orrin Witherall.' And,

Bill, the seals haven't been broken— Open it, quick! After all, you've inspected your property today—"

The denomination of the bills with which the envelope was filled stunned Leonidas.

"G-notes!" Cuff said in plaintive awe. "And I never had the chance to even *look!* G-notes!"

Leonidas, with a courtly bow, presented Cuff with one.

"For your part," he said, "in the day's entertainment. Your take. Your percentage of the gate— M'yes, I mean it. Give it to Margie to keep for you— My! How I have maligned my Uncle Orrin. This money, I suppose, was intended to tide me over until the land could be disposed of without incurring a loss. Er —I wonder, August—didn't you know about this?"

It was apparent from the look on August's face that he had not known. And Mrs. Gettridge—as Cassie said later, the woman's mouth positively watered at the sight.

"And how," Leonidas continued, "I should have welcomed this landfall during— Ah, well. That's over with. That—"

"D'you mean," Kaye said, surveying the money with some respect, "that envelope has been in Paul Gettridge's possession—and the lout never gave it to you? Bill!"

"Mr. Gettridge," Leonidas said, "was a literal-minded man. The envelope said, when I came to inspect my Dalton property, and I never did—no wonder, if he happened to know the contents of this envelope—no wonder he thought I took Orrin's bequest lightly! Now, let us hurry back to—"

"Wait," Dallas said. "Cuff's got a lot more. Deeds and things. Fork 'em over, sonny. They're Bill's—"

"Aw, gee!" Cuff said, hastily emptying his pockets. "Is it all Bill's stuff? Gee, I din't know it was yours!"

"That's quite all right, Cuff," Leonidas said. "M'yes. Now, we will get back to Rutherford. Kaye, you and Cuff take August and Mrs. Gettridge in car twenty. Dallas and Cassie and I will take the cab—"

"Will they be all right?" Cassie asked anxiously. "I mean, they can't get away, can they?"

"There's an iron bar, like," Cuff said, "in these prowl cars. We'll hook 'em on—"

The return trip to Paddock Street was so prosaically uneventful that Leonidas caught himself openly yawning.

"I suppose," Cassie said brightly to the cab driver as they stopped outside her house, "I suppose you're terribly curious about this, aren't you? All these goings-on? Aren't you wondering about it all?"

"Lady," said the cab driver, "when you've drove at night in this city as long as I've drove, see, you won't be curious about nothin'. It's the lovely garden spot like they say, see? But a lot of things goes on in gardens—"

Dallas laughed until Cassie shook her by the shoulders.

"Stop it!" she said. "I just saw Rutherford peering out of the little front room window— Bill, how are you going to tell him? We've got the confessions, and it all happened the way you thought. Every bit, even to the false mustaches, and the Meredith Academy dates, and the captain of the fishing boat being bribed. And the special plane and all. And— But, Bill, it's going to be awfully hard to explain this day to Rutherford! When he doesn't even know there's been one murder, let alone two!"

"M'yes," Leonidas said. "Dalton, the Garden City— Somehow, Cassie, I feel that Lieutenant Hazeltine has overlooked an excellent bet in some Garden Spot. M'yes, Rutherford presents a problem. So does Muir. But I have an idea— Ah, Kaye," he added, as car twenty came to a stop behind the cab. "Everything all right? Fine. Cuff, you continue to guard these two, please. Cassie, suppose you see if Margie is all right at Brett's. Kaye, I need your uniform— Driver, you stay put!"

"You left me out," Dallas said.

"You go into Cassie's living room," Leonidas said, "and be decorative. In case that boat becomes finished before we are quite ready for Rutherford. To the cellar, Kaye—and, Cuff, may I have the sergeant's badge that Margie gave you?"

"Aw," Cuff said. "Aw, Bill!"

"Come on, fellow," Kaye said. "I'll buy you another—"

"Honest?" Cuff said.

"Honest," Kaye said. "Say, Cuff, you—you really like that badge, don't you?"

Cuff sighed. "I always wanted to be a G-man," he said. "Or a cop. Margie wants I should try the exams. But—will you get me another badge? A real one?"

"I will," Leonidas promised, "if he doesn't. Watch things, Cuff—"

"You know, Bill," Kaye said as he and Leonidas entered Cassie's cellar, "we might do something about that. Cuff would be handy on the force. I think he'd be a lot more vigilant than some of Rutherford's flatfeet. He'd know more what to be vigilant about— Bill, how the hell do we break this to Rutherford? And to Muir? I sort of hate to think of Muir, particularly. It's just possible Muir may still resent my left—"

"Get his uniform together," Leonidas said, "and get into your clothes, and we will see if my idea works. It may. It worked for Hazeltine once—"

Muir still lay on the floor of the preserve room. That he was still bound and gagged was clearly through no fault of his. Muir, Leonidas guessed, had spent many weary hours fighting those bonds. He seemed almost too weary to be very angry.

"Muir," Leonidas said, "my name is Witherall. This is Stanton Kaye. Listen carefully, please, because I'm going to tell you rather a strange story, which begins with an alley cat last night—"

The sergeant's eyes opened wide as Leonidas launched into his story. They were popping when he finished.

"Now, Muir," Leonidas said, "I have here in my hand two confessions. Outside in car twenty are August Barker Brett and Mrs. Gettridge. I hope you are a reasonable man. Because if you are, you will don your uniform and then march upstairs to Colonel Carpenter and report that there have been two murders, which you have solved." He paused. "If you are not reasonable, Muir, we shall take several bottles of that excellent whiskey on Cassie's top shelf, apply it to you internally and externally, and then summon the colonel here. We will point out to him— Well, what we will point out is obvious. Now, you will observe that I present no ultimatum. You have a choice—"

"And remember, Muir," Kaye said, "about the quality of mercy. When mercy seasons justice— Well, I forget the exact wording, but mercy is an awfully swell thing, Muir."

"M'yes," Leonidas said. "What about it, Muir? Are you going to be reasonable?"

Muir nodded.

"Undo him, Kaye," Leonidas said. "I think he may wish to stretch—"

Kaye cut the clothesline which bound Muir's ankles and wrists. Before he could touch the gag, Muir's left shot out. It was a blow he had been considering in his mind for many hours, and it was as effective as Kaye's left had been, earlier in the day.

Kaye went down like a log, and Muir started to turn around to Leonidas.

It surprised the sergeant, several minutes later, to find that he and Kaye were coming to, simultaneously, on the floor.

Leonidas, with his little gun resting on his knees,

surveyed the pair from his seat on an empty orange crate.

"If you want to know, Muir," he said, "that was a can of clam broth which hit you from behind. Not jiu-jitsu, although Lieutenant Hazeltine and I have gone rather thoroughly into the matter of jiu-jitsu. The clam broth was not cricket. I admit it. But it seemed hardly the time to put my jiu-jitsu theories into practice— Muir, are you going to be reasonable?"

Muir drew a long breath as he removed his gag.

"I never," he said thickly, "seen anything like this day! Yes."

"You talk about seeing things!" Kaye said. "You, who spent the day in the peace and solitude of this quiet preserve room! Man, you burn me up!"

Cassie returned from the Brett house just as Leonidas, Kaye and Muir entered the living room.

"Everything's all right," she said. "Oh! Muir! How are you, Muir? Are you—er—"

"That Muir, Cassie?" Colonel Carpenter boomed down from the little front room. "Tell him to come up and see this boat— All of you come see it! We're through!"

"Come along, Muir," Leonidas said. "Admire the boat, and— Here. Take these confessions. And remember your lines!"

The little front room was a mess of balsa wood shavings, cement bottles, razor blade knives, string, thread, and countless little pots of paint.

"There, hah!" Rutherford said, pointing with pride to the jaunty little ten-inch "Santa Maria." "There she is, by George! Isn't she a beauty? Came out fine. Jock, just a dab more of that ochre on the poop— That's right. How's everything, Muir, running smoothly?"

"Sir," Muir said. "I have to report two—" he gulped. "I have to report two murders, sir. Next door, sir. At the Brett house."

"Murders?" Rutherford said. "Watch that poop, Jock. Don't hit the railing. Murders, you say, Muir? As more than one?"

"Yes, sir," Muir said. "Two, sir."

"Two?" Rutherford sounded dazed and incredulous. But Cassie looked at him sharply. Rutherford was, she thought, just a little too dazed and incredulous. "When did— Hah! Two! When did you put Plan Five into effect? Did it work out satisfactorily?"

"Sir," Muir said, "the murderer and his accomplice are outside in car twenty, sir. I have their confessions for the colonel. Here, sir."

"Splendid, Muir!" Rutherford said. "What I expected, of course. Always wondered how you'd get along by yourself. Hah. Jock, that mizzen mast won't do. Got to fix that. Muir, take 'em to the station. I'll be over presently. No place to discuss murders, in Cassie's little front room. Fine work, Muir. Proud of you. Credit to the force, and all."

Leonidas prodded Muir.

"Now," he said.

"Sir," Muir said, "may I ask the colonel's permission to—"

"Speak up, speak up—there's a piece over on the table, Jock. That'll do. Hah!—what is it, Muir?"

"Sir, I was assisted today by a young fellow named Cuff Murray. He—er—" Muir faltered.

"Whose record," Kaye prompted in his ear.

"Whose record is not clear, sir," Muir went on, "but I wonder if, in view of his aid today, the colonel might consider adding him to the force?"

"He has shown," Leonidas prompted in the other ear.

"He has shown resourcefulness, sir, a co-operative spirit, and ingenuity, which, coupled with his fine physique, should make him an excellent addition to the force."

Rutherford looked up from his apparently absorbing task of sandpapering the new mast. The vaguest shadow of a smile played around his lips.

"Fellow must be a jewel," he said. "Like Cassie's maid. Never heard you run on so about anyone. Hah. Bring him over tomorrow. Need good men. Now, Jock and I've got to fix this mast. I want to change the rudder, too, Jock. It's lopsided. Muir, I shall see you presently and go into this with you. Jock—"

"Let's go out and tell Cuff right away," Kaye said as the group went downstairs. "And he swallowed it, Bill! The old boy swallowed it!"

"I wouldn't gloat," Cassie said. "Would you, Bill?"

Leonidas shook his head.

"He never suspected a thing!" Kaye said. "Not a thing! Muir, you'll get to be a lieutenant— Come, come, don't look so dazed, fellow! Take your prisoners back, and then send people to Brett's. We'll catch you up on the loose ends before Rutherford gets too curious. Come on, let's tell Cuff about—"

He broke off as Jock came bounding down into the living room.

"When did he find out, Jock?" Cassie asked.

"Gee whiz, Gran," Jock said, "I don't know! I didn't guess he knew till he looked out the window a little while ago— I guess you were coming back from somewhere, weren't you? Anyway, he looked at his watch and said you had half an hour more, no matter what Charles Otis said and thought. That was your deadline. I asked who Charles Otis was, and Uncle Root said he was a wise and learned professor, hah."

"Did he add," Leonidas asked in a restrained voice, "when and where he had chatted with Professor Otis?"

"Some time this forenoon, I think," Jock said. "At the club. Isn't Uncle Root amazing?"

Leonidas drew a long breath, and then he smiled.

"It is an amazing family," he said. "Kaye, let's tell Cuff—"

Cuff, the accepter of facts, broke down and wept quietly as Kaye told him about his chance at the police.

"Where's Margie?" he said. "I got to— Margie, you here? Come and listen— But will they take me?"

"Muir'll see to it that they do," Kaye said. "And you dined with the police head, you know. You and the colonel are already pals."

"Gee, was he the— But I liked him!" Cuff said. "Aw, gee! Aw, gee. Aw—"

"Aw, gee!" Kaye said suddenly, "look what's coming up the street! My process server! And the lad's got a girl with him— Dallas, that is Violet, the cause of all my woe. I stood her to business school—she used to work in the factory, and she seemed bright— and the louse is using my innocent letters for a breach of promise case. And—"

"Violet?" Cuff said. "Violet? She's— Say, you just wait—"

Cuff stalked up to the girl, picked her up and shook her till her teeth chattered. Then, with a masterly thoroughness, he spanked her.

"Now, listen, Sis," he said, "you throw away that paper, see? You cut out this nonsense, see? And if I catch you hanging around Dalton tomorrow, I'll run you in, see? And you tell Ma and Pa I mean it. They put you up to this. I know. So you scram. I'm on the force, now, and I don't take nothing like this from my sister, see? Scram. And I do mean you!"

The burly gent and Violet scuttled like rabbits up the street. Cuff followed them, menacingly, for a few steps, and then returned.

"You won't have no more trouble with Sis," he said. "If you do, let me know. Gee, to think a sister of mine could act like that!"

Kaye, making a tremendous effort not to laugh his head off, thanked Cuff.

"Aw," Cuff said, "it wasn't nothing. Just my duty."

"I think," Cassie said in a strained voice, "that

J. Edgar Hoover is going to have— Bill! Bill, now look—it's her sedan, I know that—"

"It's my old school chum Estelle!" Dallas said. "He whose eye is— Ah. Sister Otis!"

Mrs. Otis got out of her sedan and marched directly to Leonidas.

"I've had a most difficult time finding you," she said, "but Charles said I must. Leonidas, on thinking the matter over, I find that your talk on Shakespeare was universally accepted. I have decided that I shall take no steps. Charles said I must tell you—"

"Dear me," Leonidas said, "your husband has—er —asserted himself?"

"Charles," Mrs. Otis said coldly, "thinks I made too much of a situation in which, although I cannot see why, he appears to find nothing but humor. In short—"

"In short," Dallas said, " 'He whose eye is on the tiger, sees not the small bird in the tree'—that's what you mean, isn't it?"

Mrs. Otis looked frigidly at Dallas.

"I have not been able," she said, "to find that quotation in any standard compendium on Eastern proverbs and sayings. I fear you made it up. Good night. Good night, Leonidas."

She marched back into her car and drove off.

"Made it up!" Dallas said. "It's practically the brightest thing I ever thought of— Well, that settles all our problems. I—"

"Except for your name," Kaye said. "Dallas Kaye is terrible, but anything is better than Tring. How's for next Saturday? Have you a date? No? That's fine. Next Saturday. That'll give the lads at the factory a week— I'll tell 'em to strike this week and get things settled, so I can get away. They're an awfully decent bunch, probably they'll be so overcome with sentimentality at the boss getting married, they'll give us an ormolu clock. Or a steak set— God, think of the steak sets—"

"Don't!" Dallas said. "Not steak sets. After today, I never want to think of steak sets again—"

"I'll tell 'em traveling clocks, then," Kaye said. "And Cassie can be best woman— You will, won't you, Cassie? And Bill can be best man—"

"Where is Bill?" Cassie said. "Where did he go? I thought he went in the house, but he didn't—"

Leonidas, having retrieved his hat, coat and stick from the maid's room, was cutting across blocks to the turnpike and the Boston bus.

It had been a pleasant twenty-four hours, on the whole, he decided. So many things had reached a satisfactory conclusion. There was only one drawback: he was two chapters behind on the manuscript of the current Lieutenant Hazeltine, and it had to be done in three weeks.

By the time he reached a bus stop, he had decided to throw away what he had written, and begin again. Rocket ships were tiresome, anyway. Lieutenant Hazeltine in a quiet suburb, a garden spot—it would be simpler to write, and it would be a change.

Not until he was hailing the big maroon bus did

Leonidas remember Orrin's money, in the envelope in his pocket, and the deeds to the Dalton land.

He didn't even have to write a Lieutenant Hazeltine, if he didn't want to!

He stepped off the curbing for the bus as a limousine turned the corner.

The next thing he heard was Cassie's voice.

"But I didn't mean to, Kaye! It was my bifocals—and besides, he can be your best man. He isn't dead —the fender just bumped him. See, he's saying something— What did you say, Bill?"

"I shall write it after all," Leonidas said dreamily. "It will have two stabbings—such a fine title!"

"He's delirious," Cassie said. "What are you talking about, Bill?"

Leonidas smiled.

"The Cut Direct," he said.

Mysteries available from Foul Play Press

Phoebe Atwood Taylor

The perennially popular Phoebe Atwood Taylor's droll "Codfish Sherlock" Asey Mayo and "Shakespeare lookalike" Leonidas Witherall have been eliciting guffaws from proper Bostonian Brahmins for more than half a century.

Asey Mayo Cape Cod Mysteries
The Annulet of Gilt, $5.95
The Asey Mayo Trio, $5.95
Banbury Bog, $5.95
The Cape Cod Mystery, $5.95
The Criminal C.O.D., $6.00
The Crimson Patch, $6.00
The Deadly Sunshade, $5.95
Death Lights a Candle, $6.95
Deathblow Hill, $6.00
Diplomatic Corpse, $5.95
Figure Away, $5.95
Going, Going, Gone, $5.95
The Mystery of the Cape Cod Players, $5.95
The Mystery of the Cape Cod Tavern, $5.95
Octagon House, $5.95
Out of Order, $6.00
The Perennial Boarder, $6.00
Proof of the Pudding, $6.00
Punch With Care, $5.95
Sandbar Sinister, $5.95
The Six Iron Spiders, $5.95
Spring Harrowing, $5.95
Three Plots for Asey Mayo, $6.95
The Tinkling Symbol, $6.00

Leonidas Witherall Mysteries (by "Alice Tilton")
Beginning with a Bash, $5.95
Cold Steal, $6.00
The Cut Direct, $6.00
Dead Ernest, $6.00
File for Record, $6.00
The Hollow Chest, $5.95
The Iron Clew, $6.00
The Left Leg, $5.95

Margot Arnold

The complete adventures in paperback of Margot Arnold's beloved pair of peripatetic sleuths, Penny Spring and Sir Toby Glendower:

The Cape Cod Caper, $6.00
The Cape Cod Conundrum (hardcover), $20.00
The Catacomb Conspiracy, $6.00
Death of a Voodoo Doll, $6.00
Death on the Dragon's Tongue, $6.00
Exit Actors, Dying, $5.95
Lament for a Lady Laird, $5.95
The Menehune Murders, $5.95
Toby's Folly, $6.00
Zadok's Treasure, $5.95

Joyce Porter

American readers, having faced several lean years deprived of the company of Chief Inspector Wilfred Dover, will rejoice in the reappearance of "the most idle and avaricious policeman in the United Kingdom (and, possibly, the world)." Here is the series that introduced the bane of Scotland Yard and his hapless assistant, Sgt. MacGregor, to international acclaim.

Dead Easy for Dover, $5.95
Dover and the Claret Tappers, $6.00
Dover and the Unkindest Cut of All, $5.95
Dover Beats the Band (hardcover), $17.95
Dover Goes to Pott, $5.95
Dover Strikes Again, $5.95
Dover One, $6.00
Dover Two, $6.00
Dover Three, $6.00
It's Murder With Dover, $6.00

Available from book stores, or by mail from the publisher: The Countryman Press, Inc., P.O. Box 175, Dept. APC, Woodstock, Vermont 05091-0175; 800-245-4151. Please enclose $2.50 for 1–2 books, $3.00 for 3–6 books, or $3.50 for 7 or more books for shipping and handling. Prices are subject to change.